A FURY OF SHADOWS

WITCH QUEEN SERIES BOOK FIVE

A.D. STARRLING

COPYRIGHT

DISCOVER AD STARRLING'S SEVENTEEN UNIVERSE AND MORE

Seventeen Series
Seventeen Series Novels
Seventeen Series Novel Boxsets
Seventeen Series Short Stories

Other series based in the Seventeen Universe
Legion
Witch Queen

Military Romantic Suspense
Division Eight

Miscellaneous
Void - A Sci-fi Horror Short Story
The Other Side of the Wall - A Horror Short Story

BLURB

They stole someone precious from her. And she will do everything to get him back.

After losing Nikolai Stanisic to the Sorcerer King and his Dark Council in a brutal attack that left her battered and broken, Mae Jin resolves to rescue the man who's come to mean so much to her. But just when she's unravelling a new form of magic that could help Nikolai recover his memories, Mae and her friends come under attack from Oscar Beneventi and a new breed of devils led by Barquiel.

The unexpected allies that come to their aid bring with them a perturbing development. Dietrich Farago, the Immortal long affiliated with Barquiel, is not only modifying devils, he has helped the Sorcerer King devise a way to control Mae.

Meanwhile, Nikolai Stanisic slowly adapts to his new life in the Dark Council and the horrid reality of having been a puppet under the Witch Queen's powerful illusion. Bent on proving his worth and his loyalty, he places his powers at his father's disposal to help him find and unlock the elusive *Book of Shadows*.

Time is ticking and the Sorcerer King is drawing closer to achieving his goals. Can Mae and her friends rescue

Nikolai and foil his father's evil plans, as well as those of the treacherous demon who serves him?

Join Mae Jin and her friends in A Fury of Shadows, *the penultimate book in the thrilling urban fantasy spin-off series* Witch Queen, *by the author who brought you* Seventeen *and* Legion. *Follow our intrepid witch on yet another dangerous adventure full of magic, monsters, mayhem, and steak in this riveting fifth installation in the action-packed series fans cannot get enough of.*

Witch Queen is the third series set in the bestselling Seventeen universe and follows on from the Seventeen and Legion series. It contains references to characters in the other series and the odd cameo appearance.

CHAPTER 1

THE AIR SIZZLED WITH MAGIC. STATIC RAISED THE HAIRS ON Mae Jin's arms as she dove to her left.

She missed the curving whip threatening to wrap around her left leg by a hairbreadth, used Hellreaver to block the powerful spell bomb arrowing toward her as she twisted in mid-air, and landed on her side with a grunt. The whip hissed close to her cheek as she rolled and came up on one knee. She studied the witch who'd attacked her with a faint frown.

Karin Everheart sneered. "Come now, demon. Is that all you've got?!"

The Siamese cat pacing the ground at the High Priestess's feet hissed and spat, her eyes aglow with the orange magic dancing on her mistress's fingertips and weapon.

"You give her too much credit," Derrick Adlington said coldly. Gold sparks danced along the length of the double-ended spear spinning lazily in the High Priest's hands as he trod the floor to Mae's right, his stare predatory. "We both know she's nothing but a fake."

Wow.

Mae grimaced at the insult and climbed to her feet. She hadn't anticipated they'd be quite so annoying in the grip of Anya's Illusion Sorcery.

They're almost as bad as that brat Abraham was when he was under the influence of her magic, Hellreaver grumbled in her hand. *Let me at them, my witch!*

Mae tightened her grip on the weapon as he struggled to break free.

"Down, Cujo!" she snapped. "You know that's not part of the plan."

Hellreaver growled, annoyed.

She was distracted by a calm voice.

"How's that counter spell coming along?" Enrique Cortes said from the shadows of the empty warehouse in Brooklyn where the mock battle was taking place.

Anya Mendes stood beside the Columbian sorcerer, her pupils and those of her Harpy Eagle Sable lighting up the gloom with the blue flames of the power pouring out of them.

Karin and Derrick were oblivious to her and Cortes's presence.

Now that Mae had gotten used to sensing Anya and her familiar's cores, she could feel their eerie magic throbbing against her flesh. It still set her teeth on edge even though she knew they were no longer her enemy.

She glanced at Cortes. "I know you said I shouldn't use my full powers during these sparring sessions, but it would be a lot easier to focus if I wasn't getting my ass handed to me. How about we try something—?!"

Movement out of the corner of her eye had her cursing.

She was too late to dodge the attack hurtling toward her. Heat seared her right thigh when it glanced off her flesh, wringing a gasp from her lips. Though the wound healed almost instantly, it still stung.

Derrick curled a mocking lip. The sorcerer looked like he was enjoying himself, as did the hawk on his shoulder.

It was Cortes who'd suggested the High Council assist Mae with her training. They'd been initially reluctant to do so. Considering how the entire magic community had turned on Mae mere weeks ago after falling prey to the Dark Council's latest heinous scheme, she could hardly blame them.

Cortes had finally convinced them it was in everyone's interest that she succeed in overcoming Anya's spell.

Mae eyed Karin and Derrick glumly. *They've grown suspiciously enthusiastic now they've realized they get to kick my ass every day.*

Heat pulsed across her bond with Brimstone. *That floozie from the West Coast and the damn fool from Orlando were the same when they visited last week.* The demon fox fidgeted restlessly next to Cortes. *Allow me to intervene, my witch. I cannot sit still while these weaklings attack you!*

"No." Mae's gaze flicked to the fox. "I need to do this on my own." She paused. "And don't let Abraham hear you call Raven a floozie."

Brimstone drooped. Cortes frowned at the fox. He'd

expressly forbidden him from helping her with his demon magic.

Hellreaver sulked in Mae's hold, equally annoyed. Though she was allowed to wield him as a weapon, he was also banned from aiding her with his powers. According to Anya, the best way for Mae to learn to combat Illusion Sorcery was by relying on her own two cores. Cortes had concurred.

Though neither of them had said the words out loud, Mae knew what Anya and Cortes were afraid of. If Brimstone and Hellreaver were ever incapacitated again, as they were during her last battle against the Dark Council, she would have to rely on her own magic to defend herself against their enemy.

Mae could feel the sources of power that had recently awakened inside her deep within her belly and her chest. They throbbed with the formidable demonic energy she had been born to wield. Entwined around the bright spheres were pulsing threads of white magic.

Now that she was regularly accessing the core in her heart, the legacy Ran Soyun had bequeathed her and Na Ri grew stronger by the day.

Na Ri had been as surprised by this as Mae was. And it had caused Mae to question something that had always troubled her.

Is this what Barquiel was afraid of? That our white magic would thrive under the influence of our second core?

Na Ri had remained silent at her questions.

The Archduke of Hell who had sided with the first Sorcerer King and all who had subsequently filled that position had been keen to rip out the core in her heart whenever they had fought one another. In fact, the demon seemed pretty obsessed with robbing her of her secondary source of magic.

Mae's thoughts turned to Nikolai Stanisic as she evaded another blistering attack by the bewitched Karin and Derrick. She wondered how he was faring.

Almost a month had passed since the events in Concord, when the white magic sorcerer had fallen under the spell hidden inside the altar of the church where he, Mae, Cortes, and Vlad Vissarion had battled Oscar Beneventi and Barquiel. Though they had managed to free Anya and end the Illusion Sorcery that had seen Mae become the most hated figure in the magic community, they had all ultimately failed to grasp the Sorcerer King and his Dark Council's secret intention to capture Nikolai.

With his ability to access ley lines and his newly acquired Hellfire Magic, the sorcerer's power was a crucial key in Vedran Borojevic's scheme to achieve his goals. Chief among those was unlocking the *Book of Shadows* so he could get his hands on the soul of the first Sorcerer King. What he intended to do with it no one knew, although Mae had her suspicions on the subject.

That lapse in judgment had cost them one of the most valuable assets they had in the war they would soon have to wage against Vedran, his army of black magic users, and the demonic forces Barquiel commanded.

But Nikolai Stanisic wasn't just a tool to be used in the upcoming conflict. He was the man Mae had fallen in love with.

Her chest grew heavy with an all too familiar ache as

she countered a barrage of spell bombs with *Devour*. She'd just retracted her magic when Hellreaver shot out of her grasp, startling her. He deflected Derrick's spear as it crossed her blind spot and let loose an unholy growl.

The voices of the demonic souls that dwelled within him echoed menacingly across the warehouse. Karin and Derrick flinched.

"Don't get distracted!" Cortes barked.

Mae clenched her jaw. *He's right. Moping over a broken heart isn't going to help anyone. And it sure won't give me the satisfaction of punching Barquiel's lights out the next time we meet.*

That's the spirit, my witch! Brimstone said fervently.

Mae focused her attention on the battle at hand and the presence within her. *Are you any closer to figuring out a way to break the spell?*

Na Ri replied just as Mae cut down Karin's whip and Derrick's spear with Hellreaver and unleashed *Wind Fury* upon the witch and the sorcerer.

No. And I've tried any combination of the spells our father bequeathed us since we started these practice sessions.

They had decided beforehand that Mae would concentrate on the physical aspect of their training sessions, while Na Ri directed their magic at coming up with a way to undo Anya's illusion.

Mae's stomach sank at the frustration underscoring her first incarnation's voice. *So, nothing's working?*

I'm afraid not.

CHAPTER 2

UNEASE PRICKLED MAE'S SCALP. *THAT'S NOT GOOD. WE need to be able to undo this magic if the Dark Council uses it again.*

Na Ri hesitated. *There was one spell that had a brief effect on Anya's Illusion Sorcery today. Ice Fortress.*

Brimstone's ears perked up at that.

Mae wrinkled her brow where she levitated near the ceiling. Karin and Derrick were cursing up a storm beneath her as they tried to break free of *Wind Fury.*

Ice Fortress?

Yes. It slowed Anya's magic for scant seconds, but it was enough for me to discern its structure.

Surprise jolted Mae. She remembered what *Ice Fortress* had looked like the first time she'd used it in the New York coven's infirmary, deep beneath the headquarters on Madison Avenue. They had been able to make out the runes of the spells it had trapped within its frozen cage.

Hope quickened her pulse. *Maybe if we get Ice Fortress to pin the spell down for longer, we can figure out how to deconstruct it!*

That is an interesting idea, Brimstone observed.

Na Ri mulled it over. *It might work.*

Mae smiled fiercely. "Let's do it!"

"Who are you talking to?" Cortes narrowed his eyes at her before directing a suspicious stare at Brimstone. "He's not helping you, is he?"

"No," Mae said guiltily.

Cortes's jaw set in a hard line.

She sighed. *I'd forgotten this guy's like a dog with a bone when he wants an answer.*

Few people knew that Na Ri's soul lived inside her. There hadn't been an ideal opportunity to reveal her secret to Cortes and Anya yet.

"I mean, it's not as if I can just bring it up over dinner and drinks," she mumbled under her breath.

A sound had her looking down. Karin and Derrick were almost free of *Wind Fury.* Determination tightened her limbs.

It's now or never, she told Na Ri.

I'm ready.

Mae took a deep breath and zeroed in on their two cores. Magic and Na Ri's life force warmed her blood as they invoked the spell.

Ice Fortress!

A giant cage of ice exploded into view inside Mae's consciousness. Her heart stuttered. She could see the blue runes of Anya's magic within it.

Ice Fortress started to dissipate.

Mae dug her nails into her palms. She and Na Ri drew on their demonic powers. The spell solidified again. An idea struck her then.

Instead of deconstructing the Illusion Sorcery spell, how about we use a second incantation inside Ice Fortress to shatter it?

She sensed Na Ri's surprise.

Her first incarnation pondered her suggestion. *We have nothing to lose.*

Let's invoke Negate.

They strengthened the link between their souls and voiced the spell. Anya's magic did not so much as flicker. They attempted *Devour* and *Nullify* next. The Illusion Sorcery held.

Mae's jaw ached from grinding her teeth. She could sense Na Ri's aggravation. They were close to a breakthrough. She was certain of it.

We should give Sever a go, Na Ri said abruptly.

Mae blinked.

It was the spell they had used on Nikolai in Prague to break the link between his and Alastair's cores and a familiar who'd been consumed by Fire Magic. *Sever* had also released Jared from Anya's illusion a few weeks back.

She stiffened in the next instant.

Ice Fortress was quivering violently.

They had mere seconds left to attempt the next incantation.

Karin and Derrick escaped *Wind Fury* and launched a volley of attacks at her.

"*Shield!*" Mae barked.

Crimson runes exploded into life around her, forming a barrier that few things could pierce. Karin and Derrick swore when it easily deflected their attacks. Mae ignored the scowling pair and inhaled.

Na Ri's voice reverberated inside her mind as they invoked the spell.

SEVER!

Anya's magic flickered.

Karin and Derrick froze. Awareness bled into their expressions.

Cortes straightened where he'd been leaning against the wall. Relief brought a weak smile to Anya's face.

Elation had Mae's heart singing. *Yes! This is it! We—!*

Mae! Na Ri warned.

Ice Fortress was fading. The blue runes of Anya's magic brightened once more.

Mae's gut twisted. "No! We were almost there!"

My witch! Brimstone yelped.

By the time she realized she'd inadvertently dropped *Shield*, Karin and Derrick's magic was upon her. *Bind* locked her limbs. Hellreaver cursed when he was wrenched from her grasp. The world tilted violently around Mae as she was swung about by unseen shackles and sent smashing into the roof. She crashed onto the ground with a harsh grunt.

"Mae!" Anya shouted, alarmed.

She ended her spell and dashed across the warehouse with Cortes. Karin and Derrick shook their heads groggily as they awoke from the witch's Illusion Sorcery.

Brimstone reached Mae first. She groaned as the fox licked her face and nudged her all over with his wet snout, checking for injuries. Sorrowful sounds rumbled from his chest.

Hellreaver whipped into view above them.

I'm sorry, my witch. The weapon sagged. *I couldn't protect you.*

"It's not your fault, Hell," Mae mumbled while he worriedly poked her cheek with a blade. "I should have paid more attention to the fight."

Cortes squatted beside her, brow furrowed. "Are you okay?"

"I could be better." Mae winced as he pulled her to her feet. "Yeah, I'm pretty sure I cracked a couple of ribs."

Anya's face fell. Sable leaned over and nuzzled Mae's cheek with a regretful squawk. By the time Karin and Derrick approached, Mae's wounds were already healing.

"You guys really got into it at the end there, huh?"

Derrick scratched his cheek awkwardly at her faintly accusing stare. "You can blame the spell for that."

Karin didn't look in the least bit abashed. "Look on the bright side. We felt Anya's magic waver."

"They're right," Anya confirmed. "My Illusion Sorcery weakened for an instant."

"So, how'd you do it?" Cortes asked Mae curiously.

"We—" Mae stopped and corrected herself hastily at Cortes's suspicious look, "I mean, I used *Ice Fortress* to visualize the runes that make up Anya's magic. Then I tried to break them."

This earned her a battery of stares.

"What?"

Cortes sighed. "It's incredible how you say the most astounding things like you're talking about the weather."

Mae squinted. "Why do I get the feeling that's not a compliment?"

Anya's lips twitched. Karin rolled her eyes.

Cortes opened his mouth to utter what was likely going to be a sarcastic riposte. He was interrupted by a most dreadful rumble.

Derrick froze. "What was that?"

The sorcerer's stiff gaze swept the shadows around them.

Karin's fingers whitened on her whip. "Is it a demon?"

Cortes indicated Mae leadenly. "It's her."

Karin and Derrick's expressions grew pinched.

Mae patted her stomach guiltily. "Sorry. I skipped lunch." She glanced at the fading light streaming through the dirty skylights before leveling a pointed stare at Cortes. "*And* it's almost dinner time."

"It's a miracle you haven't fainted," he said uncharitably.

Mae's attention was diverted by a pair of whiny voices.

When do we eat, my witch? Hellreaver groused.

I want steak in black bean sauce, Brimstone demanded.

"You realize we're only guests at Vlad's place, right?" She studied the pair coolly. "We can't keep asking the guy to cook steak for you two every night."

I can eat mine raw, Hellreaver contributed helpfully.

Brimstone sniffed. *I don't mind mine rare.*

Mae's mouth flattened into a thin line.

Derrick leaned toward Cortes.

"I didn't realize she'd hooked up with the incubus," the High Priest hissed out the corner of his mouth.

"It's...complicated," the Columbian replied.

"Like, threesome complicated?" Karin asked shamelessly. The High Priestess arched an eyebrow. "So, she's going to take both of them as consorts?"

"No," Mae protested. "I only moved in with Vlad because it kinda made sense at the time."

Derrick and Karin appeared skeptical at this explanation.

That's how your mother looked when you told her you'd accepted the incubus's offer, Brimstone observed unsympathetically.

Hellreaver sniggered.

Mae pursed her lips. *Thanks, like I needed reminding.*

Though Yoo-Mi was fond of Vlad, she'd seemed less keen about her moving in with him than when Mae had taken Nikolai as her tenant.

Considering the guy has the power to make women in a ten-mile radius lose their panties, I can't exactly blame her.

Popo straightened on Cortes's shoulder.

"So, you're not living in sin, former queen of my heart?" he said with a deceptively innocent expression.

"Where are you going with this?" Mae asked warily.

Popo side-eyed Cortes and Anya slyly. "In that case, you should have a ménage-à-trois with my Enrique and—*mmmph?!*"

Sable had smacked the parrot in the face with a wing.

"You totally deserved that," Cortes told his familiar coldly while Anya flushed.

Derrick grimaced. "How the heck does a parrot even know what a ménage-à-trois is?"

"Don't look at me," Cortes grumbled. "That bird was a pervert before I met him."

"He's right," Mae said thinly.

Popo spat out a feather and avoided Sable's glare.

CHAPTER 3

MAE SIGHED AND RUBBED THE BACK OF HER NECK. "HOW about we stop here for the day and resume our training tomorrow?"

A contrite expression dawned on Derrick's face. "I'm afraid Karin and I will be leaving New York after we have dinner with Bryony tonight."

Mae stared. "Oh."

"Alas, our time here is over," Karin said regretfully.

They'd decided that two members of the High Council would come to New York every week to help with Mae's training. It had been Karin and Derrick's turn this time.

"As much as we'd like to stay and knock you about every day, we have to get back to our covens," Derrick said drily. "Regina and Isabelle will be replacing us from tomorrow."

"You need to watch out for that Regina," Karin warned. "She cheats."

Regina Nox was the High Priestess of the Las Vegas

coven, a larger-than-life character Mae had met at the Annual Grand Meeting of covens in Philadelphia. She was close friends with Barbara Nolan, the head of the Chicago coven, as well as the divine allies Mae had yet to meet.

"Enrique told me Vlad is a potential consort for the Witch Queen," Anya said quietly as they made their way out of the warehouse to the town cars waiting for them.

The unexpected question sent a jolt of surprise through Mae and sobered her up. "He is." Her belly knotted at the thought of the man she had rejected in favor of Nikolai. "He was."

Anya's tone grew apologetic. "I'm sorry. I don't mean to pry. It's just—"

She faltered. Her gaze darkened as it locked on Cortes's back. Sable crooned softly and brushed the witch's cheek with her feathers, no doubt sensing the tumultuous emotions reflected in her eyes. Anya squared her shoulders and finally met Mae's stare.

"Considering I'm the one responsible for what happened to Nikolai, I want nothing more than for you to break the spell I put on him and bring him back to our side," she said steadily. "But if you were to fail. If there was no way to rescue him. Would you take Vlad as your consort?" She bit her lip. "The Witch Queen...needs someone at her side."

Her words brought all of Mae's deepest fears to life and had her stomach churning with dread. She couldn't deny that those same questions had crossed her mind. Nor that she struggled to find an answer that would soothe her soul. Try as she might, she could not.

She cared for Vlad. Deeply. And she couldn't deny the

physical attraction between them. But her heart belonged to Nikolai. And she couldn't imagine that changing for a long, long time.

"I...don't know," Mae said miserably.

Anya accepted her answer with a diplomatic silence.

The witch's question filled Mae's mind as she said goodbye and collected her Vespa from the underground parking lot of the New York coven.

They hadn't found any sign of where the Dark Council had disappeared to after they'd abducted Nikolai. The hideouts he'd told them about, including the mansion in Budapest where he'd spent most of his time as an adult while he'd still been living under his father's roof, had been deserted when the magic community sent their people out to investigate them.

Mae suspected the reason Vedran had gone to ground was to keep her away from Nikolai for as long as possible.

Which means he needs him for something. And that something is probably to do with the Book of Shadows.

By the time she pulled up in the garage beneath Vlad's building in Chelsea, night had fallen. She left her scooter next to his Bentley and took the private lift to the penthouse.

Tarang greeted them with a happy rumble when she opened the front door. He brushed against her leg and nudged Brimstone and Hellreaver toward the kitchen. Mae followed them down the hall and took a peek inside the pristine, state-of-the-art space.

There were several takeout bags on the breakfast bar. Tarang and Brimstone plopped down on their haunches beside it. Their gazes swung expectantly from Mae to the food.

Her stomach growled.

"We should wait for Vlad," she said guiltily.

A sound had her turning around. The incubus was coming down the stairs into the living area. Her mouth went dry when she clocked his half-open shirt and wet hair. She caught a whiff of his soap and shampoo.

Dammit. He smells good enough to eat.

Vlad's hands froze on the towel he was using to dry his head. A dazzling smile lit up his handsome face. "Hey. I didn't hear you come back."

Mae swallowed. "We, er, just got here."

Her gaze flitted to his chest. Her mouth parted hungrily.

Vlad's gaze grew sultry at her expression. "Like what you see?" A devilish smile curved his mouth. Incubus charm drifted from his core on a hot wave that made Mae's palms grow sweaty. He reached for a button. "Want me to show you the rest?"

"No!" Mae blurted out. "That would be a bad id—!"

She winced.

Vlad froze. His face crunched up. "Did you...just bite your tongue?!"

His shoulders trembled.

"Itth not funny."

Vlad chortled and wiped a tear from his eye before coming over to kiss her forehead. "I can lick it better, Princess."

Mae told her loins to cool it and squinted at the

incubus. "I bet you say that to all the women you want to sleep with."

Vlad cocked his head to the side. His lips quirked in a self-deprecating smile. "Possibly. But, believe it or not, I haven't touched another woman since the day we met."

An awkward silence descended between them.

Mae's chest tightened. "Vlad. I—"

She stopped and clenched her fists, angry at herself for hurting him.

Vlad watched her for a moment before sighing. "I haven't given up on becoming your consort." He pressed his lips to her brow once more, his touch as gentle as a feather. "Now, how about we eat? I can hear Hellreaver sneakily opening one of the takeout bags from here."

Hellreaver sucked in air. *That incubus has the ears of a hellbeast, my witch!*

To Mae's relief, their dinner conversation was light and warm. Vlad told her about his day while carefully omitting the gory details of what being the heir to the *Black Devils* entailed. Mae related what had happened during her training session with Karin and Derrick and how she'd come close to breaking Anya's Illusion Sorcery.

"*Ice Fortress?*" Vlad said, surprised.

Mae nodded. "*Sever* almost worked in combination with it. But the spell needs something else. What that is, I don't yet know."

"It will come to you, I'm sure," Vlad said with a confident smile. He rose and started clearing the table. "So, you given any thought to what movie you want to watch?"

Mae blinked as she got up to help him. She'd forgotten Sunday night was movie night at Vlad's place. "Not really."

In the end, they settled on a sci-fi suspense that soon turned into a full-on horror fest.

I sure would like to fight a monster like that, Brimstone enthused at the heinous alien life form ripping apart several unsuspecting and evidently too-stupid-for-their-own-good humans on the screen.

Mae grimaced. *I wouldn't. We see something like that one day, we're running the other way.*

She stiffened a moment later and looked at Vlad. "I get that horror flicks scare you, but you should really stop touching my thigh."

"That's not me. And horror movies don't frighten me." He glanced her way. "The same can't be said for Hellreaver."

The weapon twitched where he was hugging her chest.

Mae's gaze dropped farther.

Tarang had a giant paw on her leg and was giving her puppy eyes.

"No," she said firmly.

The puppy eyes got worse.

Mae steeled herself. "You're not sleeping with us," she told the tiger. "The last time you did, you almost squashed me. I even had a nightmare that I was being suffocated by some kind of Yeti."

Tarang yowled before plopping his head despondently on her knees.

I shall make sure he does not sit on your chest, my witch, Brimstone said indulgently, evidently feeling sorry for his friend.

"You and Hellreaver snored your way through the tiger trying to kill me," she reminded him.

A sandpaper tongue rasped hotly up her cheek.

Mae sighed as Tarang slobbered her with drool. "Alright, you can sleep with us. But you're staying at the end of the bed." She paused. "*And* we're brushing your teeth."

Tarang brightened, his tail picking up speed where it swept the floorboards.

"You're such a pushover," Vlad told Mae.

The movie ended with the puny humans somehow managing to outsmart the alien monsters.

"Evidently, a few of them were smarter than a jellyfish," Mae muttered as they climbed the stairs.

Vlad chuckled. "There's a sequel. Should we watch that next week?"

"Okay."

They said goodnight on the landing and headed for their respective bedrooms.

Mae mulled over the routine she and Vlad had settled into since she'd moved in with him. Although he'd made advances toward her in the past few weeks, he'd never crossed the line that would have jeopardized their friendship. It was something she would forever be grateful for. Just as she was thankful that he'd been by her side the night she'd lost Nikolai to the Dark Council. She knew she would have lost her mind had he not held her in his arms in the hours that followed their disastrous battle.

Her boss's face flitted through her mind as she slipped under the covers. Steve Hodge would be expecting a call from her soon. Despite the pressures the forensics labs in

New York had been under lately, he'd managed to convince the hospital to grant Mae the sabbatical she'd requested after the events in Concord. He'd practically told the board it was either that or he was going to hand in his notice.

Hodge didn't know she was the Witch Queen and had no awareness of the world of magic that existed alongside humankind's mundane existence. But he'd been there the night her powers had awakened and witnessed firsthand the kind of monsters the Dark Council had sent to capture her.

More than that, he was her friend. Guilt tightened her throat.

He's going to hate me when I tell him I have no intention of coming back yet.

With Nikolai's fate at stake and Vedran getting ever closer to unlocking the *Book of Shadows* and fulfilling whatever sinister intentions he had for the magic community, she didn't have time for her normal day job. Not that she would have been able to focus on it anyway.

Sleep came uneasily, the quandary of how to overcome Anya's Illusion Sorcery weighing on her mind while she stared at the dark ceiling and listened to the gentle snores of Hellreaver and the two familiars sharing her bed. She didn't know when she drifted off.

The answer came to her at 4 a.m. and had her jerking upright with enough force to send Brimstone and Hellreaver tumbling onto the floor.

Tarang woke up with a startled jerk where he'd crept onto her legs.

"That's it!" she shouted.

Brimstone picked himself up from the ground and Hellreaver woke with a snort.

Vlad burst into her room. "What's wrong?!"

His diamond swords gleamed in his hands and his crimson eyes glowed with demonic energy.

"I—" Mae stopped and swallowed as she met his tense gaze, her mouth dry. "I think I've figured out a way to foil Anya's magic!"

CHAPTER 4

NIKOLAI'S FOOTSTEPS ECHOED SOMBERLY IN HIS EARS AS HE negotiated the halls of the Dark Council. Flaming torches crackled on bare stone walls, etching his shadow on the marble floor. Despite their brilliance, the light they cast was swallowed by the perpetual gloom shrouding the castle.

It sent a chill through him.

Alastair's feathers rustled where he perched on Nikolai's shoulder, the crow just as uneasy. Which was a surprise, considering they were home where they belonged.

He was distracted by the sight of a group of sorcerers and witches approaching. The men and women stopped and moved aside to make way, heads lowered reverently and gazes averted to show him and his familiar the respect he deserved as an heir to the Sorcerer King's throne.

Nikolai frowned as their steps faded behind him.

Though the hour was late, the Dark Council remained as busy as ever. There was a buzz in the air. A palpable tension he could almost taste.

It was nearly four weeks to the day since he and Alastair had awoken from the diabolical spell the Witch Queen and her allies had woven to trick them into joining their side. They had still not gotten used to life back at the Dark Council.

It didn't help that neither of them was familiar with their surroundings. Vedran had hideouts not just in Hungary, but in countries across all five continents. Their locations were unknown to the wider magic community.

Nikolai couldn't recollect ever living in the stronghold the Dark Council was presently occupying. He clenched his jaw.

Then again, my memories are all messed up.

The Witch Queen's face rose before his eyes. Fury flooded his veins on a hot wave as he recalled her fake tears and the lies she'd spouted to try and chain him to her side when he'd last seen her, in the ruins of a church, under a blood-red moon.

I should have ripped her cold, dead heart from her chest when I had the chance.

Hellfire Magic sparked into life upon his fingertips, unbidden. Alastair made an angry sound.

"Whoa," someone said drily. "It's a bit early in the day to be showing off your powers, little brother."

Nikolai stopped and turned.

Oscar was coming up the corridor. His lynx Drabek coiled sinuously around his ankles. The familiar hissed and arched her back when they drew closer.

Alastair flapped his wings and squawked threateningly at the lynx.

"I see she still hates me," Nikolai observed.

Oscar smiled at his curt tone. "Give her another ten years or so. You'll soon grow on her." He wrapped an arm around Nikolai's shoulders as they resumed their walk, their familiars still exchanging hostile noises. "Now, how about we go see what our old man wants, huh?"

Nikolai's lips quirked faintly. He'd missed Oscar.

Vedran was examining some documents behind a large, elegant ebony desk in his office in the southwest tower. Bar the bare necessities, the space was as austere as the rest of the castle and as cold as brass monkeys.

It wasn't as if the Dark Council couldn't afford to furnish their headquarters more lavishly. They had amassed immense wealth over the centuries of their existence after all. Nikolai knew it was simply that Vedran favored power over luxury.

A beautiful blonde with gray eyes stood staring out of a window next to the Sorcerer King, the wisps of hair that had escaped her pony tail fluttering gently in the freezing breeze that accompanied the light snow flurries falling outside.

From what Oscar had revealed to Nikolai upon his return to the Dark Council, Rose Blake had been Mae Jin's best friend and a promising surgeon at Grandview General Hospital. Nikolai had no memory of the incident where Barquiel had taken over her body. According to Oscar, he and Alastair hadn't been in New York at the time.

Rose looked over her shoulder when they crossed the

room. She turned, a lazy smile stretching her lips as she raked Nikolai with her gaze. "Ah. The prodigal son has deigned to grace us with his presence once more."

Nikolai frowned at her derisive tone. "I really don't like you."

Even though he kept his gaze on the demon, he didn't miss Oscar's surprised glance.

Rose's smile faded.

Vedran sighed and looked up from his paperwork.

"How about you both calm down," he told Nikolai and the demon. "I'm getting tired of your constant bickering."

"You should just have sex and get it over with," Oscar teased.

Nikolai curled a lip. "Oh, please. I wouldn't sleep with her if you paid me in cold hard cash."

Rose's face turned into an icy mask. Crimson bloomed in her pupils.

Oscar burst out laughing. "I think you pissed off the demon, little brother."

Nikolai studied Rose dismissively, a move he knew would enrage her possessor. "I'm pretty sure the two of us could take her on."

The air trembled with the demon's fury.

Vedran tapped a finger on his desk. "You test my patience."

Nikolai glimpsed the warning in his eyes.

"My apologies, father," he murmured.

Rose crossed her arms, her expression flinty.

Vedran studied Nikolai impassively for a moment. "You're forgiven." He rose and came over. "I'm pleased to see you and your familiar are in good spirits again."

He stroked Alastair's head with a knuckle. The crow crooned happily.

"Why did you want to see us?" Oscar asked.

Vedran glanced at him before returning to his seat. "It's about our friend in New York." He propped his elbows on the desk and studied them shrewdly over his steepled hands. "It appears she's busy trying to create another spell to entrap you."

Nikolai's stomach twisted. His gaze flicked to the documents on the desk.

"Is that report about her?" he asked harshly.

"Yes." Vedran leaned back in his chair. "I have spies watching every coven she's affiliated with. Enrique Cortes, the Arcane Magic user who killed Raya, and Anya Mendes, the woman who cast the first Illusion Sorcery spell on you, are assisting Mae Jin. Anya's magic won't work on you now that we've broken it, so they're actively looking for another way to chain you to her."

Oscar's face tightened. His gaze swung between Vedran and Rose.

"Can they really do that? I thought we'd disposed of pretty much anyone who could cast that spell except for the handful who now serve us."

Nikolai masked his surprise. This was the first he was hearing about this.

Vedran shrugged. "This is the Witch Queen we're talking about." His blue eyes focused on Nikolai. "I can see why she's desperate to reclaim you. You're a precious commodity, after all." A low chuckle escaped him. "One of a kind, even."

Nikolai's scalp prickled. The Sorcerer King's stare was so zealous he feared it would pierce him.

He rid himself of the foolish notion that his father meant to harm him somehow and lifted his chin. "What's our plan?"

Vedran's gaze twinkled with amusement. "Our *plan* is to keep you safe and sound by my side, where you belong. Oscar will go to New York and deal with her."

Oscar furrowed his brow. He didn't seem to like the sound of that.

Vedran ignored his evident displeasure and looked over at Rose. "Barquiel and Dietrich have cooked up a little surprise for the Witch Queen and her friends. I'm sure they'll…enjoy it."

Malice underscored his words.

Dietrich Farago was an Immortal and genius alchemist who had been in the service of the Dark Council for the last decade. He had known Barquiel longer still, their past a mystery even to the Sorcerer King.

Frustration churned Nikolai's stomach. He ground his teeth. "I appreciate that you want me to stay close to you, father, but I'm not some weakling who needs your constant protection. Let me go to New York and settle this once and for all!"

His irate words reverberated around the chamber.

Rose arched an eyebrow. Even Oscar stared at him like he'd lost his mind.

For a heart-thumping moment, Nikolai wondered if he had. No one openly defied the Sorcerer King and lived to see another day, even if they were related to him by blood.

"It appears you are yet to fully recover from the

effects of Mae Jin's bewitchment," Vedran said calmly. "I was warned your emotions would remain volatile for a while."

"I—" Nikolai faltered. His nails sank into his palms. He felt like a hotheaded child in the face of his father's benevolent attitude. "I'm sorry."

"You have nothing to feel sorry for, my son."

Nikolai's pulse quickened. He met Vedran's eyes.

Even though his memories were muddled, he was pretty certain the Sorcerer King had never called him that before. Nor even Oscar.

A strange expression danced across his brother's face. If Vedran noticed, he didn't show it.

"You and Barquiel should have a chat," he told Oscar mildly. "And make full use of what your brother has gifted you and our council in the short time we've had him back in our fold."

A muscle twitched in Oscar's cheek at their father's command. He nodded curtly and twisted on his heels. Drabek mewled softly around his legs as he headed for the exit.

Rose cast a thoughtful look at Nikolai and followed Oscar to the door. It closed soundlessly behind them.

Vedran stood up and indicated a seating area by a window, like he'd been waiting for this moment. "Come."

Nikolai steeled himself as he fell in step behind his father. This was a part of his new daily routine he would never get used to.

They settled opposite one another.

"Show me," Vedran ordered.

Nikolai took a deep breath. Heat surged through his

and Alastair's cores as he summoned their Hellfire Magic. A dark red blaze engulfed the crow.

Excitement brought a faint flush to Vedran's cheeks. The Sorcerer King leaned closer, his gaze bright with the reflection of the flames Nikolai and his familiar had brought forth and a hunger he could not quite mask.

It took all of Nikolai's willpower to suppress a shudder when his father pressed a hand to his stomach. Black magic bloomed around Vedran's fingers, the bands so thick with corruption Nikolai felt fairly sick as they kissed his skin. He gritted his teeth when his father's powers seeped beneath his flesh, the echo of Alastair's pain stinging him more than his own. Despite his instinct to pull away, he accepted it all.

After all, this is necessary to defeat the Witch Queen.

CHAPTER 5

"DAMMIT ALL TO HELL!"

An ugly expression darkened Oscar's face. He stomped across his suite and punched the wall viciously, his magic protecting him from harm even as his fist cracked the stone.

"I can't believe my father is keeping that asshole by his side!" he raged, spit flying from his lips. "And he even called him," his mouth twisted in an expression of pure disgust, "—*son!* That guy is nothing but the dirty bastard of a whore! How *dare* he think he can take my place?!"

Barquiel watched wordlessly while the sorcerer paced the room like a man possessed, smashing several of his belongings. He recognized a jealous outburst when he saw one. It would have amused him had Vedran's order not impacted upon his own private plans.

The last thing he wanted was to reveal their hand to the Witch Queen and the High Council too early. The demon frowned.

Besides, the project isn't complete yet. Dietrich is going to have a meltdown when I tell him Vedran wants Oscar to take his new pets to New York. Dietrich's handsome yet annoyingly sycophantic face rose before his mind's eye. Barquiel grimaced. *Yeah, he's going to bitch about this for days.*

He'd picked up Dietrich on a winter's night some two hundred years ago, in a back alley in Moscow. The Immortal scientist had fallen prey to a trap set by the Immortal societies to capture and eliminate him for the heinous crimes he had committed against humans and Immortals alike. On the verge of his twelfth death, as a blizzard swept across the Russian capital and blanketed his bleeding body in a layer of snow that soon turned crimson, he'd begged Barquiel to save him, promising him his soul for all eternity in exchange.

Although the demon had been surprised the Immortal had seen through the disguise he'd adopted at the time, he'd recognized Dietrich's inherent talents for evil. He'd seen the darkness that dwelled inside his heart.

Barquiel still wasn't sure what whim had possessed him to accept the Immortal's desperate request. Seeing the man torn limb from limb and his remains scattered to the four corners of the world would have been vastly entertaining. Still, he'd agreed to help Dietrich that night.

It was a decision he had never come to regret.

Disposing of the Hunters who'd ambushed the scientist had been child's play for an Archduke of Hell. That night, Dietrich Farago disappeared from the world of man and became one of his most faithful acolytes.

The demon was distracted by the sight of Oscar

throwing a vase across the room. Drabek yowled and shot underneath a chair as it struck the wall and shattered into pieces.

A stray shard sliced a thin cut across Barquiel's cheek. This would normally have incurred his wrath and the gruesome death of whomever had dared injure him, but he really didn't have time for that right now. He wiped away the trace of blood that bloomed on Rose's skin. The wound healed with a faint hiss of his corruption.

"Are you quite done? You're acting like a child." This earned him a death glare. "Vedran intends for you to be his heir, so how about you start acting like one?"

Oscar ignored his sardonic tone, too preoccupied with the green monster eating at his insides. "I would be a fool to think the throne of the Sorcerer King is mine just because my father once promised it to me." Doubt and bitterness etched stark lines in his face. "You know how fickle he can be."

Barquiel could not deny this. The heart of the man was capricious indeed.

And they say snakes are treacherous.

"Still, Nikolai is too soft-hearted to be the next Sorcerer King. Vedran knows this." The demon shrugged. "Also, we have no idea how long Anya Mendes's Illusion Sorcery will stay in effect. Your brother is a ticking time bomb. We need him to open the *Book of Shadows* and lure the Witch Queen to Budapest before he goes off."

Oscar's eyes rounded. "Wait. Vedran still wants her at his side? Even though we now have Nikolai? I thought he didn't need her anymore!"

Barquiel masked his distaste as he observed the Sorcerer King's oldest surviving scion.

What a fool. To think Vedran even considers him as his heir is an insult to the first Sorcerer King. Davor is probably rolling in his grave.

Only he and the current Sorcerer King knew the name of the first man with whom Azazel had made a pact, when the fallen angel decided to bestow his knowledge of magic upon humankind. It was not paranoia that had kept his, Vedran, and every other Sorcerer King's lips sealed over the centuries.

The power behind the first Sorcerer King's true name was something only three people in the world were aware of. Azazel, Vedran, and himself.

And Ran Soyun, when she was alive.

Barquiel's chest tightened at the thought of the woman who had gained Azazel's favor and eventually become his wife. Oscar's voice stirred him from his dark contemplations.

"What does Mae Jin have that my father covets so?"

"She is Azazel's daughter and the most powerful witch on the planet," the demon said irritably. "Having her under his direct command will be helpful for what he has planned for mankind." He paused. "He still intends to bind her to his heir with the *Marriage of Magic*."

Oscar's expression darkened. Barquiel could tell exactly what he was thinking. A union with Mae Jin was only a means to an end. The *Marriage of Magic* was a special ritual that would allow him to use her immense powers at will.

He has no intention of treating her like his wife, the demon mused dispassionately.

Considering the humiliating defeats Oscar had suffered at her hands since their first encounter in New York, he would no doubt exact his revenge on her in ways that would make her wish she were dead.

But this fool is overlooking the fact that I did not specify which of his heirs Vedran may choose for the Marriage of Magic *with Mae. It would be far easier to get her to accept Nikolai as her partner since she already cares for him deeply. Which means Vedran might still favor Nikolai as his heir. Yet another reason for him to keep his second son chained to his side.*

"And if we still can't control her?" Oscar jutted his jaw. "Even the binding ritual you taught my father and me couldn't subjugate her. How does Vedran plan to bring her to heel if nothing works? We know Illusion Sorcery is useless against her."

"Oh, come now," Barquiel scoffed, impatience adding an edge of steel to his voice that would have had his attendants in Hell make themselves scarce for fear of being vaporized by him.

Evidently, Oscar was too much of an idiot to notice he was in half a mind to rip his foul heart out of his chest and shove it down his throat.

"Mae Jin is half human. And like all humans, she is a slave to her emotions. We can use her family against her, like we did before. Better yet, it's clear she's chosen Nikolai as her consort. If his life's at stake, she will do our bidding."

Oscar frowned. "And if that still doesn't work? She's a

doctor. More than that, she's the daughter of Ran Soyun, a woman who willingly sacrificed herself to save her people, according to your own account of the war you and the first Sorcerer King waged against Azazel. She's altruistic enough to do the same, even if her actions result in Nikolai's death."

Barquiel's fingers twitched. Hearing Ran Soyun's name on Oscar's lips made him want to tear his mouth off his face.

"Then, we'll just have to kill her," he said flatly.

Oscar lapsed into silence. Barquiel could tell from the spite burning in his eyes and the way he smirked that killing Mae Jin rated high on his bucket list.

"When do we leave?" the sorcerer asked brusquely.

"In the morning. Be ready at dawn."

Barquiel left Oscar in better spirits and returned to his own quarters in the northeast tower. Though it was strictly unnecessary, he raised a demonic barrier around the suite to keep intruders out just in case.

He shifted into his demon form, opened a rift to Hell, and stepped inside. Crimson light pulsed across his vision as he descended into the interdimensional portal, the hot wind whipping at his body carrying the distant screams of lost souls.

He and Vedran had an agreement. It was the same agreement he'd reached with the first Sorcerer King after they'd defeated Azazel, and every man who had taken his throne thereafter. He would help them rule the world as long as they stayed out of his business.

The familiar stench of the Underworld filled his nostrils when he emerged on the other side of the rift. He stilled and scanned the dark cavern around him.

Few demons ventured this deep into Hell. Still, Satanael had eyes everywhere. His gaze dropped to the creatures crawling across his boots.

Even these hellspiders could be his spies.

With that in mind, he opened a series of portals that would make even the Lord of Hell's most shrewd lackeys struggle to keep up with his location. He walked in and out of the doorways that opened all over Hell Deep seemingly at random until he happened upon a mountain in an unchartered stratum of the dimension. One he had concealed upon first discovering it, several millennia ago.

Barquiel spread his dark wings and dove off the summit of the elevation. A vertiginous drop opened up below, the bottom obscured by mist and sulfur clouds. Wind whistled in his ears as the rockface blurred past him. He spotted the breach in the cliffside, snapped his wings closed, and slipped inside.

Sulfurous fumes whirled around him as he navigated a chasm scored with lava pits. It widened after some two hundred feet. The demon's pulse quickened. He arrowed toward the vertical wall rising at the end of the shadowy gully.

The defensive shields he'd erected to obscure the mouth of the cave that stood at the base brushed across his skin as he flew inside. Barquiel landed lightly on his feet and headed into a dark tunnel at a brisk pace. One mile of underground passages later, he finally reached the innermost sanctum of the cavern beneath the mountain.

A pale light lit the gloom as he approached the space. It

brightened the closer he got. He emerged into a circular chamber he'd carved with his own hands, the radiance filling the sacred space almost blinding him.

His breath caught, as it always did.

"I'm here," Barquiel whispered reverently.

CHAPTER 6

"YOU WANT TO DO WHAT?" CORTES SAID LEADENLY.

"I want to touch your core," Mae repeated. "And I mean that in a strictly non-sexual way," she added hastily at the sight of Popo's bright eyes and Anya's frozen expression.

"That's sick," Violet Nolan mumbled.

The witch's face was full of macabre delight. She sat on a box eating a sandwich, her rabbit Trixie nibbling enthusiastically on a chunk of carrot where she perched on Brimstone's head.

Violet had finished her end-of-semester engineering exams in Chicago and returned to New York last night. Her cousin Miles was arriving later that day, after taking his last paper at Harvard Business School.

Anya's wary gaze swung from Cortes to Mae. "What exactly are you intending to do?"

Mae explained her theory. They listened to her with mounting disbelief.

"Told you they'd react that way," Vlad muttered.

He was sitting on a crate filing Tarang's claws with one of his diamond swords. His bodyguards Ilya and Milo stood close by.

The incubus had insisted he be there when she attempted the, quote, "cockamamie" idea she'd come up with the night before.

"Are you sure it's okay for you to be skipping work?" Mae said sharply.

"The *Black Devils* can cope without their heir for one day," Vlad replied dismissively. "Besides, whoever's on my kill list can probably wait."

Mae's lips pressed into a thin line. Violet rolled her eyes.

Anya paled.

"He's joking," Cortes reassured the witch.

He flashed a warning look at Vlad.

The incubus grimaced. "Does she even know what it is you do in your other job?"

Cortes's eyes shrank to deadly slits.

Confusion clouded Anya's face. Her gaze swung from Vlad to her boyfriend. "What does he mean, Enrique? I thought you were an accountant."

Vlad almost fell off his crate. Mae sucked in air.

"Enrique?" Anya repeated hesitantly.

Cortes broke into a sweat.

Something brushed against Mae's magic then.

They're here, my witch, Brimstone grunted.

The warehouse door clattered open while the Columbian was still struggling to come up with a suitable lie.

A FURY OF SHADOWS

Ilya and Milo reached for their guns. They froze at the sight of the figure that appeared in the doorway.

"Howdy, boys and girls!" Regina Nox greeted them jovially.

The Las Vegas coven High Priestess walked in like she owned the place, the spurs on her cowboy boots glinting in the light streaming inside the building.

Ilya started lowering his weapon. He stilled, his eyes bulging.

"Hey, Ilya!" Milo whispered. "Why is the crazy lady from Philadelphia wearing pantaloons?!"

All eyes focused on Regina's trousers. The handsome, black jackrabbit cradled in her arms wore a green bowtie around his neck and the determined look of a familiar pretending he hadn't noticed his witch's outrageous outfit.

Erik Nox trailed in behind them.

"I told you not to wear those," he grumbled at his mother. "They are highly unbecoming of a High Priestess."

His Rottweiler Ross padded over to greet Brimstone and Tarang.

Violet brightened. "I didn't know you were coming too."

She rose, crossed the floor, and hugged Erik.

The tension melted from the sorcerer's face. He squeezed Violet back. "I'd thought I'd surprise you." His smile faded as he looked at Regina. "Besides, someone needs to hold her leash."

"I'll pretend I didn't hear that, fruit of my loins," the witch said magnanimously.

Isabelle West appeared behind Erik. She put a hand on

his shoulder. "The Phoenix coven will always have a place for you, Erik. Just say the word."

"Hey!" Regina protested. "Why does everyone keep trying to snatch my son?"

"Because his talents are wasted in your coven." Isabelle stroked the gerbil sitting on her shoulder, her tone faintly accusing. "His only role appears to be that of your guard dog. His magic will shrivel up at this rate."

Since she could see Erik's core, Mae was pretty confident that wouldn't be happening anytime soon. She introduced the newcomers to Cortes and Anya.

Regina crossed her arms and jutted her jaw. "So, you're the woman behind the mess that got our Mae into trouble and lost us Nikolai, huh?"

Anya's face tightened with guilt. Cortes narrowed his eyes slightly.

"It wasn't Anya's fault," Mae said. "She was as much a victim of the Dark Council as we were."

Regina sniffed. "You're too nice for your own good, Witch Queen."

Isabelle broke the taut hush.

"I hear your Illusion Sorcery is quite something to behold," she told Anya kindly.

Anya's expression loosened a little. "Thank you."

"Her Illusion Sorcery is the best in the world," Cortes stated bluntly.

Anya flushed at his words.

Regina stared. A saccharine smile slowly stretched her mouth. "Oh-ho! No wonder you're acting like her guard dog. You two are playing hide the sala—*oof!*"

Isabelle had elbowed her viciously in the ribs.

"Jesus," Erik mumbled.

Mae sighed. "How about we get started?"

Regina and Isabelle looked as dubious as the others when she explained what she intended to do.

"So, you're going to combine his powers with your spell?" Erik asked uneasily.

"No. I'm going to study the structure of his Arcane Magic and create something similar. I think it might stabilize *Sever* and *Ice Fortress* enough to shatter Anya's Illusion Sorcery."

Cortes furrowed his brow. "I'm still not sure you're going to be able to pull this off. There's a reason Arcane Magic is rare."

"There's only one way to find out," Mae replied, undeterred.

"You're absolutely confident this won't pose a risk to Enrique?" Anya said in strained voice.

Sable crooned nervously on her shoulder.

"Yes." Mae hesitated. "I accessed Nikolai and Roman Volkov's cores in Prague to suppress the Hellfire Magic storm that almost destroyed the city."

An awkward silence befell them at the mention of the sorcerer who had betrayed them.

Cortes studied her for a moment longer before dipping his head curtly. "Okay. If this allows you to counter Illusion Sorcery, it's worth a try." His lips curved slightly. "Besides, even if something happens to my core, you and Nikolai should be able to fix it."

Mae's chest tightened at the faith in his eyes.

Popo bobbed enthusiastically on the sorcerer's shoulder. "I agree. I trust Mae."

Anya still looked worried.

"By the way, I've been meaning to ask," Violet interrupted. "Why is Hellreaver panting like that?"

Everyone looked to where the weapon hovered close to Vlad and Tarang. His blades shivered as he focused on the sparks erupting where the incubus's sword met the tiger's nails.

Erik squinted. "It's almost as if he's watching...porn."

Vlad's hand froze on the handle of his sword.

Hellreaver startled guiltily. *It's not!*

"He says it's not," Mae said leadenly.

"Do you believe him?"

"Would you?"

"No."

"There you go then."

I object to that vile assertion, my witch, Hellreaver protested.

"How about you wipe the drool from your blade before you assert anything?"

Vlad climbed stiffly to his feet and directed Tarang to a spot on the other side of the warehouse. Ilya and Milo cast perturbed looks at Hellreaver before following.

The weapon drooped and bobbed over to Mae.

Brimstone stamped his paws restlessly while Regina and Isabelle took up positions around her and Cortes.

I really want to help you this time, my witch.

"You can't," Mae said firmly. She looked over at Vlad's bodyguards and Erik. "It might be better if the three of you stepped outside for this. You are bound to fall for the illusion. I don't want to have to hurt you."

"It's okay," Anya reassured her. "I can control whom my magic affects. They'll be safe in here."

Regina looked begrudgingly impressed at that.

"Be careful," Vlad murmured.

Mae met the incubus's troubled gaze and dipped her head. She pressed a hand to Cortes's back. His magic warmed her palm.

"Whenever you're ready," she told Anya.

The witch licked her lips. Her eyes and those of her familiar flashed with blue fire. Their power made Mae's scalp prickle as the Illusion Sorcery took effect.

Regina and Isabelle's expressions changed instantly.

"*Witch Queen!*" Isabelle hissed, her face dark with loathing.

Regina's furious gaze flitted to Cortes. "Let go of him, you demon hag!"

"Oh boy," Violet muttered on the other side of the warehouse.

How dare she call you a hag? Hellreaver growled. *You're far too young for that title yet, my witch!*

Mae gave him a jaundiced look.

Her pulse quickened. Magic was building up inside Regina and Isabelle as they prepared to attack. Heat surged through her veins.

"*Contain!*"

Her spell filled the warehouse with a flash of red.

Regina's colorful curses reached her dimly as the two High Priestesses found themselves trapped inside giant, crimson spheres.

"That should keep them busy for a while." Mae glanced at Hellreaver. "Keep an eye on them."

He bared his fangs at their friends-turned-enemy.

Mae locked in on Cortes's core and directed her magic inside him.

The sorcerer stiffened. "This feels as…unpleasant as it did when you repaired my core."

"Bear with it."

Her breath caught when she brushed the source of his powers and finally perceived his Arcane Magic.

CHAPTER 7

THE COMPLEX GOLDEN RUNES TWISTED AROUND HIS CORE, intricate, moving bands that swarmed, multiplied, and dissolved as they dove in and out of the vivid orb that was the origin of his powers.

They were akin to the tumultuous flares of energy on the surface of newborn stars and unlike anything she'd ever seen before.

His power is incredible.

Na Ri's presence rose within her.

No wonder there are so few Arcane Magic users around, she observed guardedly as she studied Cortes's core. *His magic is constantly destroying and remaking itself. Not many humans would be able to withstand that kind of pressure on their core.* Her tone hardened. *Let's get to work, Mae. This is going to take a while.*

Mae braced herself as they projected their consciousness inside Cortes. The warehouse disappeared. Darkness surrounded her.

There was a sensation of speed.

She squinted when the sorcerer's core blasted into view once more. It grew rapidly in size and brightness until it rose before them, a mountain made of pure white light.

Mae's heart slammed against her ribs.

The heat reflecting off the mysterious golden runes was palpable.

There! Na Ri pointed.

Mae snapped out of the hypnotic daze she'd started falling into and looked where her first incarnation was indicating. Her eyes widened.

Glittering chains linked the symbols making up the writhing Arcane Magic before them, the connections appearing and disappearing almost as fast as the runes.

Mae stared. *They look like chemical bonds.*

I think we can study his magic if we immobilize one of them, Na Ri said excitedly.

Mae hesitated. *Will it hurt him?*

We won't break it.

Mae swallowed. She watched the closest chain dissolve. Na Ri's power swelled inside her when it materialized again. They pounced on it, crimson bubbling around their fingers.

The chain whined and fought their grasp.

Cortes's core throbbed.

The sorcerer grunted, his pain echoing around them on a pulse of gold. His familiar made a pained sound.

Anya's trembling voice reached Mae faintly. "Enrique! Popo!"

"It's okay." Cortes ground his teeth. "We can take it."

Guilt churned Mae's stomach. She was distracted by Brimstone's voice.

My witch, the demon fox warned.

She caught a glimpse of what was happening outside through her bond with Hellreaver.

Regina was attacking *Contain* with her sword while Isabelle fired projectiles of pure blue magic at the sphere trapping her from the pistol in her hand. Faint cracks appeared in the barriers.

You need to hurry, Brimstone said. *They'll be through soon.*

Mae clenched her jaw. *I'm counting on you, Hell.*

I have your back, my witch.

She drew on her cores and raised *Shield* around her and Cortes.

"Fuck," Cortes mumbled.

Mae bit her lip. *He can probably sense our demonic power inside him.*

The man has been through worse, Na Ri said. *Now, focus.*

An endless void exploded inside Mae's mind as she and Na Ri opened the repertoire of magic Azazel had gifted them. Pale runes swam in and out of view deep within it.

Mae took a deep breath and dove inside the grimoire with Na Ri.

Complex magic formulas formed before her inner vision as she and her first incarnation manifested their intent. They reached for the ones that called to them and started breaking down Cortes's Arcane Magic fraction by slow fraction.

Mae lost track of time as she and Na Ri patiently unraveled the puzzle of the golden runes. She was faintly aware of Hellreaver engaging Regina and Isabelle at one point.

They must have broken through Contain.

Sweat was pouring down her physical face by the time she and Na Ri had finished deconstructing Cortes's magic and copied its blueprint into their own fathomless repository. Mae let go of the golden chain that connected the runes they'd immobilized and yanked her and Na Ri's consciousness out of the sorcerer's body.

Cortes sagged and swayed, legs trembling and chest shuddering with his breaths. Mae looped an arm around his waist to steady him. He blinked at her, the color slowly returning to his face.

"You look—like how I feel!" he mumbled.

Mae smiled shakily. "Thanks."

There was no more time to think. A fracture had just appeared in *Shield*.

Hellreaver cursed and deflected another coordinated attack from Regina and Isabelle.

They're strong, my witch, Brimstone grumbled.

Irritation and admiration pulsed in equal measure across their bond.

They aren't High Priestesses of their covens for nothing, Mae observed. She ignored the exhaustion sapping at her limbs and steeled herself. *Ice Fortress!*

The spell bloomed inside her and Na Ri's joint consciousness, a glittering, frozen cube that exposed Anya and Sable's magic to the naked eye.

The crack in *Shield* started to expand.

Alarm tightened Mae's shoulders. "Hell, can you buy me twenty seconds?!"

Of course, my witch! the weapon replied smugly.

Shock rounded Anya's eyes.

Cortes's pupils flared with surprise as he stared at Mae. "You've done it? You've deconstructed my magic?!"

"Yes."

Sparks exploded when Regina's sword met Hellreaver's blade. Isabelle bared her teeth and fired at the weapon. Hellreaver dodged her magic bullets at breakneck speed.

Mae's breathing sounded loud in her ears as she tapped into her cores. Cortes shivered when her demon magic washed across his skin. She incanted the second spell.

Sever!

The blue flames inside *Ice Fortress* shuddered.

Anya blinked. Regina and Isabelle faltered mid-attack.

Ice Fortress trembled.

Mae ground her teeth and drew on all of her and Na Ri's power.

Doing this without Brimstone and Hellreaver is more taxing than I thought it would be!

Na Ri grunted in agreement.

They reached for the formula to Cortes's Arcane Magic and weaved it into a new spell. The golden runes fused with *Sever* just as *Ice Fortress* started to come apart.

Regina and Isabelle charged her and Hellreaver.

The conjuration's name finally came to Mae and Na Ri. They invoked it as one.

"DISSEVER!"

Anya's spell shattered on a wave of crimson and gold that made the air tremble. The witch gasped, the blue flames in her pupils and those of her Harpy Eagle winking out.

Regina and Isabelle stumbled to a halt a few feet from Mae and Hellreaver. They blinked as they emerged from the illusion.

"Shit," Cortes muttered hoarsely. "You actually broke Anya's magic."

Violet and the others approached swiftly, Brimstone scampering ahead of them. The demon fox pressed against Mae's leg and nuzzled her cheek where she bent over with her hands on her knees, her breaths coming hard and fast.

Hellreaver hovered close by, a happy hum buzzing off his blades.

Vlad smiled. "That was pretty amazing, Princess."

Mae panted and grinned. "Told you I could do it."

She straightened and wiped the sweat from her chin.

The incubus's expression softened. "I never doubted you."

Her belly flip-flopped at what she read in his eyes.

Regina scratched her cheek.

"Uh. Is it weird that I'm still feeling a lingering sense of distaste for you?" she asked Mae sheepishly. "Like, I still want to punch that pretty face of yours."

"It should fade in a moment," Anya said distractedly. She clasped Mae's hands, her cheeks flushed and her eyes bright. "That was incredible!"

Mae's heartbeat finally slowed. "I couldn't have done it without the two of you." She squeezed Anya's fingers and addressed Cortes. "Your magic was the key to—"

She froze mid-sentence. The hairs were lifting on the back of her neck.

Vlad's smile faded as he watched her expression change. "What's wrong?"

Mae's pulse accelerated all over again. "I'm…not sure."

She scanned the warehouse for the source of the eerie sensation that had just glanced off her senses. Brimstone's low growl raised goosebumps on her flesh. Hellreaver vibrated agitatedly beside her.

Whatever it was that was making her skin itch, they'd picked up on it too. Except she wasn't sure what it was she was actually feeling right now.

Dread knotted her belly. She could only think of one thing that would make her and her bonds instinctively uneasy.

"Nullify!"

The air swelled with tension. Vlad and the others exchanged wary looks. They knew what that spell meant.

"Is it the Dark Council?" Cortes asked in a hard voice.

The sorcerer had stepped in front of Anya. He unleashed his whip and sword, his wary gaze and that of his parrot familiar aglow with golden magic as they swept the shadows. Though Anya's Illusion Sorcery was powerful, she and Sable were vulnerable to physical attack.

Demonic power bloomed in Vlad's pupils. The diamond stud in his left ear dropped into his hand and transformed into a second blade.

Purple disks formed around Violet's wrists as her ring extended into an arming sword. Erik shifted closer to her, his eyes and spear brimming with an aquamarine light.

Violet shot a worried glance at her. "Mae?"

Mae clenched her jaw. Instead of the black magic cores she'd expected to find close by, all she could feel was a whole load of nothing. She stiffened in the next instant.

Something had just moved on the edge of her mental map of the area around the warehouse. She focused.

The sinister sensation from before returned ten-fold. It came in growing waves, a foul energy that felt akin yet different to the black magic and corruption she was used to feeling from their enemy.

Is it him?! Na Ri ground out.

Mae knew she meant the Archduke of Hell who had killed her and Ran Soyun. Frustration churned her insides. She still couldn't figure out what the hell this was.

"Brim?"

The demon fox sniffed the air. His pupils flashed red a moment later.

He bared his fangs. *This is something from the Underworld. I am certain of it!*

Ilya and Milo startled when he shook himself out into his nine-tailed form.

Crimson throbbed around Hellreaver. The weapon dropped defensively in front of Mae. *I agree, my witch. I can practically smell Hell's stink from here!*

Mae's heart pounded heavily against her ribs. "Brimstone and Hellreaver say it's something from the Underworld."

Isabelle cast a fraught look at Regina. "Didn't you fight things from the Underworld once?"

"Yeah." Regina's expression grew pinched. "It was about as fun as being sober at a covenstead."

"Stay behind me," Vlad instructed Ilya and Milo curtly.

The bodyguards traded nervous looks. In a fight against the powers of Hell, they wouldn't stand a chance.

Cortes glanced at Mae. "Can you tell which direction they'll come from?"

Mae frowned and extended her magic outward. Her stomach plummeted when a trace of Hellfire Magic flickered against her consciousness. Hope stole her breath.

Wait! Is he—is Nikolai here?!

CHAPTER 8

"*He isn't, my witch.*"

Brimstone's voice reverberated in her ears, dashing the suffocating feelings that threatened to swallow her whole and causing Vlad to direct a puzzled look their way.

"*Do not be fooled by—*" The demon fox's eyes flared. His hackles rose. He lowered his head and let loose a savage sound, his tails vibrating so hard the eddies raised debris around the warehouse. "*Devils!*"

Icy fingers danced down Mae's spine. She recalled the creatures who'd attacked them in the crypt under the church in Prague, where Barquiel and the Dark Council had laid a trap for her and her allies while they'd been hunting down Roman Volkov's whereabouts.

Violet paled. "Did Brimstone just say devils?!"

Anya's voice trembled a little. "What are—devils?"

"They are creatures from Hell who answer to Barquiel," Cortes explained in a deadly tone. "They ambushed us in Europe, two months ago."

"They're nasty little sons of bitches," Vlad grunted.

My witch, we are being surrounded, Hellreaver warned.

Mae's nails sank into her palms. She squashed the longing bubbling inside her. Thinking about Nikolai was not going to get them out of whatever mess they'd just gotten themselves into.

And if devils are around, then that asshole is definitely skulking somewhere close by.

But try as she might, she could not detect even a whiff of Barquiel's corruption. Her flesh heated up as she drew on her cores, Na Ri's fury a hot taste on her tongue that bolstered her weary body. Demonic magic burst from her pores and lit up her skin. She blinked.

Underlying it was a sheen of dazzling light.

"Is that—?!" Violet started.

"—white magic?!" Isabelle gasped.

Na Ri's presence filled Mae's consciousness. An invisible wind whipped at her hair and clothes as she rose within a giant, crimson sphere laced with ivory threads, the power they'd inherited from Azazel and Ran Soyun making her very bones tremble. She lowered her brows, raised her hands at her sides, and hurled her magic outward as far as she could.

"Negate!"

Hellfire Magic immediately clashed against her own, shattering the spell that would have eaten away at the demonic energy closing in on them.

Mae scowled. *Nikolai may not be here. But his magic sure as hell is!*

Something flickered on her mind map before she

could give further thought to how he'd managed to counter her spell. Her eyes widened.

The whole load of nothing she'd sensed before was moving toward the warehouse at breakneck speed. Bile burned the back of her throat when she realized her mistake.

Shit. It was a concealment spell?!

Her alarmed gaze met Vlad's. "Brace yourselves!"

Incubus energy solidified in a thick veneer around the Black Devils' heir and his familiar at her warning. The others raised their defenses.

Mae barely had time to create a second version of *Shield* around them before the warehouse door blasted open and the skylights and windows exploded inward. A dark mist burst inside the building amidst the falling shards as the door tumbled across the floor, bringing with it the stench of Hell.

Fiends with red eyes and arrowhead-tipped tails emerged from the inky clouds, along with a horde of black magic users.

They all converged on her.

"*Wind Fury!*"

The tempest that roared into life across the building at her command lifted half the sorcerers and witches hurling spell bombs in her direction inside a vortex from which there would be little chance of escape.

The next incantation left Mae's lips on the same breath. "*Devour!*"

Scarlet spheres exploded around her shield. They swallowed the multiple attacks arrowing toward her.

"Watch out!" Vlad yelled.

A shadow fell across her. She looked up and narrowed her eyes.

A devil had landed on top of her barrier. Another alighted to her right. A third one crawled across the surface on her left. They started striking her defenses.

Mae flinched when their claws pierced *Shield*. She caught a glint of metal on their talons, and in their hide and eyes.

What the heck is that?!

Brimstone batted the devils away, his wrath making the air boil and his tails vibrating so hard the storm they raised tore part of the roof from its supports. More landed on him. He snarled.

Horror twisted Mae's belly at an echo of pain across their bond. "Brim!"

The monsters' talons were drawing blood from the nine-tailed fox's flanks.

That's impossible! Her heart thumped violently against her ribs. *They shouldn't be able to get through his demon magic!*

Regina's curse had her gaze swinging down distractedly.

A group of devils and black magic users had surrounded Vlad and the others. Sparks exploded where the monsters' strange, metal-tipped claws punctured the barrier she'd erected. The Dark Council sorcerers and witches focused on the breaches, blasting them with wave after wave of powerful spell bombs.

Violet stabbed her sword into the edge of Mae's *Shield*. Sweat beaded her forehead as she focused her magic and the energy she'd absorbed from Artemus

Steele and the divine beasts in Chicago into the crimson wall.

The expanding cracks froze.

Anya whimpered, eyes wide and body rigid with fear. Mae knew the witch was recalling the horrors she had suffered at the hands of the Dark Council mere weeks ago.

A dark foreboding chilled her to the bone. There was something strange about these devils. Unfortunately, she didn't have the luxury of figuring out what that was right now.

She glanced at Hellreaver, her pulse racing. "Go!"

He shot out of *Shield* on an ululation that rooted the legs of the sorcerers and witches bombarding the barrier enclosing Violet and the others to the ground. Blood coated his blades as he rapidly cut down the enemy.

The only ones who avoided his serrated fangs were the devils. They flickered in and out of view, their movements faster than when she'd last fought them.

Mae's stomach roiled as they pounced on Hellreaver in a coordinated attack that brought him to the ground. "*Hell!*"

Vlad's voice jolted her out of the panic threatening to overwhelm her.

"Drop your shield, Mae!" the incubus shouted, a ball of demonic magic hovering above his hand. "The three of you can't fight them and protect us at the same time!"

Cortes scowled. "He's right. Let us help you!"

Mae raised her hands to the sky, too far gone in her fear and rage to care about anything but the monsters attacking the familiar and the weapon bonded to her and Na Ri's souls.

"DECIMATE!"

Her savage bellow was swallowed by the detonation that ripped the air above her head. An orb brimming with dark red lightning materialized with a sizzle of ozone. It swelled rapidly, sapping her strength as it grew. Black currents laced with crimson shot out of it. The arcs multiplied, moving at speeds and angles that defied gravity as they sought her foe.

The devils atop Brimstone and Hellreaver screeched and reared back when the lightning found them, their flesh darkening with fresh burns. Brimstone and Hellreaver escaped their clutches and returned to her side.

Mae's scalp prickled.

The devils were still standing.

They aren't disintegrating!

She didn't realize she'd mumbled the words out loud until someone spoke behind her.

"How smart of you to notice."

Mae whirled around. A red-haired sorcerer levitated inside a sphere of pungent black magic some twenty feet from her. His lynx's obsidian eyes were full of hate where she bobbed at his side.

She glared. "Oscar!"

Demonic power drenched the air as Brimstone and Hellreaver moved closer to her.

Oscar smirked. Darkness bubbled on his fingertips. *"Disperse."*

To Mae's shock, his spell ended *Wind Fury*, releasing the Dark Council magic users she had entrapped. The sorcerers and witches rose inside globes of inky magic.

Their hands brimmed with spell bombs as they surrounded her.

How the hell did he do that?!

The answer came to her at the same time Na Ri spoke.

It's Nikolai. The Dark Council must have figured out a way to counter your spells with his Hellfire Magic. That's what we're sensing.

Mae's throat tightened at her first incarnation's bitter tone. Though they knew Nikolai was acting under an illusion, his betrayal still stung.

"Release us, Mae!" Vlad barked.

"He's a noisy little man, isn't he?" Oscar looked at the incubus dismissively before meeting her gaze. "Now, how about you be a good Witch Queen and come with us? We won't have to kill your friends if you do."

Adrenaline flooded Mae's veins on a surge of heat that rid her of her exhaustion. *Wait. So, this is about capturing me again?!*

Brimstone gnashed his teeth. *It seems so, my witch!*

Mae squared her shoulders and jutted her chin at Oscar. "How about I rearrange your face instead?!"

The sorcerer's expression grew ugly.

"Get away from her!" Vlad slammed a fist on *Shield*, his murderous gaze locked on the sorcerer. "She's not going anywhere with you, asshole!"

A vile light lit Oscar's eyes. Black magic exploded around him on a wave that drew a gasp from Mae's lips and shoved her back some half a dozen feet.

He lifted a hand at the incubus. *"Rot."*

The barrier protecting Vlad and the others dissolved with a hiss of corruption.

The incubus grunted and fell to his knees before he could counterattack, the demonic magic coating his dark swords and flesh fizzing into nothingness. He clutched his chest with a hand, his face crunched up in agony and his knuckles whitening where he clawed the ground.

"No!" Mae screamed.

The denial tore through her, threatening to break her heart all over again. Desperation knotted her belly as she invoked *Soul Shield.*

The spell shattered the moment it met Oscar's magic.

CHAPTER 9

Milo lunged toward Vlad. "Boss!"

Violet blocked him. "Stop! You don't know what that magic will do to you!"

Ilya restrained the younger bodyguard as he struggled to reach Vlad, the older man's face a rigid mask of anger and despair. Regina, Isabelle, and Erik raised fresh shields to protect Anya and the bodyguards.

Cortes laid a hand on the incubus's shoulder. "Vlad."

He flinched, *Rot* burning his palm. Arcane Magic detonated in his eyes as he attempted to counter the spell.

Mae looked wildly at Oscar's loathsome expression.

He's crushing his heart! Blood thumped painfully inside her skull. *This isn't just Nikolai's power! It's Vedran's black magic!*

Dark lines bloomed under Vlad's skin. Tarang whimpered, the crimson in his pupils flickering as he pressed against his sorcerer. The tiger swayed.

Anya and Violet caught him as he collapsed. Brimstone

and Hellreaver's wrath scorched Mae's mind. Tarang was their best friend.

Oscar recoiled when the dark globe protecting him shook violently. Brimstone swatted it with his powerful tails before clawing at it with his talons.

The voices of a thousand demons filled the warehouse, the din making Mae's ears ring. Even the devils flinched at the unholy sound.

Hellreaver slammed into Oscar's barrier again and again, his fangs and blades shredding and piercing the shield layer by layer. He slipped through a crack and hurtled toward the sorcerer, his rage a red cloud that obscured his deadly form.

He would have pierced Oscar's heart had Drabek not jumped in his path. The familiar screeched as the weapon sliced a deep cut across her face and eye.

"Drabek!" Oscar cried out.

His black magic sphere imploded under one of Brimstone's strikes. The sorcerer shrank back.

"*You are mine!*" the demon fox snarled, eyes a fierce scarlet and flecks of drool dripping from his jaws.

Oscar retreated, his face full of fear and spite, a bleeding Drabek clutched in his arms. The Dark Council sorcerers and witches surrounded him in a defensive formation.

Mae turned to Vlad. "*Negate!*"

The incubus gasped as the power squeezing his heart was consumed by her magic.

The spell resisted her. She bit her lip and drew on her cores. A gasp left her when she finally won the battle.

The color started flooding back into Vlad's face. He

raised his head weakly, his lips tilting in a tremulous smile. "Thanks, Princess! I thought I was—"

The incubus froze, his eyes rounding.

Evil saturated the air with a suddenness that robbed Mae's lungs of air. The acrid scent of ozone filled her nostrils and washed across her tongue.

No!

Panic bled across her bond with Brimstone. *"My witch!"*

The demon fox leapt toward her.

Hellreaver overtook him.

"MAE!"

Horror underscored Violet and the others' desperate screams.

She looked up in time to see Barquiel slam into *Shield.* The barrier broke, weakened by the damage the devils had inflicted upon it and the toll *Dissever* had taken on her magic.

The demon barreled into her and took her to the ground.

Na Ri roared inside Mae, a sound of incandescent fury. Mae clenched her teeth as her first incarnation took over their cores.

The power of the Witch Queen hardened her flesh and bones a second before she struck the dirt with her back. Air locked in her throat at the impact.

Sparks exploded inches from her face.

Hellreaver had blocked the obsidian sword that would have skewered her left eye. Metal scraped and groaned as he fought the demon Archduke glowering down at them, his blades vibrating and his fangs holding on tightly to the dark sword so their enemy could not cut her.

Brimstone plowed into Barquiel with a roar of pure fury. The demon went flying off Mae with a grunt. He snapped his wings, darted beneath the fox's swinging tails, and grabbed him by the throat.

Mae's chest constricted painfully as he hurled her familiar across the warehouse with a mighty bellow.

"BRIM!"

Brimstone twisted and landed on his feet like a cat. He skidded backward, abandoned crates and boxes exploding around him as his claws raked deep grooves in the ground. A murderous sound left his throat when he came to a stop. His muscles bunched for another attack.

He sprang at the same time Hellreaver shot toward Barquiel.

Mae sat up shakily, her heart thundering so fast against her breast she felt dizzy. She ignored the pain and numbness shooting through her body and raised a trembling hand to the winter sky. Heat ignited her cores.

"ECLIP—!"

Something snapped around her throat and choked off the rest of the spell. Magic burned her skin. Mae cried out and clawed at her neck.

Her fingers found a metal collar. She tried to rip it off. It shifted into a liquid form that slipped through her grasp.

Violet sucked in air. "That's—!"

The witch cursed and fended off an attack from a devil with her blade. Regina and Isabelle blocked a barrage of spell bombs with their magic.

Erik slammed his spear into the ground as the Dark Council resumed their assault, eyes aglow with a dazzling, viridescent light. His power made the air throb as a fresh barrier materialized around him.

It expanded to shield the others.

Mae gritted her teeth, still struggling to free herself from the ring around her windpipe. She could feel Nikolai's Hellfire Magic in it.

An amused chuckle reached her. Metal clinked. She froze. A chain was attached to the collar. She followed it with her stunned gaze, her heart in her throat.

Oscar was holding the other end. The sorcerer smirked at her expression.

"That look fits you perfectly, Witch Queen." He snapped the chain, causing her to jerk and fall awkwardly onto her forearms. "How about you come over here and lick my boots? I might just let your friends walk out of this place if you do."

The sorcerers and witches around him laughed nastily.

Mae knew he was lying.

Na Ri's voice sounded inside her skull, cold and deadly. *He will never let them leave this warehouse alive.*

Pain thrummed across Mae's bond with her familiar and weapon, startling her.

"*My—!*" Brimstone grunted.

—witch! Hellreaver moaned.

Her head whipped around. Her eyes widened.

Collars similar to the one around her neck now bound Brimstone and Hellreaver. Barquiel held their chains, a smug look on his face.

Fear drenched her in a cold sweat. The spell in the metal was stopping Brimstone and Hellreaver from accessing their demonic powers.

Mae swallowed convulsively, despair a living beast inside her chest. *It's not just Nikolai's magic. I can smell Vedran's power too!*

She sensed Vlad's stare and turned her head to meet his tortured gaze.

"Don't," the incubus whispered.

Mae closed her eyes, her breaths rattling her ribs. She knew what he was asking of her. That he was telling her giving in was not the right answer. That she should fight and that he would fight alongside her, come what may.

But she couldn't see a way out of their situation. Not one where he and the others would emerge from this alive. From the frustration wringing her insides, neither could Na Ri.

Nikolai's magic throbbed against her flesh along with the Sorcerer King's insidious power, an unpleasant reminder of her recent failure. Vedran wanted her. He had no need for anyone else.

Mae's nails scraped the dirt as she fisted her hands. She pushed off the ground slowly. There was only one thing she could do.

Better that we swallow our pride and beg Barquiel for mercy, than watch them die before our eyes.

Na Ri's bitter silence told her she felt the same way.

"Come now, Witch Queen, is that how you show your respect to your new master?" Oscar sneered. He yanked viciously on the chain, strangling her breath and sending her face down in the dirt again. "That's right." Glee lent a manic pitch to his voice. "Crawl to me like the worm that you are, Mae Jin! Learn your rightful place in the new world order the Dark Council shall bring about. Once we locate the *Book of Shadows*, the Sorcerer King will be invinci—!"

"Oscar!" Barquiel barked.

The sorcerer cast a puzzled glance at the demon.

Mae barely had time to register his shocking revelation before a whistling sound tore across the warehouse from her left.

Oscar looked around. His eyes bulged. He cursed, let go of her chain, and raised a shield.

A rocket-propelled grenade slammed into his barrier and sent him hurtling across the building. The sorcerer smashed straight through the wall and vanished from view, his gurgled scream swallowed by the sound of the explosion.

The boom died down.

Mae blinked, her pulse drumming rapidly in her ears.

The sorcerers and witches who'd accompanied Oscar beat a hasty retreat toward the other side of the building. The devils straightened, strange clicks leaving their throats as they cocked their heads from side to side, as if they were puzzled by something.

"That guy is such a tool," a woman said in a voice laced with distaste.

"Yeah," a man agreed leadenly. "If I'd listened to him for one more minute, I would have hurled my breakfast."

Mae twisted around. Her stunned gaze found the

figures framed by what used to be the warehouse entrance.

There were sixteen of them, all dressed in dark combat suits that glittered in a mysterious way. They were holding an array of deadly weapons and wearing even deadlier expressions.

"Se—*Serena?!*" Violet squeaked.

CHAPTER 10

VIOLET WAS STARING AT THE BEAUTIFUL, DARK-HAIRED woman who'd spoken.

"Hi, Vi."

"Lou." Erik's shoulders slumped. He smiled weakly at the powerfully built, red-haired man standing beside the woman. "You guys sure are a sight for sore eyes."

"Hey, Erik." Lou's gaze twinkled as he observed Regina. "You're looking mighty fine there, old gal."

Regina simpered.

Isabelle leaned toward the witch. "Who the heck is this guy?!"

The man who'd fired the rocket launcher at Oscar lifted it off his shoulder like it weighed nothing.

He beamed at Violet. "You're all grown up, little witch."

Violet's expression turned sullen. "Oh. I forgot you were part of the package."

Someone snickered behind the man.

"You're hurting my feelings, little witch," he protested.

"Shut up, Tom," Serena said.

It was obvious she was the leader of the group.

Evil filled the air with a force that pressed against Mae's eardrums. She turned, dread chilling her skin.

Barquiel had let go of Brimstone and Hellreaver's shackles. He hovered above them all, his black wings open and his crimson eyes blazing with wrath as he glared at the strangers.

"Who are you to interfere with my plans, you insects?!"

Serena curled a lip. "Oh, please. I've been called worse things by some of your friends in Hell's Council."

She removed a gun from the holster on her thigh and shot Barquiel. The bullet burned a hole through the demon's right wing.

Mae's jaw dropped open. *How?! His skin is harder than diamonds!*

Barquiel recoiled, just as stunned. He recovered and howled his rage. Mae stared unblinkingly while the building shook around her on a powerful wave of corruption.

Dark blood was oozing from the demon's flesh.

He's not healing, Na Ri exulted.

Mae inhaled sharply. A faint, golden light was fading from the edges of the wound. Understanding dawned.

"It's divine energy!"

Na Ri's surprise echoed within her.

Brimstone's groan had Mae jerking around. The fox was crawling toward her. Hellreaver shuffled in the dirt beside him.

Mae scrambled shakily to her knees. Motion above

checked her movement before she could take a step toward them. Her eyes widened.

The light was fading from the section of sky visible through the torn roof. Dark clouds bloomed into life and merged into a familiar, sickening, spinning dance.

Black lightning cracked the heavens.

Mae reached for her magic and tried to invoke *Eclipse.* The manacle around her neck tightened, throttling her breath and blocking the spell before it could take life. She directed a frantic look at Serena and her group.

"Watch out! That lighting will—!"

"It's alright." Serena met her alarmed gaze, her blue eyes calm. "It won't hurt—"

Inky currents brimming with millions of volts of electricity struck her and her friends. The explosion seared Mae's sight and made her ears ring. She fell onto her bottom.

"No," she mumbled hoarsely.

The dark spots swarming her vision cleared.

Horror had drained the blood from Isabelle and Anya's faces. Cortes and Vlad stood with their jaws clenched and their hands fisted, Ilya and Milo frozen behind them. Only Violet, Erik, and Regina looked strangely unaffected by what had just transpired.

The smoke and static cleared. Mae's eyes bulged.

Serena and her friends were still standing.

"Did you feel something?" a woman asked a man curiously behind her.

"You mean that tickle?"

"Yeah?"

He shrugged. "Barely felt it."

"*How?!*" Barquiel raged, spit flying from his mouth.

"As I was saying before the moron with the wings interrupted us," Serena told Mae, "that lightning won't hurt us. We are super soldiers. And these are third-generation, nanorobot, liquid-armor suits."

A vicious smile stretched Lou's lips. "Lightning actually powers us up."

Tom flipped a middle finger at Barquiel. "Thanks for the extra juice, dumbass."

Barquiel's face reddened until Mae thought his head would burst. She swallowed a hysterical giggle.

"*Kill them!*" he bellowed. "*KILL THEM ALL!*"

Serena sighed. "You bad guys need to come up with a more original line."

Eerie shrieks echoed to the broken rafters as the devils stormed across the warehouse. The super soldiers charged toward them, expressions undaunted.

The only thing that allowed Mae to keep up with the men and women's speed was magic. Even so, she struggled to see their movements.

Sparks flared where the super soldiers made contact with the devils. It took but a moment for her to realize they could more than hold their own against the fiends.

They're strong! she marveled.

It isn't just their physical strength, Na Ri observed animatedly. *They have something in common with those devils.*

Mae swallowed. *You mean, that strange metal we saw?*

Yes!

A noise drew their attention.

Oscar was stumbling back inside the building through the hole his passage had made in the wall. He straightened

81

with some difficulty. Blood oozed from a nasty gash in his head. He was holding Drabek with one arm, the other hanging limply at his side.

His furious gaze swept the warehouse and landed on the sorcerers and witches cowering near the back.

"What are you waiting for?!" The sorcerer pointed a trembling finger at Vlad and the others, his chest heaving with labored breaths. "Get them!"

Purple magic detonated in Violet's eyes. "Drop your shield, Erik."

The witch's voice dripped with ice. Erik took one look at his girlfriend's expression and hastily withdrew his barrier.

Vlad's hands tightened on the handles of his swords as he confronted the sorcerers and witches surrounding them, demonic energy brightening his eyes to a deep vermilion.

Cortes cracked his whip.

Regina and Isabelle assumed defensive stances.

Anya stepped past them all, determination radiating from every line of her body. The fear had vanished from her face. Blue fire ignited her and Sable's eyes with an audible thump. Illusion Sorcery washed across Mae's skin.

The Dark Council sorcerers and witches faltered. Their faces took on the peculiar look she'd come to recognize. One that said they'd fallen under Anya's spell.

They squatted, flapped their elbows, and started squawking.

Everyone stared. Oscar spluttered incoherently.

Regina turned to Anya. "Oh, come now, that's cheating!"

"Yeah, we wanted to kick their ass," Erik protested.

Cortes sighed.

Anya's eyes flashed. "They're lucky I'm not having them eat their own shit."

Sable made an irritated sound. Violet snorted.

"Babe," Cortes mumbled.

"Trash talk doesn't suit you," Vlad told Anya.

"You guys, there's plenty of devils left if you want some exercise!" Tom yelled as he dashed past them. He skidded to a stop, ducked beneath the talons of the devil chasing him, kicked the monster in the gut, and slashed its throat. Dark blood splashed onto his armor. He cringed. "Eww! Hell cooties!"

"Hey, watch the suits!" Lou shot a fiend in the head and stabbed the one trying to eat his arm in the heart. He lowered his brows at Tom and the other super soldiers. "Gideon will have my guts for garters if anything happens to them."

"Your husband is a pain in our ass," a woman grumbled.

She lifted a devil in the air and slammed it into a pile of crates before dusting off her hands.

"Yeah," Tom agreed with a vigorous nod.

"My husband signs your paychecks," Lou snapped.

Tom decided to overlook this. He blocked an attack by a devil and squinted at Cortes.

"By the way, isn't that guy Enrique Cortes, the *Bacatá Cartel's* second-in-command?" he asked Lou as he kneed the monster in the groin.

Cortes froze. Anya sucked in air.

Regina's eyes sparkled with horrified delight as she looked from the mobster to his witch girlfriend.

"*Abort! Abort!*" Popo warned his sorcerer in a stage whisper.

"Er." Tom scratched his cheek awkwardly at Cortes's murderous look. "Was that meant to be secret?"

"I swear, I'm going to shoot him one day," someone murmured next to Mae.

CHAPTER 11

Serena was standing beside her. The super soldier dropped down on her haunches and reached for Mae's throat.

Mae recoiled.

Serena's hand stilled inches from her flesh. "I'm just trying to get that collar off you."

Mae met the super soldier's steady gaze. She swallowed and dipped her chin. Golden light shimmered on Serena's fingertips and in her eyes. She took hold of the collar, studied it with a frown, and crushed it.

Air flooded Mae's lungs on a sweet wave as the debilitating magic suppressing her powers faded. Her bond with Brimstone and Hellreaver brightened her world.

She looked at the fox and the weapon, her pulse quickening. "Can you—?!"

"Sure."

Serena rose and offered her a hand. Mae took it

gratefully and allowed the super soldier to pull her to her feet. She raised *Shield* around them and scanned the warehouse warily as they headed over to Brimstone and Hellreaver.

There was no sign of Barquiel.

"He disappeared through a rift the moment he gave his command." Serena observed Mae's demonic barrier with a thoughtful stare. "That's pretty neat. It's probably as strong as Sebastian's divine shield when you're at max power."

Mae could feel her strength returning in leaps and bounds as her cores healed her wounds. She recalled the little that Violet and Miles had reluctantly revealed about their allies in Chicago.

"Is Sebastian the Sphinx?"

"Yeah."

Mae could feel Na Ri watching Serena curiously. The super soldier's divine energy brushed against their magic, a warmth that tasted of gold.

Hellreaver growled when Serena squatted beside him and Brimstone. The demon fox bared his fangs.

"It's okay," Mae said hastily. "She's a friend."

Serena looked unfazed at the hostile display. She smiled faintly at Brimstone. "Smokey says hi."

The demon fox blinked. He lifted his head and took a careful sniff of her hand. *"I smell the Hellhound's scent on you."* Brimstone looked around eagerly, his ears flicking back and forth. *"Is he here?"*

"No." Serena destroyed his and Hellreaver's collars as if they were made of candy. "His bond sent me."

Pressure thickened the air.

Serena took her gun out and fired at the demon charging out of the portal behind them before Mae could react.

Barquiel blocked the bullets with his sword.

Serena narrowed her eyes. "Clever."

She lowered the weapon.

Brimstone rose from the ground, eyes flashing a bloody red as he towered protectively above them. Hellreaver slammed into Mae's waiting palm.

"You wanna take the demon or the weasel?" Serena asked Mae conversationally.

Mae followed her gaze past Barquiel to where Oscar was attempting to make his escape. She lowered her brows. "I have a bone to pick with the weasel. Think you can handle the demon?"

Serena's mouth tilted in a half-smile. "It's been a while since I fought a demon general." She holstered her gun, cracked her neck and knuckles, and unsheathed the daggers strapped to her thighs. "Hey, Lou! Want to help me with some pest control?" she called out over her shoulder.

"What kind of pest?" the super soldier grunted as he fought a pair of devils some twenty feet away.

Serena arched an eyebrow at Barquiel. "A giant flying rat with an attitude problem."

Outrage distorted the demon's face. He bolted toward them on a scream of rage, his corruption distorting the air on a sickening, dark wave.

Heat surged through Mae as she prepared to invoke *Eclipse*.

She froze mid-incantation, Na Ri's surprise echoing

her own. Barquiel had gone flying backward into a steel column and bent it clean in two.

Mae's pulse raced when she clocked Lou's new position. *Shit. I didn't even see him move!*

The demon blocked the boot curving toward his face, still looking shocked at having been caught off guard.

He scowled. "You missed, weakling!"

Lou grinned. "I don't think so."

Serena blurred in front of Barquiel and punched him in the solar plexus. The demon gasped out a fine spray of blood.

The column sheared. Part of the roof came down on top of him.

Serena and Lou jumped clear of the debris and bumped fists.

They've got this, Na Ri said.

Mae closed the distance to Oscar with Brimstone and Hellreaver. *Devour* swallowed the spell bombs the sorcerer cast their way. She glanced around the warehouse.

The Dark Council sorcerers and witches who had escaped Anya's spell had enough on their hands dealing with Vlad and the others without having to come to the defense of their wounded leader too.

Mae released Hellreaver. The weapon zoomed ahead and blocked Oscar's path as he came in sight of a back door, his blades sending crimson ripples through the air.

A horrified gurgle escaped the sorcerer. He whirled around, his frantic gaze scouring the warehouse for another escape route. Drabek mewled softly in his arms.

Brimstone snatched a devil out of the air, crushed its

head with his jaws, and cast the gory remains at Oscar. Blood splashed the sorcerer's clothes.

He jumped back. "No! Stay away from me!"

He turned and bolted for a gap between towering piles of crates.

Mae brought them crashing down with *Wind Fury.*

Oscar raised a shield to avoid the debris and turned to confront her, sweat and blood trickling down his face.

Mae scowled at the taste of Nikolai's magic and Vedran's corruption in his barrier. "What did you do? Why can I feel Nikolai's Hellfire Magic inside you when he isn't even here?!"

A trace of defiance brightened Oscar's wild eyes. "Like I'd tell you, bitch!"

"Then you leave me no choice." Mae raised a hand. "*Ice Fortress!*"

Oscar gasped as the black magic sphere surrounding him froze. His breath misted in front of his face. Frost formed on his lashes.

Drabek went limp in his arms, her fur turning white with ice particles. A horrified sound left the sorcerer.

Mae stopped in front of him. "Your blood will freeze in your veins in a minute or so." She looked dispassionately at the lynx. "Of course, your familiar will die first." Brimstone and Hellreaver crowded around her as she met Oscar's panicked gaze. "Tell me what I want to know if you want to live."

The sorcerer ground his teeth and closed his eyes. Shivers racked his body as Ice Fortress raced across his skin. For a moment, Mae thought he would talk.

Oscar opened his eyes and glared at her, mutinous to

the end even as his lips turned blue. "I'd rather die than betray my father!"

Mae fisted her hands. She was about to invoke *Purge* when Na Ri spoke.

Wait! I have a better idea.

Mae's pulse accelerated as she listened to her first incarnation's suggestion. "Hell, Brim? I need your help!"

Anything for you, my witch, Hellreaver hummed.

He slipped into her hand when he grasped her intent.

Brimstone lowered his head and pressed his brow to Mae's back. *"We are yours to command, my witch."*

Mae took a shallow breath and opened herself up to their demonic magic. The power of three ignited her cores with a thump that seared her senses. She focused their magic into Hellreaver and thrust him through *Ice Fortress* and into Oscar's belly.

The sorcerer's mouth rounded on a stunned O. He grabbed frantically at the weapon lodged in his body, his grip turning slippery with blood. Crimson oozed out of the corner of his mouth. He blinked furiously at Mae, the track slowing as it congealed under the effect of *Ice Fortress*.

"What—what are you doing?!" he gasped.

Mae swallowed. "That which you would have done to me."

Fire licked her veins as she attempted to penetrate the barrier Vedran had erected around his son's core. It resisted her.

Mae lowered her brows, her heart thundering in her chest as she called upon everything she had. Blood washed across her tongue.

Brimstone grunted. Hellreaver vibrated violently in her grip.

His blade pierced Oscar's core.

The sorcerer jerked. Once. Twice. Three times.

An oppressive miasma darkened the interior of the building as his eyes rolled back in his head. Mae's stomach lurched. An inky doorway whooshed into life behind Oscar. She yanked Hellreaver out of his body as he fell backward into the Sorcerer King's portal.

Vedran's glacial voice reached her when the doorway started closing on his heir. "You test my patience, witch."

Na Ri's wrath burned through Mae.

"I'm coming for you, asshole," she growled.

A deafening silence fell around her when the rift vanished.

She turned, her heartbeat loud in her ears. Barquiel had vanished along with the devils and the Dark Council sorcerers and witches who had survived the battle.

Mae met Vlad's relieved gaze, her breaths rattling her lungs.

A sound had everyone whirling around and raising weapons and spell bombs.

"Whoa." Miles put his hands up hastily where he stood in the gaping opening that used to be the entrance of the warehouse. The sorcerer stared, his boa constrictor familiar Millie tasting the air curiously with a forked tongue from where she'd draped herself across his shoulders. "What the hell happened?"

CHAPTER 12

Curious glances landed on Mae and her companions when they walked inside the headquarters of the New York coven on Madison Avenue two hours later.

"It looks like the cat is officially out of the bag," Violet muttered as they crossed the foyer. "Jared is gonna be so pissed."

Mae swallowed a sigh.

Jared Dickson was an NYPD Lieutenant working as a liaison between the Immortal societies and the U.S. Special Affairs Bureau, or, as Violet liked to call it, the U.S. Supernatural Affairs Bureau. He had been tasked with keeping the otherworldly disturbances in New York from the eyes of the public and the curious media.

Though the magic community had tried its best to stay under the radar of the authorities over the decades they'd operated in the state, the rise in magical incidents following Mae's awakening and the battles they had been forced to wage against the Dark Council in the past year had attracted more attention than they would have liked, including that of City Hall.

From the whispers they could overhear, rumors of what had transpired at the warehouse had already spread among the magic users in the city. Mae suspected the cops who'd turned up in the aftermath of the attack in Brooklyn had something to do with that. Some probably had family members who'd been born a sorcerer or a witch, making them aware of the existence of the not-so-secret coven in New York.

Jared had showed up in Brooklyn that morning. The Immortal had sighed wearily when he'd stepped out of his car onto the icy pavement and seen them.

"My horoscope said I was going to have a shitty day. I should have known it would be because of you guys." He'd frowned when he'd spotted Serena Blake and her team. "What are you doing here?" He'd slowed and looked around warily. "Wait. Don't tell me Artemus and the pooch are here too?"

"They aren't," Serena had replied drily. "Artemus will be thrilled to hear you talk about him that way, though. Specially since he made that sword for you and everything."

Jared had flinched guiltily. "I didn't mean it like that. It's just that guy is—"

"A trouble magnet," Serena had interrupted with a weary grimace. "I know. I live with him."

Everyone had looked at Mae then.

"What?" she'd said defensively.

Serena had glanced at Brimstone and Hellreaver. "Looks like you share a common trait with Artemus beside your demonic bonds."

They'd left while Jared was dealing with the local cops and had dropped Regina, Erik, Isabelle, and Anya off at their hotel.

Cortes and Vlad had reinforced security in and around the building. Though the chances of the Dark Council attacking them again were slim, everyone had agreed it would be better to take extra precautions than be caught off guard.

As for Anya, the witch had maintained a frosty silence around her boyfriend ever since the accidental revelation of his exact role in the infamous Columbian cartel.

"I really want to shoot that guy," Cortes muttered for the twentieth time as they rode the elevator to Bryony Cross's office.

He glared at Tom Bright. The super soldier shuffled guiltily behind Lou Flint.

"She was going to find out sooner or later," Vlad told Cortes.

Mae pursed her lips. Despite the sabbatical the mobster's superior had granted him to decide where his alliances lay, his reputation preceded him wherever he went.

"To be honest, I'm surprised your secret lasted so long," she said critically. "I mean, what do the two of you talk about in bed?"

"We don't do a lot of talking in bed," Cortes replied gruffly.

Violet sucked in air. Lou raised an eyebrow.

Popo puffed his chest out proudly. "My Enrique is a—"

"Don't say it," Cortes growled.

Mae studied the parrot and Cortes leadenly. "Sure. Just rub it in, why don't you?"

"You're living with an incubus," Cortes said stonily. "If you want some action, all you have to do is ask."

"Yes, former queen of my heart," Popo enthused. "You must obey the call of your loins."

Lou made a face. "The call of your loins?"

A sinful smile curved Vlad's mouth at her surreptitious glance.

"You know you only have to say the word, Princess," he drawled. "I'll satisfy your every wish."

Mae's cheeks warmed. She caught Serena's shrewd look.

"It's not like that," she protested.

"I didn't say a thing."

They entered the meeting chamber of the New York coven a moment later. The tension melted from Bryony's face when she saw them. The witch rose and came around the conference table, her cat Penley padding silently beside her.

"Serena." She hugged the super soldier. "It's good to see you again."

Serena smiled. "It's good to see you too."

Bryony acknowledged the men beside her with a brisk tilt of her chin. "Lou, Tom. It's been a while."

"Bryony." Lou strolled to the large windows overlooking Madison Avenue and Central Park. He whistled softly. "This is some view."

Tom plopped himself in an armchair and crossed his

ankles on a coffee table as he looked around the impressive space. "Man, if I'd known you had such nice digs, I would have dropped in for a visit earlier."

Bryony and Serena looked pointedly at his boots. He took his feet down hastily.

Abraham Whitworth frowned. From the guarded look he was giving Serena and the two men, it seemed Violet and Bryony had been as scant with the truth with the aide as they had been with Mae.

The chamber doors opened. Brimstone perked up.

A retinue of kitchen staff came in with serving carts. Half were laden with steak and other raw meats, as well as platters of fruit and seeds for the non-carnivorous familiars.

Brimstone, Hellreaver, and Tarang headed briskly over. To Mae's relief, the tiger looked to have fully recovered from Oscar's debilitating spell.

She became aware of a stare. Bryony was watching her with a worried expression.

"What's wrong?" Mae said.

The High Priestess waved a vague hand at the gourmet lunch her staff were laying out on a dining table. "Your stomach would normally have growled at least half a dozen times by now. Are you okay?"

Mae grimaced. "I have acid."

It was only after they'd finished eating that she finally got to ask the super soldiers the burning questions that had occupied her mind all morning.

"How did you know we were going to be attacked?" She fixed Serena with a sharp stare. "You said Artemus

Steele sent you. How did he find out Oscar and Barquiel were going to be in New York today?"

The super soldier took a leisurely sip of her coffee before replying. "We have our own seer."

Cortes stiffened. Mae knew he was thinking of Raya Medeiros, his aunt and the woman who had shattered his core and killed his first familiar when he was sixteen in a bid to dethrone him from his rightful role as the next High Priest of the Medellin coven.

Raya had been the Sorcerer King's seer. Cortes had killed her with his own hands a few months ago, in Prague.

Serena glanced at the Columbian. "She's not that kind of seer. Lily is of divine lineage. She inherited her powers of prophecy from the archangel who gave rise to the Immortal races."

Goosebumps broke out on Mae's skin. Violet had hinted at what the woman who led the Immortals could do. She was destined to be a major player in the war at the End of Days, just as Mae and Artemus Steele were.

Serena must have seen the trepidation in her eyes.

"We should technically not be assisting you," she admitted quietly. "Artemus and his companions had to fight their own battles before the Immortals revealed themselves to them." A cynical smile curved her lips briefly. "And us." She looked over at Lou and Tom. "We had to overcome our demons too. It seems our path was predestined to cross Artemus's and that of the people who rescued us from a fate worse than death when we were but children."

97

The super soldier met Mae's tense stare. "To answer your question, Lily had a vision of us fighting alongside you in New York and Europe. That's how she knew this was inevitable. And she was pretty adamant that you not fall into your enemy's hands."

CHAPTER 13

Serena removed something from her jacket and passed it to Mae.

Mae stared. It was a thin, metal bracelet. She took it, puzzled.

The jewelry was plain and made of a material she'd never seen before. One that warmed her palm and glistened as if it contained a source of light deep within it.

"What is this?"

Hellreaver nudged the bangle curiously with the edge of a blade.

Brimstone took a careful sniff of it. *I smell divine energy in this, my witch.*

"Lily asked Artemus to forge it for you," Serena said. "It's an artifact that will allow you," she glanced at Brimstone and Hellreaver, "and them to resist the magic-infused, nanorobot collars they wanted to enslave you with."

Mae's eyes widened.

"So I was right." Violet's expression had grown flinty. "That thing Oscar put around Mae's neck was made of nanorobots."

"Jeez," Miles muttered. "Looks like I missed quite the party."

Mae's pulse quickened as she studied Serena. "The devils we fought today. They had nanorobots inside them too, didn't they?"

Abraham drew a sharp breath.

"What?!" Bryony mumbled.

Mae explained what they had witnessed that morning.

"Those devils should never have been able to get through my magic the way they did, however tired I was. And they shouldn't have been able to pin down Brimstone and Hellreaver. They were faster and deadlier than the ones we encountered in Prague." She faltered, her tone turning bitter. "There's something else." She met Bryony's stunned gaze. "I sensed Nikolai's Hellfire Magic and Vedran's black magic in those collars and inside Oscar. That's why my spells didn't work on him."

Vlad cursed under his breath. Cortes furrowed his brow.

Mae fisted her hands. "I think Vedran has found a way to use Nikolai's powers against me."

A stark silence fell in the wake of her words.

Bryony's complexion had turned ashen. "Oscar canceled out your magic?!"

"Yes. He and Barquiel were trying to capture me."

"They told Mae they would let us go if she went with them," Violet said darkly at Abraham and Bryony's confused stares.

A wave of incubus energy pulsed across the room and brushed Mae's skin. She met Vlad's furious gaze.

"Do you think Vedran still means to enslave you with the *Marriage of Magic?*"

Mae bit her lip. She couldn't deny that the thought had crossed her mind. The incubus's face darkened.

Serena's puzzled gaze swung between them. "*Marriage of Magic?*"

"It's a ritual that allows one marriage partner to command the magic of the other," a pale-faced Abraham explained distractedly.

"That sounds…unpleasant," Lou murmured.

Bryony regained her composure. "If Vedran is indeed still intent on matching you with Oscar, then there's a good chance he has yet to achieve his goal of securing the first Sorcerer King's soul."

Oscar's face rose before Mae. She shuddered. "I agree. Oscar mentioned something this morning. It looks like they haven't found the *Book of Shadows*."

Tom looked lost. "The book of what now?"

"It's a tome that is said to house the soul of the first man Azazel taught magic to," Serena said quietly before anyone could reply. "It was the price he had to pay for the gift he received from the Third Leader of the Grigori." The super soldier shrugged at their blank stares. "Sebastian is a collector. He knows all kinds of stuff."

"Why did they go after Fire Magic users and try to capture Roman if they hadn't found the *Book of Shadows?*" Violet asked dubiously.

Mae hesitated. "My best guess is they wanted to be ready for when they did."

Cortes leaned his elbows on the table and steepled his hands under his chin. "If I were in Vedran's shoes, I would choose Nikolai as my heir."

Mae's breath caught. The sorcerer watched her closely in the aftermath of his bombshell statement.

"It's not just because his Hellfire Magic could probably open that book," he said in a matter-of-fact tone. "It would be easier to get you to accept a man you love than one you loathe with every fiber of your being."

A muscle jumped in Vlad's cheek.

"However much I hate to agree with Enrique, he has a point," the incubus said reluctantly. "Nikolai is the logical choice for the position of the next Sorcerer King right now."

Mae scowled at her fisted hands. She could only imagine how utterly devastated Nikolai would be if he emerged from the spell controlling him to realize not only what his father had made him do to her and their friends, but what he intended for him. The last thing the sorcerer would want was to assume the title of the man responsible for his mother's death.

She looked up and found herself the focus of a battery of stares.

"Can you fight him?" Bryony asked, troubled. "Really fight him?" She paused. "If it comes to it, can you kill Nikolai?"

"It won't come to that."

Abraham lowered his brows at her curt tone. "You still haven't been able to undo Anya's Illusion Sorcery. Vedran could just order him to subjugate you again."

"Oh." Violet offered him a contrite look. "We forgot to

tell you what with everything that went down today. Mae succeeded in breaking Anya's spell."

Bryony went still.

Abraham's eyes bulged. "She did?!"

"Yeah." Mae started telling the witch and her aide how she'd used Cortes's Arcane Magic to make *Dissever*. She stopped mid-explanation at the sight of their leaden expressions. "What?"

"Like I told you before, you say the most incredible things with the most blasé attitude," Cortes muttered.

Serena's lips twitched.

A familiar energy resonated against Mae's core a second before a rift split the air behind the super soldier. Serena and her companions were on their feet in a heartbeat.

Alicia Calvarro stepped out of the portal. She looked up into the barrels of three guns and froze. Her pupils flashed crimson. Shadows fluttered into life around her as she prepared to transform.

"Wait!" Mae jumped up and stepped between Alicia and Serena. "She's a friend."

Alicia blinked. Recognition dawned in her eyes.

"Oh." Serena lowered her gun. "It's you. I'm sorry, I didn't recognize you for a second there."

"You know this chick?" Lou said suspiciously.

"She's the Queen of the Soul Reapers."

Lou sobered. Tom paled.

Mae squinted. "You guys have met?"

Alicia studied Serena with a faint frown. "You're the super soldier from that time I came to Chicago with Astarte, for that birthday…party…"

Serena and Alicia's faces glazed over a little.

"Shit," the Reaper Queen mumbled. "I did my best to forget what happened that day."

"Don't," Serena groaned. "I still have nightmares about it."

"Oh yeah. We were out of town that week," Violet commented. "Wasn't that when the chicken fought a helldragon? And someone broke Artemus's favorite antique clock?" She grinned. "Also, didn't Haruki accidentally flame the grounds when he was performing a party trick for the kids?"

"A chicken fought a helldragon?" Vlad said dully.

"She's an undead chicken," Miles explained, as if that made all the difference.

"An undead chicken?" Cortes repeated woodenly.

Brimstone's ears twitched with interest.

"Her name is Gertrude." Miles shuddered. "Don't mess with her if she ever crosses your path."

"I hear ten fire engines turned up at the mansion after Haruki nearly burned the whole place down," Violet continued with barely suppressed glee. "Aunt Barbara got an earful from the mayor afterward."

"Oh." Bryony pursed her lips. "I heard about that party."

"We have—*demons* coming to Earth for birthday parties now?!" Abraham spluttered.

"Sebastian and Naomi insisted." Serena sighed and holstered her gun. "Since Artemus and Callie agreed to be the godparents to their first child, they wanted Drake and Astarte to be godparents to their second born." She grimaced. "I've never seen a kid so happy to get gifts and cards from Hell."

Hellreaver vibrated enthusiastically. *My witch, we should go to one of these parties.*

I want to meet that chicken, Brimstone said adamantly.

"I don't," Mae muttered.

Alicia eyed the super soldiers curiously. "What are you doing in New York?" Her gaze dropped to their weapons. "And did Artemus make those? They carry the smell of holy water and Heaven's powers."

"Yeah." Serena tapped her gun lightly with a hand. "He got these babies ready for us in time for this mission."

Mae recalled the shot that had pierced Barquiel's wing. "Wait. Artemus Steele created your weapons and those bullets?!"

"He's a metalsmith." Serena shrugged at her stunned expression. "The best one on Earth. He will forge the weapons we will need to fight the forces of Hell at the End of Days."

A somber silence befell them at that stark statement.

"So, why are you here?" Alicia repeated quizzically.

They told her about that morning.

The Reaper Queen's lips pursed. "The devils you fought had nanorobots inside them?"

"Yes," Serena replied. "We can handle them with our speed and sheer brute strength, but they're hard for these guys to take on, even with magic."

She indicated the witches and sorcerers in the room. Frustration tightened Cortes's face.

"We can't deny that," Violet said bitterly.

Alicia ran a hand through her hair and blew out a heavy sigh. "Then Astarte was right."

Mae stiffened at her tone. "Right about what?"

"Some of her demons encountered a new breed of devils in Hell Deep. She said they could smell alchemy off them. That's why I came here, to find out if you guys knew anything about it."

Mae's stomach lurched. "Alchemy?" She shot an uneasy look at the others. "Could it be—?"

"Dietrich Farago." The lines around Bryony's eyes deepened. "He must be the one behind this."

"Gideon Morgan, the head of the mercenary corps we belong to, accepted a contract on Farago's head two days ago," Serena informed them quietly. "We are to bring him in, dead or alive." She directed a hard look at Mae. "That's the other reason we're coming to Europe with you."

Mae met the super soldier's undaunted gaze, her heart thudding wildly against her ribs. "Alright."

"The Dark Council will know we're coming after them," Lou observed.

A thought came to Mae then. "Shit."

Serena tensed. "What?"

"I better call my boss."

Serena stared at her, nonplussed. Cortes rolled his eyes. Bryony muttered something under her breath.

"Princess, you're gonna give me a heart attack," Vlad grumbled.

CHAPTER 14

TREPIDATION QUICKENED NIKOLAI'S STEPS AS HE MADE HIS way to Oscar's chambers. The sorcerer who had come to seek him out and give him Vedran's message hung back as they approached the suite.

Black magic made the ground tremble when they reached the doors. Nikolai clenched his jaw. Vedran's anger was thickening the air with a pressure that made it hard to breathe.

Alastair let out a nervous sound on his shoulder.

Nikolai touched the crow gently, his stomach roiling as he used his white magic to dampen the brutal effect of the Sorcerer King's power on their bodies. "It's okay."

Alastair relaxed. He ruffled his feathers and bumped Nikolai's hand gratefully with his head.

The sorcerer who had accompanied them swallowed audibly.

"You can leave," Nikolai said curtly.

The man sagged, relief pasted across his pale face. He

turned and scampered back in the direction they had come. He cast a fearful glance at them before disappearing around the corner.

Nikolai could practically hear his thoughts. *Better you than me!*

He steeled himself and opened the door. A wall of black magic pushed him back a foot and wrenched a gasp from his lips. Alastair braced his wings, feathers brushing Nikolai's hair.

White magic throbbed through their cores. It brightened the air around their bodies and eased the suffocating force bearing down on them. A sour taste filled Nikolai's mouth.

Dammit. If this is him annoyed, I don't want to be around when he completely loses it.

His heart pounded heavily as he stepped inside the suite. The source of the oppressive power battering him and Alastair was coming from Oscar's bedroom. He crossed the floor to the partly open door, each step a battle of will against the Sorcerer King's corrupt magic.

The sight that met his eyes when he entered his brother's room rooted his legs to the ground.

Shit.

Oscar floated above his bed inside a translucent sphere of black magic. Vedran stood beside the unconscious sorcerer, his brow furrowed in a scowl, oblivious to his surroundings. Oily bands of corruption writhed around his fingers where he pressed his hands to Oscar's belly.

Oscar jerked and twitched, mouth slack and face deathly pale. Drabek mewled softly where she lay next to his pillow.

Nikolai could tell his brother and the familiar were in pain. He registered the wounds on their bodies before looking at the demon on the other side of the bed.

The Archduke of Hell had assumed Rose's form. She stood watching Vedran and Oscar with her arms crossed and a heavy frown clouding her pretty face.

"What happened?" Nikolai said in a low voice.

Rose glanced at him. "Some unexpected visitors turned up."

Nikolai's hackles rose at her dismissive tone. He bit back a nasty retort. His gaze found Oscar.

"Who did this to him?"

Rose sneered. "Your ex-girlfriend." Crimson flashed in her pupils. Her mocking smile faded. "We almost had her. If those bastards hadn't interfered—"

She flinched at Vedran's warning glare. The Sorcerer King switched his attention to Nikolai.

"I can't undo this magic," he grated out. "It's all twisted around his core." A muscle jumped in his jawline. "Help me."

Nikolai's mouth went dry. He'd never seen his father so agitated.

He must be desperate if he's asking for my help.

He swallowed and approached the bed. The hairs lifted on the back of his neck.

He could feel the wrongness inside Oscar.

The anger that surged through him felt as familiar as his own breath. *Mae Jin, what have you done?!*

Vedran took his hands off the unconscious sorcerer and retracted his shield. Oscar floated gently down onto the sheets.

Nikolai sat gingerly on the edge of the bed. He hesitated before touching Oscar's stomach.

"Can you sense it?" Vedran said sharply.

Blood thumped in Nikolai's ears. "Yes."

The Witch Queen's magic lashed at his hands, strong and hot. *Was she always this powerful?*

He recalled the broken woman he'd left in that church, four weeks ago. Nikolai's chest tightened at the unwelcome feeling suddenly clogging his throat. It wasn't his first time experiencing the conflicting emotion tugging at his heart.

He'd kept it a secret from Oscar and Vedran so far, too ashamed to admit that the devious spell Mae Jin had created to enrapture him and chain him at her side still had a hold on him.

But sometimes, in the darkest hours of the night, when his rage and his frustration at having been lied to and manipulated by the Witch Queen kept him awake, a small, insidious voice told him there was another reason why he had not revealed this weakness to his father and brother.

Irritation had him grinding his teeth. *There is no other reason. It's just the effect of that witch's evil spell.*

He focused on his brother. It took a moment to make out the crimson orb pulsing deep inside Oscar's body. His pulse quickened.

Vedran is right. Her magic is embedded in his core.

Alastair pressed against his neck as Nikolai called on their powers. A pale haze detonated around them.

Rose drew a sharp breath.

The room trembled when his and Alastair's white magic clashed with that of the Witch Queen.

Surprise jolted him in the next instant. "Wait." Dread filled Nikolai's veins with ice at what he could perceive within the chaos that was Oscar's core. "I—I think she put some spells inside him. They are suppressing his powers!"

Vedran's wrath stirred the oppressive air in the room on a wave that made Nikolai's eardrums throb. "Can you undo them?!"

Nikolai's stomach hardened with determination. "I'll try my best."

Vedran took a step forward. "I'll lend you my strength."

"Don't." Rose fixed the Sorcerer King with a glare. "Hellfire Magic is something, but his white magic is incompatible with yours." A muscle twitched in her cheek. "You *know* what happens when a pure black magic core tries to work with a white magic one."

Nikolai frowned at the strained look the demon exchanged with his father. *What are they talking about?*

"Alright," Vedran agreed reluctantly. He clasped Nikolai's shoulder tightly before falling back. "Do your best to save your brother, my son."

Nikolai's throat constricted. He nodded.

We should try to use our Moon Magic.

Alastair squawked in agreement.

The sphere clinging to Oscar's core shuddered and shook when they poured the magic he'd inherited from his mother into it. For a moment, he thought it would shatter.

The Witch Queen's power hummed mockingly in his skull as it wrapped ever tighter around his brother's core. A tortured scream escaped Oscar. His spine bowed off the bed. Drabek fainted.

"What's happening?!" Vedran barked.

Nikolai's eyes shrank to slits. "Give me a minute!"

He reached for his and Alastair's Hellfire Magic. Dark red flames bloomed around them. He threw everything they had at the Witch Queen's magic.

Several things happened in rapid succession.

The sphere trapping Oscar's core opened up like a puzzle, revealing the spell subduing it. Nikolai crushed it with his powers.

The spell vanished immediately.

What?! He froze. *Wait! That—that was too easy!*

His heart stuttered as a complex sequence of golden runes interlaced with demonic and white magic flashed into life under his hands.

Alastair screeched out a warning.

Fuck!

The hidden spell raced all the way up the path he'd created between his and Oscar's cores before he could lift his fingers from his brother's flesh. Nikolai gasped as it blasted him and his familiar clear across the room. Pain bloomed on his back when he struck the far wall. He tasted blood on his tongue as he and Alastair slumped to the ground.

The Sorcerer King's shout reached him dimly through the ringing in his ears. Darkness encroached on the edges of his vision. With it came a flurry of memories that faded along with his consciousness.

CHAPTER 15

VLAD STARED, HIS PULSE ACCELERATING. "YOU DID WHAT?"

"I put a few spells inside Oscar before Vedran rescued him at the warehouse," Mae repeated.

Hellreaver hummed smugly against his witch's chest. Vlad exchanged a startled look with Cortes and the Nolan cousins.

They were in the back of a van taking them to the airport. Lou was driving, with Tom riding shotgun.

"I didn't know that was possible," Violet mumbled.

Miles appeared similarly dumbfounded beside her.

Cortes lowered his brows at Mae. "I suspect she's the only one who could do that."

"Yeah, well, I didn't know it was possible until that moment either," she muttered.

"What do the spells do?" Serena asked curiously in the stilted hush.

The super soldier had chosen to sit with them near the

rear doors. The rest of her team chatted among themselves where they crowded the rest of the vehicle.

Vlad masked a frown. He'd done some research on the mercenary group run by Gideon Morgan that afternoon, before their scheduled pick-up. Considering the circles he belonged to, he was surprised he hadn't heard the guy's name before. He'd ended up having to ask his uncle Yuliy about him after he'd come up with a handful of vague rumors.

It was Gustav Luchok, Yuliy's secretary and Vlad's former tutor, who'd finally uncovered the unsavory truth from one of his trusted sources.

Gideon Morgan and his employees had operated in the shadows for over a decade. They were suspected to be behind some of the most baffling incidents to have rocked the criminal underworlds and political arenas of a range of countries, across several continents. Enabling and reversing coup d'états. Rescuing hostages trapped in regions of the planet no one would send their special forces to. Finding persons of interest who had gone so deep underground to hide from the authorities they might as well be dead.

Assassination.   Intimidation.   Blackmail. Cyberespionage. Counterintelligence.

They operated above the law and under circumstances most governments would not tolerate. Which had led Vlad to one undeniable conclusion.

A greater power supported the super soldiers. One that was even more secretive than Gideon Morgan's group. One every government in the world was wary of.

Vlad clenched his jaw. *The Immortals.*

He didn't know how he felt about a shadowy society of supernatural beings playing with the fate of mankind as if they were chess pieces on an invisible board. It left a sour taste in his mouth, even though he wasn't completely human himself.

From the guarded way Cortes occasionally watched Serena and her team, it seemed the Columbian had gleaned the same unpleasant facts he had. He looked as thrilled with his findings as Vlad was.

It didn't matter that Violet had reassured them the Immortals were working for the betterment of humanity. Evil acts were more often than not performed in the name of the greater good.

Besides, he and Cortes were used to being the sharks in their respective oceans. Finding out an apex predator they'd known nothing about had been waltzing about in their territories was unsettling.

Vlad focused on what Mae was saying.

"*Seal* shuts down someone's access to their magic," she told Serena. "It's a nasty spell."

The super soldier raised an eyebrow. "It sounds like you have prior experience of it."

Mae shuddered. "Yeah, well, someone tried it on me a short while back. They got pretty close to scrambling my brains in the process."

A low growl left Brimstone. The fox was no doubt recalling the incident at the U.S. Army facility on Staten Island, when they had been taken prisoner by the New York coven and the Dark Council.

Mae stroked the familiar's head soothingly. His hackles settled.

"And you—" Serena waved a vague hand, "just copied the spell?"

"Yes."

The super soldier clocked Violet and Miles's uneasy expressions.

"I get the feeling you're making something very complicated sound very simple," she told Mae drily.

"She is," Cortes grunted.

Mae avoided the sorcerer's piercing stare.

"What about the other spells?" Serena asked.

"*Reveal* lets me track down anyone with demonic powers or black magic if they are close enough for their energy signature to hit my radar."

Serena narrowed her eyes slightly. "By radar, you mean you can see stuff? Like a GPS?"

Lou glanced at them in the rearview mirror. The super soldier was frowning.

Vlad's shoulders tightened. *Looks like we're going to have to add keen hearing to their abilities.*

"Sort of," Mae said, either oblivious to the fact that the super soldiers in the van were paying close attention to her words, or not really caring that they were. "But it only applies to magic and demonic energy." She paused and scratched her head awkwardly. "I, er, can however see all the magic cores in New York without that spell."

Lou's frown deepened. A wary stillness came over some of the super soldiers.

Serena was silent for a moment. "And the third spell?"

"That's the one I'm hoping will do the most damage." A fierce expression brightened Mae's face. "It's reserved for Nikolai."

Cortes stiffened.

Vlad's stomach lurched. *Wait. Don't tell me she—?!*

"You put *Dissever* inside Oscar?!" Violet gasped.

Mae smiled savagely. "Yes."

"Whoa," Miles mumbled.

Cortes pressed his lips together. "You think Nikolai will trigger your spell and it will somehow counter the Illusion Sorcery he's under?"

Mae nodded.

"How can you be so sure?" Vlad couldn't mask his doubt either. "For all you know, Vedran could free Oscar on his own."

Mae's jaw set in a mutinous line. "He's already using Nikolai's powers to overcome my magic. He will do so again. I'm certain of it."

If Serena detected the underlying tension thrumming between him and Mae, she gave no indication of it.

She leaned her elbows on her knees, her expression calculating. "Does that mean Nikolai Stanisic will be freed from the magic that is currently obscuring his mind?"

Mae hesitated for the first time.

"I don't know," she admitted in a small voice. Some of the fight drained out of her. "My magic will be affected by Oscar's core to an extent, as well as the distance between us. There's a good chance the Illusion Sorcery Nikolai is under won't shatter completely, even if he comes into direct contact with my spell."

A tense hush fell in the wake of her words.

"You'll have another opportunity when we find him," Serena said quietly.

Mae smiled faintly at the super soldier's confident

tone. "Thanks."

Vlad's gut twisted. He looked away.

Shit. I should be the one comforting her.

He knew the reason he was acting like an asshole right now. He didn't want to lose Mae. And he was petrified he would the moment she undid the spell on Nikolai.

From the shrewd look Serena shot his way from under her lashes, the super soldier could guess what was on his mind. This irritated him even more.

Tarang stirred where he sat on the lap of three super soldiers busy braiding his fur. He made a worried sound, in tune with Vlad's emotions as always.

"By the way, did you and Anya make up?" Mae asked Cortes.

The sorcerer's expression turned sour. "She promised she'd listen to me when I come back."

Popo bobbed his head. "I'm sure the queen of our hearts will welcome us with open arms and hug us to her generous bosom when we—"

Cortes clamped his beak shut with a hand.

"Not one more word out of your trap," he threatened.

Lou grimaced. "That parrot is a pervert."

Serena observed Tarang. "He looks handsome with plaits."

The tiger huffed, pleased. Vlad narrowed his eyes at his familiar.

Tarang pretended he hadn't seen his accusing look and rumbled something at Brimstone. The demon fox raised his head where he was lying by Mae's feet. His ears cocked to and fro.

Mae's expression grew pinched. "No. We're not

dropping by Artemus's mansion just so you and Tarang can 'hang out' with the Hellhound."

Brimstone drooped. Hellreaver hummed.

Mae took on a long-suffering air. "I don't know why the chicken is undead, Hell. We'll find out when we go to Chicago one day."

"The chicken was the victim of…unforeseen circumstances," Serena explained diplomatically. She studied Hellreaver with the look of someone who wasn't sure if the other party had a screw loose. "He wants to meet Gertrude?"

"Yeah."

"Does that idiot have a death wish?" Violet muttered.

Hellreaver vibrated indignantly against his mistress's chest.

The van slowed and stopped, bringing the impending argument to a close. The super soldiers spilled out the side doors and started unloading their belongings. Which didn't amount to much compared to the arsenal they were packing.

Serena opened the rear doors and jumped out. Vlad stepped onto the tarmac after her. His eyes widened.

He'd been expecting a functional, military aircraft for their trip to Europe, the type mercenaries were renowned for using. The sleek airplane before them was anything but that.

Miles's eyes shone as he stared at its graceful lines. "That's cool."

Suspicion clouded Cortes's face. "Isn't that the newfangled Gulfstream that's expected to hit the market next year?"

Serena looked somewhat resigned as she grabbed a duffel bag from the van. "Yeah."

"Wait." Violet was staring at the golden lion symbol painted on the tail. She pointed a stiff finger at the aircraft. "Is this Sebastian's new jet? The one he and Callie kept arguing about and making bets on who'd land a contract for it first?!"

Realization finally dawned as Vlad studied the emblem.

"Sebastian? As in Sebastian Theodore Dante Lancaster?" He turned to Serena. "The man who owns half of England?!"

"Lancaster is the Sphinx?" Cortes said guardedly.

"I'm afraid so." Serena grimaced at their accusing looks. "He rented the jet to Gideon for this mission."

"Charged him double what it's worth, the cunning bastard," Lou muttered darkly.

He headed past them with a backpack and several bags of ammo.

"It's not like Gideon can't afford it," Tom said cheerfully, lugging three crates of assault rifles behind him like he was taking a dog for a walk.

Lou scowled at the super soldier. "How about I ask him to deduct your salary from our expenses?"

Tom's face fell. "I thought you were my friend."

The aircraft door opened to reveal an affable flight attendant. His expression glazed over a little when he saw the arguing super soldiers. He ignored the pair and beamed at the rest of them.

"Welcome aboard the *Dante 3*."

CHAPTER 16

A MUSCLE JUMPED IN VEDRAN'S JAWLINE AS HE WATCHED Nikolai and Oscar.

The brothers lay in adjacent beds in the Dark Council's infirmary. They and their familiars had remained unconscious since Nikolai had attempted to free Oscar of the Witch Queen's magic.

A bevy of sorcerers and witches scurried about the chamber. They'd tried all kinds of magic, potions, and medicines to revive the Sorcerer King's heirs, so far to no avail. Their fearful gazes kept darting to the man observing their efforts with a heavy scowl.

Barquiel swallowed a sigh.

Vedran's wrath was making the air burn with a coldness that would soon freeze the blood in the veins of the men and women attempting to save his sons.

"How about you calm down?" the demon murmured.

Vedran whirled around and glowered at him.

The corruption that detonated across the infirmary

rattled the windows and made the lights flicker. The Dark Council healers covered their heads with their arms and dropped to the floor with terrified whimpers. A few passed out.

"Don't tell me what to do, demon!" Vedran spat, his eyes bubbling with darkness.

Barquiel brushed the specks of dirt drifting from the ceiling off his shoulder and met the Sorcerer King's glare, undaunted. "Throwing a hissy fit isn't going to help your sons." He waved a hand vaguely. "Time will."

Vedran flinched. Though the movement was infinitesimal and he recovered his composure in an instant, it surprised Barquiel nonetheless.

It also gave the demon hope.

"They—aren't dying?" Vedran grated out.

"No." Barquiel shrugged. "I would know." He glanced at the motionless men on the beds. "You should be able to tell if you touch them. Oscar is on the mend. And Nikolai should wake up soon. Whatever Mae Jin put inside Oscar just stunned him."

Vedran hesitated. His nails sank into his palms.

"You believe neither of them will suffer any permanent damage from that witch's magic?" he asked in a more measured tone. "I can still sense some of it inside Oscar."

"No, they won't."

Barquiel wished to an extent that his answer were a lie. He could just about tolerate Oscar in small doses. Seeing the sorcerer meet his demise would not upset him.

Vedran's shoulders loosened fractionally. Barquiel could tell how much the question had cost him. The Sorcerer King was a man used to having all the answers.

Having to rely on me when he is at his weakest is probably sticking in his craw.

Of all the Sorcerer Kings he'd worked with since the first man Azazel gifted with magic, Vedran was the one he trusted the least. Not just because the demon couldn't get a read on the guy.

Vedran Borojevic had been born with the kind of twisted soul that would have made him a perfect commander in Hell's army. Satanael himself would have been impressed by his ideas and deeds.

Barquiel had realized a long time ago that it wasn't just that the man was evil. He had an insatiable appetite. For power. For authority. For absolute dominion over all humankind.

To put it simply, Vedran wanted to be a god.

Anyone who didn't know him would assume he was the product of a miserable childhood, unloved and rejected by those he had held dear. That couldn't be further from the truth.

Vedran had been born the fifth son of a wealthy, noble couple. His parents and siblings had doted on him from the moment he opened his eyes and had gifted him with everything he had ever wished for. Not a single member of his family had been a sorcerer or a witch.

Which had made killing them with magic child's play.

Vedran had been thirteen at the time, nearly an adult in the eyes of the sixteenth century European society he had grown up in. He had also been a Dark Council member and an apprentice to the incumbent Sorcerer King for three whole years.

When his master had asked him why he murdered his

kin, his reply had chilled the air in the Dark Council chamber.

"Because they weren't needed. Their existence was a shackle that would only have gotten in the way of my plans."

That day, Barquiel had realized something fundamental about the boy who would become the next Sorcerer King. For the young Vedran, executing his family had been a matter of expedience and another way to show his devotion to his master.

Now that he sat on the throne, he expected the same from his followers, as well as his own flesh and blood. Hence the *Trial of Blood*, the custom he had revived and which had seen Oscar and Nikolai emerge as the sole survivors of a brutal ritual that had claimed the lives of all their siblings.

Barquiel suppressed a grimace.

The magic community had always believed that the Sorcerer King was a direct descendant of the previous ruler. This was yet another lie, one often perpetuated by the sorcerer who occupied that role at the time.

The fact of the matter was that only those powerful enough to survive the secret rite they had to undergo to inherit the mantle of the Sorcerer King could be considered candidates for the throne. For that purpose, several potential heirs were chosen, not just from the current king's bloodline if they satisfied the stringent criteria, but from the wider magic community at large. Succession didn't adhere so much to a hereditary monarchy as it did a meritocracy.

A sound drew Barquiel's gaze and had Vedran's head snapping around. Oscar moaned softly.

The Dark Council sorcerers and witches scattered in Vedran's path as he stormed across the room. Oscar blinked his eyes open when his sire stopped beside his bed.

"Fa—father?" he mumbled.

Pain scored deep lines in the sorcerer's pale face.

"It's okay," Vedran said stiffly. "You're safe now."

The Sorcerer King touched his son's forehead. Oscar swallowed. His eyelids fluttered closed.

Those in the infirmary might assume what they were witnessing was the love of a father for his children. Barquiel knew otherwise. The only person Vedran cared about was himself. His sons were just a means to an end.

The demon couldn't help but feel a sliver of admiration for Mae Jin as he observed the motionless sorcerers. *Say what you want about the girl, she knows how to fight dirty when she needs to.*

Vedran stood unmoving for a moment. His frowning gaze swung to Nikolai. He fixed his second son with a long stare before whirling around and striding past Barquiel.

"Let's go," he ordered curtly.

Barquiel followed him reluctantly. He knew that look. His worst fears were realized when Vedran headed into the bowels of the castle.

"It's not ready yet," the demon protested as they descended a flight of stairs.

"It's ready when I say it's ready." Vedran shot him an irate look. "What are you so afraid of?"

That you'll mess this up.

Barquiel swallowed the bitter words threatening to spill past his lips.

"That you will ruin your chance of getting your hands on that which you seek," he said instead.

"How nice of you to care." Vedran's tone turned mocking. "Why, you almost sound like you cherish me, demon."

Barquiel fisted his hands.

There was only one reason he had served Davor and all the Sorcerer Kings who had come after him. He took a deep breath, quelled his rage, and focused on the goal that had been his since the aftermath of the war where he had vanquished Azazel.

Just a little bit more. Then I'll be able to bring you back.

CHAPTER 17

A DOOR APPEARED AT THE END OF THE SEEMINGLY ENDLESS flights of stairs and winding corridors. It was clad in iron and steel and reinforced with enough protective spells and demonic energy to repel an entire army.

"It would be nice if Dietrich could work in an airy tower full of light one of these days," Vedran muttered as they approached it. "Must he always skulk in dark corners?"

Since Barquiel usually rifted to this place, he'd never particularly paid attention to the ambiance. "You know he lives in fear of the Immortals ever catching a whiff of his scent."

Vedran furrowed his brow. "Once we rule the world of man, we'll have to do something about those Immortals."

Barquiel didn't respond to this. Partly because he had no interest in that plan, but mostly because Vedran was insane if he thought he could take on the Immortal race.

The Immortals weren't powerful just because of their

ability to survive death. They possessed gifts on par with the magic Azazel had passed on to mankind. Gifts bestowed upon them by one of Heaven's oldest and most powerful warriors.

The acrid stench of sulfur and the nefarious chemicals Dietrich usually worked with washed over them when Vedran opened the door to the lab. The Sorcerer King grimaced. He erected a thin barrier of black magic around himself to repel the toxic fumes and crossed the threshold.

The chamber they entered would have been ice cold and dark if not for the furnaces that Dietrich kept burning at all times. The Immortal alchemist didn't react to their presence. He was working on something at the far end of the chamber, too focused on his task to pay heed to anything else.

Barquiel's heart sank. An erratic, dark light outlined Dietrich's silhouette in the golden glow of the fires.

Dammit. Is that what I think it is?!

Vedran's eyes flared. His steps quickened, only to falter when he caught sight of the corpses dotting the ground.

His lips pressed together. "You should tidy this place up. We didn't lend you those demons for decoration."

The fiends feasting on the remains of Dietrich's victims shrank back into the shadows at the sight of Barquiel, gristle and blood dripping from deformed jaws and talons.

The Immortal flinched and whirled around at the sound of Vedran's voice. His eyes rounded.

"Oh. I'm sorry." Dietrich cut his eyes to Barquiel before giving the Sorcerer King a flustered look. "I didn't know you were coming to visit."

Vedran lowered his brows. "Do I need permission to go somewhere in my own castle?"

"I—" Dietrich hesitated and shook his head, "no, of course not."

Barquiel's disquiet grew. He could tell from the Immortal's disheveled appearance and glassy expression that he had not slept in days.

He only gets like that when he's close to completing a project.

The demon cursed himself all over again for not having the foresight to distract Vedran and stop him from coming to the lab.

At this rate, he may very well ruin our plans.

Dietrich was the only person in the entire world who knew what the demon truly wanted. Having promised his soul to Hell, the man had nothing to gain from betraying him. Not that he had ever wanted to do so. The Immortal revered Barquiel.

It was clear from the tightness of his shoulders and the furtive glance he gave him that he didn't like their current situation either. This only deepened the demon's dismay.

Vedran seemed oblivious to their silent exchange. He stopped next to the Immortal and stared at what floated above the stone workbench. The bursts of radiance it emitted made his eyes gleam with a sinister brilliance.

"Is this it?" he said with a quiet intensity that belied his excitement. "Is this the precursor to the alternative compass?"

Barquiel's stomach churned as he joined them. He studied the boiling, inky mass. Something was reforming and imploding on itself within the maelstrom of crackling shadows, its shape still undefined.

It had taken months for them to get to this point after countless failed experiments. Vedran's confident assertion that there were other ways to find the *Book of Shadows* when he'd confronted the Witch Queen in Philadelphia during the Annual Grand Meeting had proven to be disastrously wrong.

After spending weeks using his dark magic and countless malevolent artifacts attempting to locate the book, the Sorcerer King had finally admitted defeat. He had instead tasked Dietrich with finding a way to make an artificial compass that could mimic the *Book of Light*.

The Immortal genius had deduced early on that they would need Fire Magic to open the artifact he was attempting to recreate. Their failure to capture Roman Volkov, the most powerful Fire Magic user in the world, in Prague had ended up being a mixed blessing. Because it had revealed an even more explosive alternative in the form of Hellfire Magic, as well as the sorcerer who had seemingly mastered it in no time at all.

Vedran's interest in his second son had been roused after witnessing his white magic and his ability to tap into ley lines in Philadelphia. Bringing his wayward offspring back into the fold became his singular pursuit after the events in the Czech Republic.

Deceiving Nikolai with Anya Mendes's Illusion Sorcery while isolating and attempting to subjugate Mae Jin at the same time had been an ambitious plan, one that the Sorcerer King deemed a success even though they'd failed to catch the Witch Queen.

It was only in the last month that Dietrich's attempts to fuse alchemy, magic, and the souls of humans and ghouls to produce an artificial compass had started to bear fruit. What Barquiel was looking at was the best version he'd seen yet.

Judging from Vedran's zealous expression, he thought so too.

"Well?" he said impatiently.

"Yes." Dietrich swallowed. "I just need to add the last ingredient to see if it will work."

Barquiel's pulse raced as the Immortal walked over to a cold cabinet. He removed a vial from a shelf. It contained a minute amount of dark red liquid. It was the last of Mae Jin's blood, which they'd obtained in Philadelphia and in New York.

Dietrich extracted a drop of it and returned to the bench.

"You might want to stand back for this," he warned nervously.

"I have a better idea," Vedran muttered.

Dietrich tensed when the Sorcerer King raised a black magic shield around him.

"You're my most prized scientist and the weakest one among us," Vedran said coolly at his surprised look. "I can't let anything happen to you."

The Immortal looked doubly skittish at that. He steeled himself and released the scarlet droplet. Barquiel's gaze followed its descent into the storm cloud of alchemy and magic, his heartbeat loud in his ears.

The Witch Queen's blood glowed a dazzling crimson as it struck it.

For a moment, nothing happened.

A silent implosion rocked the chamber with enough

force to make the air quiver and shake the ground. Glass shattered all around them. The demons screeched.

Vedran grunted as he was pushed back half a dozen feet. Barquiel clenched his jaw and dug his heels into the floor. The forces battering the lab abated with a suddenness that made the demon's ears ring.

The seething shroud of darkness above the bench began to dissipate. A circular object emerged from the fading maelstrom, its surface shining dully.

Dietrich drew a sharp breath. Barquiel fisted his hands, elation and frustration tightening his chest in equal measure.

It was a metal compass without a needle. One that looked identical to the *Book of Light* in all respects bar the absence of the complex runes that had scored the original version.

"Thank you."

Vedran approached the bench with a rapt expression. He reached out and took hold of the compass, barely aware of their presence.

For one wild moment, Barquiel was tempted to rip his throat open.

"Rest assured. You shall be rewarded generously for this feat," the Sorcerer King told Dietrich in a grave voice, his eyes still locked on the artifact.

A muscle jumped in the Immortal's jawline. He bowed his head. "I live to serve you, my liege."

His gaze flickered to Barquiel, his regret and bitterness on full show for a scant second.

"What of our devil troops?" Vedran tore his gaze reluctantly from the compass and fixed Dietrich with a hard stare. "Are things progressing well with your nanorobot experiments?"

"Yes, they are." The Immortal paused. "New York was a useful test. I should be able to fix the flaws the super soldiers exposed in my devils."

Dietrich's involvement in the secret super soldier program a rogue branch of the U.S. Army had funded for over half a century had ended up being more useful than even Barquiel had thought it would be. The project was abruptly terminated when the Immortals got involved and the most advanced subjects of the decades-long research now lived in the wild under their protection.

Barquiel was aware Dietrich would sacrifice a limb to get his hands on one of those super soldiers. Somehow, he suspected the Immortal might soon have that opportunity.

Mae Jin is bound to come to Europe to try and rescue Nikolai. The demon frowned. *And if the super soldiers got involved in New York, then it means the Immortals have finally made their move.*

CHAPTER 18

ARE WE THERE YET? HELLREAVER WHINED.

Mae's eye twitched. "For the hundredth time, no!"

Vlad pinched the bridge of his nose. Serena's hands slowed on the gun she was cleaning, her shoulders knotting. One of the super soldiers said a choice swear word.

Cortes slugged down his whiskey and slammed his glass on the table where he sat with Mae and Vlad.

Violet pursed her lips at the Columbian from across the aisle. "Are you sure you should be doing that? I mean, we're about to potentially walk into a war zone."

"I'm drowning my sorrows." The sorcerer scowled at Hellreaver. "I either drink or I'll shoot him."

"You and me both, pal," Lou muttered three rows ahead.

Hellreaver sniffed.

"Now, now, my Enrique." Popo stroked Cortes's cheek

soothingly with a wing. "All this tension is bad for your blood pressure. Never mind your manly vigor."

"Stop that," the sorcerer snapped. His jaundiced gaze swung from Hellreaver to Mae. "He wasn't like this on our last trip," he said accusingly.

Mae's expression grew pinched. "That's because no one gave him any sugar."

Everyone looked at Miles.

"What?" He shrugged. "It was only Skittles."

Hellreaver zoomed down the aisle with a *Wheee!*

"He's used to a high-protein diet."

"Well, now you know what happens when he has processed carbs," Miles said helpfully.

Mae tensed when she spied the weapon slinking innocently toward the flight deck. "That little—!"

Lou snatched a recalcitrant Hellreaver by the blade before she could jump to her feet and stop him.

"How about you park your sorry ass by your mistress?" the super soldier said thinly. "Ain't nobody wants a replay of what happened two hours ago."

Several people groaned. A headache thrummed between Mae's temples as she recalled the incident in question.

Hellreaver had waltzed into the cockpit to find out where they were while no one was looking and scared the bejeezus out of the pilot and co-pilot. Five bladder-loosening minutes later, aided by *Wind Fury* and the buffering spells Cortes, Violet, and Miles raised, the men had finally regained control of the nose-diving aircraft some thousand feet before it hit the surface of the Atlantic.

Everyone had needed a drink after that, including the pilot and the co-pilot. Chris the flight attendant had finished a bottle of wine all by himself.

A crimson aura bloomed around Hellreaver. *Unhand me this instant, you naked monkey!*

Mae's headache intensified to the point where she suspected an imp with a war hammer was pounding the inside of her skull.

Serena put her gun down, rose, and took Hellreaver from Lou before she could intervene.

"Listen here," the super soldier said coldly, nose to knuckleduster. "Either zip your blades and sit down quietly for the rest of this flight or I'm throwing you off this aircraft."

Hellreaver quivered belligerently. *Oh yeah? I can float, lady!*

Serena narrowed her eyes. She looked at Mae. "Did he just say something asinine like he can float?"

Mae blinked. "How'd you know?"

Serena's frown deepened. "Because I live with a Hellhound who can be just as idiotic." Her gaze shifted to Brimstone and Tarang. "You two. Come here."

The fox and the tiger got up and padded over.

"Whoa," Violet muttered. "It's like her words are wired to their brainstems."

Mae was similarly impressed. Vlad on the other hand looked like he had words to say on the subject of someone else commanding his familiar.

Serena put Hellreaver on the floor.

"Sit on him," she ordered Brimstone and Tarang.

The demon fox's tail drooped a little.

I don't know about that, he said warily. *What if he bites us? He looks pretty bitey to me.*

The tiger rumbled his own doubts.

Serena rolled her eyes. "You have fangs. Just bite him back if he bites you."

Hellreaver tried to heave her off him, to no avail. *Argh! Why is this damn woman so strong?!*

"Because I have divine powers," Serena muttered.

"Because she has divine powers," Mae said thinly at the same time. She paused and squinted at the super soldier. "Are you sure you can't read minds?"

Brimstone and Tarang gingerly squished an annoyed Hellreaver. There were audible sighs all round.

"If you're a good weapon, I'll give you plenty of demons to eat," Serena said.

Hellreaver stilled. *You will?*

"Yes."

Alright, he said reluctantly.

He hugged the floor, as quiet as a mouse.

"Thank God for that," Cortes muttered.

"Can you people do something about her?"

They turned.

Chris the flight attendant was struggling to hold a floppy and distinctly green-looking Millie in his arms. "I found her being sick in the toilet."

Miles rushed over and took the boa constrictor off him. "Sorry, she's not good with altitude."

He murmured comforting words to his familiar while she coiled around his waist like a limp, ten-foot-long linguine.

"The boa constrictor can go to the toilet?" one of the super soldiers remarked with a healthy dose of skepticism.

"She's very smart," Miles said proudly.

"She tried to eat the food offering at Mr. Ho-Nam's funeral," Mae reminded him coolly.

"It was only because we skipped breakfast," Miles protested.

Violet snorted. "That funeral was hilarious."

Mae cut her eyes to her.

The witch sobered. "Sorry."

"Was that the one where a widow punched you?" Cortes shrugged at Mae's pinched look. "Abraham blabbed."

"A widow punched you?" Serena said.

"She had a mean left hook," Mae grumbled.

Vlad watched Chris the flight attendant head back into the galley with a resigned air. "That guy has nerves of steel considering what he's been through so far today."

"He's been on a plane with Smokey before," Serena said sourly. "Having to entertain a bored Hellhound in a confined metal space thousands of feet in the air builds character."

A crunching sound drew everyone's stare.

Tom had his feet up on the backrest of a chair and was eating a bowl of popcorn with gusto.

"This is the best trip ever!" he said with a grin.

Lou furrowed his brow. "You're such an ass."

Someone threw an empty carton of juice at Tom.

"Hey!"

He responded to the attack with a barrage of popcorn. Things went rapidly downhill after that. Tarang grinned at the growing mayhem. Brimstone wheezed, eyes shrinking into merry slits.

Hellreaver tried to wriggle out from under them. *Lemme see! Lemme see!*

Mae rubbed her temples and started counting.

Vlad curled a lip as miscellaneous projectiles whooshed above his head. "Jesus."

"Shoot me," Cortes groaned.

Much to his annoyance, Popo bobbed on his shoulder and called out encouragement and suggestions to the brawling super soldiers.

Violet bit her lip. "Sebastian's gonna be pissed if we ruin his new jet."

"Sebastian is the least of their problems," Serena growled. Her dagger appeared in her hand. "I swear, I will cut you guys if you don't pipe down *right now!*"

Lou cracked his knuckles, ready to knock some heads together. Chris emerged from the galley at the sounds of the commotion. His expression turned glassy. He twisted on his heels and disappeared.

The sound of a cork being popped followed.

"Is that guy okay?" Miles asked worriedly.

"This is ridiculous." Mae threw her hands up in the air, sighed, and rose to her feet. "How about you all calm down and behave like adu—?"

A piece of popcorn hit her in the eye as she turned.

"Oh." Tom flashed her a sickly smile. "Sorry."

Mae lowered her brows. Magic flared around her. Everyone's eyes locked on the crimson spell bomb above her right hand.

Popo squawked worriedly.

"Want me to put them in time out?" Mae asked Serena between gritted teeth. "Just say the word."

Calm down, my witch, Brimstone urged.

By the time the *Dante 3* landed in Budapest, Chris the flight attendant was mildly inebriated, Cortes had a migraine, and Mae's jaws ached from grinding her teeth.

"I'm never getting on a plane with them again," Vlad grumbled.

They were standing near the jet, waiting for their ride. The incubus's expression was pinched as he watched the super soldiers innocently stacking crates and bags of ammunition a short distance away.

Lou grunted. "They grow on you."

"So does fungus," Cortes muttered.

A cold wind blew across the tarmac. Mae shivered.

It was nearly dawn.

She stilled a moment later, her unfocused gaze on the pale band brightening the horizon.

Vlad's tone turned wary. "Mae?"

Mae's pulse quickened. Heat surged through her bond with Brimstone and Hellreaver as she extended her magic outward as far as she could.

My witch, the fox warned.

Her heart sank at what she couldn't sense. "I know."

"What's wrong?" Serena asked guardedly.

"I can't pick up Oscar's core with *Reveal*."

Violet traded a troubled look with Cortes and Miles. "What does that mean?"

Serena frowned at the hazy lights of the city to the north as a convoy of dark SUVs with tinted windows appeared on the edge of the airfield. "It means we're going to struggle to find the weasel."

A light snow flurry spiraled down from the overcast sky, mirroring their somber mood.

CHAPTER 19

NIKOLAI WAS DREAMING. HE WAS STANDING IN AN amphitheater, at the top of a palace. Marble pillars spanned the vast space around him, pale giants rising to support a domed roof with a ceiling open to a cloudless night sky.

A crowd occupied the arena.

Their chants echoed in his ears, a relentless sound that matched his racing pulse. Though he could not make out the faces of the men and women filling the packed seats, Nikolai knew they hated him.

Alastair trembled on his shoulder. The crow's claws dug into his flesh as he clung desperately to him. His familiar's fear and distress resonated inside him.

Nikolai startled. The crow looked young.

No! It's not just Alastair!

He realized he was in the body of his sixteen-year-old self.

Movement opposite drew his eyes before he could

make sense of what was happening to him. Dread squeezed his chest.

Moonlight shone on a young man wrapped in a haze of black magic and wielding a wicked sword dripping with blood. A lynx sat beside him, her eyes aglow with a venomous light.

It was his brother, Oscar. Except he couldn't recall ever seeing him with that look on his face. A look that said he wanted to rip Nikolai's heart out of his chest and crush it with his bare hands.

It was then Nikolai realized that he too was covered in blood.

His breath stuttered. He looked down and witnessed the crimson stains on his spear and clothes. *What—what is this?!*

A whimper had him whirling around. Bile burned the back of his throat.

Bodies covered the south end of the arena. Though he could barely discern their bloodied and battered features where they were piled atop one another, he knew they were his siblings.

A girl no older than ten raised her hand weakly toward him where she lay amidst the gruesome stack, her broken legs askew and the gash in her left temple exposing a smashed skull.

"Help...me...brother!" she mumbled.

Her breath left her lips on a puff of air that misted briefly in front of her face. Her arm flopped limply over the chest of the dead boy she rested upon, her frozen gaze locked on something only she could see.

Nikolai knew that she had just passed from this world. *Please! Dear God, no!*

He didn't realize he'd uttered the words out loud until Oscar laughed.

"God?! Are you insane, little brother?!" the sorcerer scoffed. "There is no God here tonight!" His tone hardened with a fury that threatened to scorch the air. "There are only the eyes of our king." He jutted his chin. "Now, bow before me. I shall grant you the mercy of a swift death if you crawl to me on your hands and knees and lick my boots."

Riotous guffaws erupted from the rows of onlookers watching the gory ritual.

Nikolai's gaze found the silent man on the throne at the head of the arena. Flanked by his guards and the concubines who served him in bed, the Sorcerer King observed him with a cold, dispassionate stare. Several of the women were sobbing quietly, their bereft gazes fixed on their dead children.

Guilt paralyzed Nikolai. Even though he couldn't recall what happened, he knew he was responsible for some of the murders. His heart thumped painfully with his next breath.

Vedran's right hand was clamped around the wrist of a dark-haired woman sitting beside him. Tears streamed down her beautiful, gaunt face.

Nikolai's mind went blank.

"Mother?!" he said hoarsely.

Moon Magic flickered weakly in Gabriela Stanisic's eyes as she watched him, pain rendering her pale. Vedran's black magic scorched her flesh where he thwarted her attempts to rise from her seat, his powers suppressing her core.

Rage flooded Nikolai's veins. *"Let her go, you bastard!"*

He didn't realize he'd charged toward the Sorcerer King until Oscar blocked his path. Metal glinted on his left.

Nikolai ducked beneath his brother's sword and slashed his thigh with his spear. Oscar scowled and cast a spell bomb at him.

Nikolai deflected the black magic orb with a snap of his wrists and sent it flying into the crowd. Someone screamed. He didn't even bother to look to see who had been struck down by the wayward attack, his attention fully focused on his foe.

An ugly expression twisted Oscar's face. He moved.

Nikolai ground his teeth as he parried the blistering blows his brother delivered with blade and magic. Oscar pushed him back again and again, their wild dance taking them across the amphitheater and drawing enthusiastic shouts and jeers from the crowd.

A faint sound had him glancing toward the dais where Vedran sat with his mother. Gabriela had bitten her lip until she'd drawn blood. She swallowed another groan.

Horror chilled Nikolai to the bone when he saw her broken wrist.

Vedran held the twisted limb in a tight grip, heedless of his favorite concubine's suffering. His gaze bore into Nikolai like a black hole seeking to suck in all his hope.

Heat seared Nikolai's core at the same time Alastair's fury scorched his mind, the crow releasing a screech that silenced the baited audience. A pale haze bloomed around them as they drew on the power the Sorcerer King had forbidden them to use. The white magic that lived in their souls, a gift from Gabriela Stanisic.

"No," his mother mumbled.

She shook her head numbly, her gaze beseeching him not to do the unthinkable. Nikolai shut his eyes. There was no way out of this and they both knew it.

Resolve knotted his belly. He opened his eyes and glared at Oscar.

The sorcerer grunted as he started fighting back with a relentlessness born of desperation. Rage thickened the black aura around him when he was finally forced to cede ground for the first time in their battle.

He raised a hand, his lip curling in a distasteful sneer. *"Rot."*

Black magic overwhelmed Nikolai, bringing him to his knees and robbing him of breath. Alastair swayed and fell. Nikolai caught the crow and clutched him protectively to his chest as Oscar's powers started crushing their flesh.

Black spots swarmed his vision. The taste of iron filled his mouth. He coughed up blood, his consciousness flickering.

Gabriela's scream roused him in the next instant.

Nikolai turned his head with agonizing slowness, the muscles in his neck feeling like they were tearing as he resisted the debilitating force holding him prisoner.

"No! Please! *I beg of you!*" his mother pleaded with the man beside her, her shattered wrist forgotten. "Spare him! I will do any—!"

The spell bomb struck her left temple, killing her instantly.

Nikolai stopped breathing. Vedran's pupils flared.

The crowd fell silent.

Oscar's cold voice rang around the amphitheater in the frozen hush. "She distracted me."

This...isn't happening!

Nikolai blinked dazedly, disbelief making his head spin.

A woman laughed, one with red hair and hateful gray eyes that matched those of the sorcerer before him. She stopped when Vedran cut his gaze to her.

Black magic exploded around the Sorcerer King. He stood up, his fingers still clasped around the wrist of the dead woman slumped in the chair beside him.

"Why did you do that?!"

His vengeful roar shook the arena and brought dust down from the ceiling. The spectators shrank back in fear. The pressure crushing Nikolai started to ease.

Oscar swallowed and retreated a step, his expression uncertain. "I—"

A forlorn sound rent the air. Nikolai looked down, his heartbeat a heavy sound that filled his wretched world. Alastair was crying, deep shudders quaking his tiny body.

Nikolai's vision blurred with unshed tears as the agony of their loss threatened to drown him in an ocean of dark despair.

The rage that swelled deep within him with his next breath ignited his belly with a power that would not be denied. Alastair's eyes flashed white, his core responding with a wrath that matched his own.

The crow lent him his power as he climbed shakily to his feet.

Light filled the arena, drawing cries from those it blinded. Nikolai's gaze did not waver as he headed for the one he blamed for his mother's death and the misery that had been visited upon him and all his dead siblings.

The Sorcerer King lowered his brows, his sight unaffected by the white magic pulsing across the amphitheater. *"You mean to kill me, son?"*

"I am not your son!" Nikolai snarled. He raised his arm to lob the blazing spell bomb floating in his palm. *"And you are not my father!"*

Vedran's gaze shifted past him. "Don't kill him."

In that instant, Nikolai realized he'd forgotten about the other monster in the arena with him. Oscar's sword lanced his back, leaving a trail of fire.

Black magic seared his senses as the sorcerer grabbed him by his neck. He lifted him up with a savage sound and slammed him face down into the floor. Pain locked the air in Nikolai's lungs. He felt his jaw and nose break.

Oscar clutched his hair and bowed his head so far off the ground he thought his spine would snap. He smashed Nikolai's skull down, again and again.

Blood stained the marble, a crimson mess Nikolai could barely make out. Shadows blanketed out parts of his vision. His body started going numb. Sight and sound faded.

He thought he heard a woman's voice as he fell into a void from which he feared he would never emerge.

CHAPTER 20

THE SUV DOOR OPENED.

Lou climbed in with a large paper bag.

Brimstone perked up where he sat in the passenger footwell. *I smell meat.*

Lou closed the door and removed a pair of foot-long subs dripping with fat from the carrier. Hellreaver drooled against Mae's chest. The weapon transformed and inched closer to Lou.

The super soldier handed the food to him and Brimstone. "Don't make a mess."

His warning was lost amidst the sound of scarfing. He frowned as food debris pelted the interior of the vehicle.

"I'm sorry," Mae said. "The only place they mind their manners is at my mom's."

"She must be a powerful witch if she succeeded in putting the fear of God into them," he grunted.

She grimaced. "She's a South Korean matriarch."

"Oh. One of those." He took more packages out of the bag. "I got us some subs too."

Mae's stomach growled at the delicious aroma of bacon and sausage wafting from the bread rolls.

"Thanks," she said gratefully.

They ate their breakfast in companionable silence and watched the rundown place twenty feet south of where they were parked, on a busy street in Budapest's District 7. Serena had disappeared inside it an hour ago.

It housed a ruin bar, a style of drinking establishment that had become popular in the city in the past decades. With a predilection for vacant, pre-war buildings, they boasted eclectic interiors and a bohemian atmosphere that appealed to people of all ages.

Though it was mid-morning, the place was already seeing a steady footfall with a stream of diverse clientele heading in and out the arched doorway.

According to the super soldiers, the bar was popular among some of the city's less reputable counterintelligence agents. Since the Dark Council had dealings with crime syndicates and gangs in practically every metropolis in Europe, they hoped they would find a clue to their enemy's possible whereabouts from one of those sources.

Serena and Lou had dispatched the rest of their team to the known hideouts that had already been cleared by the magic community. Vlad, Cortes, and the Nolan cousins had split up and gone with them. As Serena had observed, it made sense to divide the magic users among them in case they encountered a Dark Council witch or sorcerer.

Mae suspected they wouldn't. She'd already used *Nullify* on a few occasions that morning. Bar the cores of the normal magic users in the city, she hadn't picked up on the magic that would indicate the presence of their enemy.

There were either no Dark Council members in Budapest right now or their cores were being concealed by the Sorcerer King, just like in New York. Except Mae had yet to detect any trace of Nikolai's Hellfire Magic or the *Reveal* spell she had carved into Oscar's core. She'd be surprised if Vedran had managed to undo all her conjurations in such a short amount of time. Which only confirmed her first assumption.

"Here she comes," Lou said twenty minutes later.

Mae straightened in her seat.

Serena crossed the road briskly, her hands tucked in the pockets of her bomber jacket. The black disk that contained her nanorobot combat suit rested against her chest in the guise of a pendant.

No one followed her out the building.

She got into the back of the SUV and handed Lou a piece of paper. "Plug those into the GPS and share them with the others."

Lou stared at the list of places written down on it. "What are they?"

"The last ten places the Dark Council was spotted."

Mae wrinkled her nose. "They just gave this to you?"

"Of course not. I bribed them."

Lou groaned.

Serena's smartband buzzed. She frowned when she saw the name on the display and answered the call.

"Haruki? What's wrong?"

"Mommy!" a little boy squealed.

Serena froze. "Kristopher? What are you doing with Uncle Haruki's phone?"

Lou checked the clock on the dash. "Isn't it two a.m. in Chicago?"

"Mommy, we miss you!" the little boy chanted.

"Is Kristopher her—?" Mae started.

"Son," Lou confirmed.

A little girl's voice came through the speakers. "Mommy, Kris did a big poop today!"

She giggled.

"Did not!" the boy protested.

"Did too!" the girl sang.

"That's Sienna, his twin," Lou explained at Mae's questioning look.

"Mommy, when are you and daddy coming home?" Sienna asked.

"Daddy's on an important job right now, honey," Serena replied gently through gritted teeth. "So is mommy."

"Are you chasing bad people?" Kristopher said innocently.

"Very bad people." Serena drummed her fingers on the armrest. "Now, how about you go get your Uncle Haruki, sweetheart?"

Mae eyed the vein throbbing in the super soldier's temple warily. "I get the feeling this Haruki guy's in trouble."

"You have no idea," Lou muttered with the long-suffering air of someone who'd seen this shit before and had the receipts to prove it.

A man picked up the phone. "Serena?"

Her eyes became slits. "Hey, asshole! Why are my kids still up?!"

The man's tone grew cool. "Is that any way to speak to your favorite babysitter?"

"My favorite babysitter is Callie, followed closely by Nate, Lily, and Naomi," Serena snapped. "The only reason Drake and I defaulted to you this week is because the others are away. Why are Kris and Sienna not tucked up in their beds?"

"They were," Haruki admitted. "Leah came into my room. The kids, er, heard us fooling around."

The armrest cracked under Serena's hand.

"What was that sound?" Haruki said suspiciously.

"Shit," Lou mumbled.

Mae pursed her lips. "Isn't this a rental?"

Hellreaver and Brimstone peered curiously around her.

Serena finally regained her ability to speak.

"I thought that hussy had gone to an art exhibit in New Orleans with Sebastian and Naomi!" she growled.

"She came back early because she missed me." Haruki sniffed. "Also, I would appreciate it if you refrained from calling my fiancée a hussy."

Serena said something unsavory.

"You're on speaker by the way," Haruki said reproachfully. "The kids can hear you."

On cue, the twins started chanting the curse word their mother had just inadvertently voiced in their presence.

"I'm gonna kill you," Serena said stonily.

"Violence is not the answer to everything, Serena," Haruki chided.

The chanting got louder. Sienna added poop to it for good measure.

Hellreaver sniggered. *That rhymes.*

Brimstone observed Serena's reddening face. *She looks like she's about to blow.*

Mae hushed them.

A woman's voice became audible on the line. "Whoa. I only went away to make hot cocoa. Why are the kids cursing?"

Mae could only presume this was the infamous Leah.

"Kris and Sienna got hold of my phone and called their mother," Haruki explained to his fiancée.

"Why, you little geniuses you," Leah gushed. The children tittered. "Here, drink up."

"Thanks, Aunt Leah!"

Serena's voice dripped with ice. "You guys know I'm still here, right?"

"Oh, hey Serena," Leah said innocently. "How's New York?"

"We're in Budapest!" Serena snarled.

"Isn't it morning there?" Haruki said.

Serena pinched the bridge of her nose and started counting to ten.

"This is making me wish it were five o'clock so I could drink," Lou said morosely.

Mae shrugged. "Like my grandma says, it's five o'clock somewhere."

Serena cut her eyes to them.

"Sorry," they murmured.

"I'm afraid we have to go," Leah said breezily. "The kids are getting sleepy. They say they wanna hear the story of how their favorite Lion bagged her Dragon."

"Should you be taunting her like—?" Haruki started worriedly.

The call disconnected.

Mae bit her lip. Lou sighed.

A murderous light brightened Serena's eyes. "I'm gonna skin that lizard and his lion and feed them to Vannog," she vowed fervently.

"Who's Vannog?" Mae asked Lou quizzically.

"He's a helldragon."

CHAPTER 21

WAKE UP.

A silent scream wheezed out of Nikolai as he bolted upright, a woman's voice fading in his ears. Pale sheets tumbled past his waist. He grasped them with a white-knuckled fist and looked around wildly, his heart thundering against his ribs.

He was in an infirmary.

His pulse slowed when he recognized the walls of the castle the Dark Council was currently occupying. His gaze landed on the figure in the bed next to him.

It was Oscar. He was fast asleep, his lynx Drabek curled next to his pillow. Fury burned Nikolai's throat. His muscles bunched as he prepared to lunge at the sorcerer. A vice-like pain gripped his skull with his next breath.

He gasped and winced, hands rising to clutch his temples. The frenzied wrath bubbling through his veins faded. A different memory from the one that had tormented him in his sleep rose before his mind's eye.

It showed him Mae Jin killing his mother. He flinched.

Yes. Nikolai swallowed. *That's how—that's how she died. The Witch Queen killed her. What I saw just now was only a nightmare!*

His nails sank into his flesh as he tried to separate his bad dream from the reality he knew to be true. Alastair stirred beside him. The crow made a worried sound.

"You're awake," someone said in a voice full of relief.

Nikolai twisted around. A sorcerer had gotten up from the table where he'd been writing some notes.

He approached the bed briskly. "How do you feel?"

"My head hurts," Nikolai muttered.

"That's to be expected. You've been asleep for over twenty-four hours. I'll bring you a light meal and something to make you feel better."

The man walked off. Nikolai's stomach flip-flopped. He looked out the lancet windows behind him. Pale clouds peppered a bright blue sky.

Shit. I was asleep for a whole day?!

Blood pounded viciously inside his head. He recalled what had happened in Oscar's room. The shape of the spell the Witch Queen had hidden within his brother danced before his eyes.

What kind of magic was that?!

Alastair jumped into his arms and huddled against his chest.

"Did you have the same nightmare?" Nikolai mumbled.

The crow trembled. Nikolai furrowed his brow when he sensed his familiar's confusion.

He wished he could blame whatever wicked conjuration Mae Jin had concealed inside Oscar's core for what he and his familiar had just relived. His stomach lurched at that unbidden thought.

Nikolai swallowed convulsively. *Relived? Is that really what I think just happened?!*

His headache intensified with a vengeance. Alastair crooned wretchedly, the pain afflicting the crow echoing across their bond.

Nikolai's gut told him there was more to this than just the Witch Queen's magic. It was as if something was stopping them from exploring their past memories in greater depth.

He was distracted by the arrival of the sorcerer. The man handed him some pills and a glass of water. The medicine tasted bitter on Nikolai's tongue. He gulped it all down and wiped his mouth.

The sorcerer offered him a bowl of steaming soup next.

Nikolai shook his head. "I'm not hungry."

The man hesitated. "Shall I inform the Sorcerer King that you're awake?"

"*No!*"

The vehement denial left Nikolai's lips before he could help it, shocking him as much as it did the sorcerer. He glanced at Oscar. His brother hadn't stirred.

Nikolai took a shallow breath.

"No," he repeated in a calm voice that he hoped disguised the emotions churning his insides. "I wish to rest some more. If my father asks, I'm in my chambers."

He swung his legs onto the floor and stood up, Alastair

in his arms. A wave of dizziness swept over him. He clenched his jaw and forced himself to move.

He didn't remember how he got back to his suite. He stumbled inside his bedroom, closed the door, and headed into the bathroom. It took him seconds to strip off. Alastair joined him when he stepped under the shower, the crow stretching his wings to wash his feathers.

The hot water cleaned away the stale sweat clinging to Nikolai's skin.

He pressed his head against the tiles and closed his eyes, wishing it would wipe away his muddied thoughts too. Because he had a nasty feeling he couldn't tell what was real and what was fake anymore. Judging from what he sensed from Alastair, neither could his familiar.

One thing they were both conscious of. They could not trust their own memories.

Nikolai curled his hands into fists as a fragment of his nightmare flitted before his inner vision. *That palace. It exists somewhere. I'm certain of it!*

Dusk was painting purple streaks across the sky when the Sorcerer King came to find them. He entered the suite without preamble, Barquiel trailing in his wake in Rose's form.

"How are you feeling?" Vedran asked briskly.

Alastair flinched on Nikolai's lap. They sat in the gathering gloom by the windows, where they'd been staring out over the forest and lake that surrounded the castle.

Nikolai looked around. He'd thought he would have an epiphany when he met his father's probing stare. All he felt was…

Nothing. I don't feel a thing for this man.

"I'm much better, thank you," he replied, his voice composed.

Vedran closed the distance to him, his intense gaze never wavering. Nikolai couldn't help but feel like an insect being carefully dissected under his scrutiny. He realized he did feel something in his father's presence then.

Dread.

"Come, join us for dinner." Vedran laid a hand on his shoulder, unaware of the ice forming in the pit of Nikolai's stomach. "It won't do you any good brooding in the shadows, my son."

A denial tore through Nikolai's mind. The same denial he'd screamed in his nightmare.

I am not your son!

He bit the inside of his cheek and squashed the protest bubbling up his throat. He glanced at Rose's figure where she lurked in the background.

"The demon is joining us for dinner?"

Barquiel did not respond to his taunt. If anything, he was watching Nikolai with the same intensity as the Sorcerer King, as if he were attempting to unravel a puzzle he could not decipher.

"Yes," Vedran said. "So is your brother."

A pain that was new and yet terrifyingly familiar seared Nikolai's back at his words, nearly robbing him of breath. His fingers clenched on his knees as he buried a gasp.

Alastair pressed against him, body shivering slightly.

How could I not remember my scar?!

160

The old wound burned his back, the puckered length of skin throbbing angrily as it crossed his spine. It took everything he had to maintain a neutral expression as he rose and accompanied the Sorcerer King and the demon.

It was as if his body were intent on punishing him for everything he had forgotten.

Or been made to forget.

That notion made his shoulders knot.

To his surprise, Vedran led them to his private quarters. It was an area of the castle no one was allowed access to bar his personal attendants and Barquiel. By the time they reached it, the stinging on Nikolai's flesh had faded to a dull ache.

Though larger, the suite was just as austere as his and Oscar's accommodations. A dining table with candelabras had been set up by a pair of French doors overlooking a terrace. Beyond it, mountains rose like soldiers against a darkening horizon.

A man and two women dressed in the livery of the Sorcerer King's retainers stood beside the serving carts next to the table.

The light from the candles cast eldritch shadows on Oscar's pale face where he was already seated at the table. He raised the glass of wine he had just been served to his lips, only to falter when he saw them.

CHAPTER 22

Nikolai suppressed an instinctive shudder of distaste when he met his brother's pale gaze.

"It's good to see you up and about," he greeted Oscar calmly as he made his way to the table with Rose and the Sorcerer King.

A muscle twitched in Oscar's cheek. He forced a smile. "Likewise."

Nikolai caught the faint frown Vedran flashed at Oscar. He took the seat his father indicated, his senses on alert. Alastair straightened on his shoulder, just as vigilant.

One of the servants uncorked a bottle and poured him some wine.

"It's your favorite," Vedran said when Nikolai looked quizzically at the half-empty bottle on the table. "It shouldn't interfere with the medication you took earlier."

Nikolai's stomach tightened. *So he knows I've been up for a few hours.*

He reached for the glass. His fingers stilled fractionally on the stem before closing around it.

He wouldn't poison me, Nikolai thought bitterly. *Not when magic is an easier and more painful alternative.*

He barely tasted the food Vedran's attendants placed in front of him during the interminable dinner. It wasn't until they had finished their meal and the servants had left that the Sorcerer King removed an object from his pocket and placed it on the table.

Nikolai's scalp prickled at the sight of the metal compass sitting innocently on the pale linen. *Shit.*

Oscar licked his lips, his unblinking gaze fixed on the artifact. "Dietrich managed to make an alternative compass?!"

"Yes. He succeeded in recreating it while the two of you were…incapacitated."

Nikolai cursed himself. He'd forgotten that the Immortal alchemist was working on reproducing the *Book of Light,* even though Oscar had mentioned it in passing a couple of weeks ago. The implications of Dietrich's experiment had escaped him until this moment.

His heart sank when he finally dragged his eyes from the artificial compass. His father was studying him with a zealous expression.

"Open it," the Sorcerer King ordered.

Nikolai saw Rose stiffen slightly out of the corner of his eye. His mouth went dry.

"What?" he said hoarsely, unable to mask his shock.

"Fire Magic is the key to making this compass work," Vedran said impatiently. "Your Hellfire Magic should serve that purpose."

That's why I'm here. Awareness chilled Nikolai to the bone at this sudden realization. He observed Vedran's predatory look with a sick feeling. *Because I'm a pawn he desperately needs!*

He looked around the chamber, stalling for time. "It might be better to do this elsewhere."

Irritation darted in Vedran's eyes.

He sighed and pushed himself up on to his feet. "You're right. Let's take a walk."

Nikolai followed his father out of the suite, Oscar and Rose following in their steps. His heartbeat grew louder as they navigated the gloomy corridors of the keep to the main stairs leading to the entrance hall, the Dark Council members whose paths they crossed falling back reverently at the sight of their king.

He felt the gazes of the sorcerers and witches guarding the grounds upon them when they exited the stronghold.

Vedran led them down a winding path to a coppice. The outlook opened up after a minute. A pier lined with lanterns appeared. They shed an orange light on the dark body of water surrounding the island.

The lake was as still as a grave.

For one second, Nikolai entertained the crazy notion of jumping into it and swimming for his life. Alastair crooned softly, a warning that brought him to his senses.

We wouldn't make it to the other shore.

"This should do," Vedran said in a tone that brooked no argument.

Nikolai swallowed down bile when his father handed him the compass. The metal was heavy and cold to the touch. Every instinct he possessed screamed at him not to open the damn thing.

Mae Jin's face flitted before his mind's eye. His belly knotted.

Though he still felt animosity toward the Witch Queen, he realized he could now segment that emotion to an extent and stop it from clouding his every judgment and action.

What would she do in my stead?

Alastair butted his cheek gently with his head.

Nikolai clenched his jaw at the answer his familiar gave him, a cold smile tugging at his lips. *You're right. She would see this through to the bitter end and turn the tables on her enemy at the earliest opportunity, like the crafty witch she is.*

He tapped into his core with that singular thought in mind. Heat flared inside his belly and surged through his veins, Alastair's energy resonating with his own. Hellfire Magic blossomed around them with a force that cast ripples across the water.

He focused it into his hands.

A keyhole opened in the compass where none had been before.

Oscar gasped. Vedran leaned forward, his expression rapt. A muscle jumped in Rose's jawline.

The compass shuddered violently in Nikolai's grip.

It was trying to resist him.

He scowled, drew on his and Alastair's combined powers, and blasted the artifact with the full strength of their magic on a roar that made birds take flight from the surrounding trees.

The air exploded in front of him with a *whoomph* that

stole his breath and doused the lanterns on the pier and the flaming torches across the castle grounds.

Waves swelled on the lake. They surged toward the opposite shore, invisible but for their foam-tipped edges. The trees on the island groaned, roots poking through the soil under the weight of the violent storm sweeping across them. The cloud cover broke on an outward ripple that exposed a star-bright firmament and a gibbous moon.

The Moon Magic he'd inherited from his mother responded to the bright orb, augmenting the Hellfire Magic he was pouring into the compass.

A black hole some two-feet wide materialized above the artifact. Nikolai's pulse stuttered. The edges of the rift fluttered in the destructive maelstrom it was wreaking upon this world.

Something danced into view inside it.

He blinked. *Is that a—?!*

"Take it!" Vedran barked. "Take the book!"

Nikolai shot a glance at his father.

The Sorcerer King's features were twisted in a hungry grimace that was overshadowed by the fanatical light in his eyes. Oscar stood ashen-faced and slack-jawed beside him. But it was the woman standing behind them that captured Nikolai's attention in that instant.

Rage lit Rose's pupils with an unholy red light.

The black hole whined, drawing Nikolai's startled gaze.

"Take the goddamn book!" Vedran bellowed.

Nikolai ground his teeth and reached inside the rift, unable to disobey his father's command. An icy void wrapped around his flesh. His fingers closed on something smooth and dry. He yanked the object out a second before the portal shuddered and closed.

The lake stopped churning. The branches in the trees stilled, the last of their broken twigs and leaves fluttering to the ground. The whole world seemed to hold its breath as Nikolai stared dazedly at the object in his hands, his heart pounding against his ribs.

It was a black book. One that looked like hundreds of others in the Dark Council's library.

Is this thing really the fabled Book of Shadows?!

Vedran snatched the artifact from his grasp before he could react. He flipped it open and stilled. Confusion rounded his pupils. He stood frozen for a timeless moment.

A shudder finally shook him. His arms dropped slackly by his sides, his eyes dead. The pages of the book fluttered in his hand.

Nikolai's chest tightened. They were empty.

The truth struck him like lightning as he watched the Sorcerer King's thunderous face. "It's a fake, isn't it?"

Oscar jerked at Nikolai's low mumble.

Rose closed her eyes, her shoulders sagging.

Black magic detonated around Vedran. He opened his mouth and howled out his fury.

Corruption swamped the island, an oppressive force that caused the guards atop the castle walls and in the grounds to faint. Oscar choked and clawed at his throat. Even Rose flinched.

The only thing that stopped Nikolai's knees from hitting the ground was the Moon Magic and white magic barrier his core had automatically erected around him and Alastair.

He felt something give deep inside his head as the Sorcerer King cursed and raged. Pain assailed him from within, drawing a tortured grunt from his lips. Alastair screeched.

Dizzying images flickered across Nikolai's inner vision. He clutched his temples and shuddered as more memories scorched his mind.

CHAPTER 23

I̲T̲ ̲W̲A̲S̲ ̲R̲A̲I̲N̲I̲N̲G̲ ̲W̲H̲E̲N̲ ̲T̲H̲E̲Y̲ ̲R̲E̲A̲C̲H̲E̲D̲ ̲T̲H̲E̲ ̲F̲I̲N̲A̲L̲ ̲A̲D̲D̲R̲E̲S̲S̲ Serena had procured from her contact, a little after midnight. The SUV beams cut through tightly packed trees as they took a sharp corner up a mountain, a few miles west of Budapest.

The light glanced off a moss-covered stone marker mostly hidden by the undergrowth overhanging the side of the road.

Serena braked. "This is it."

Headlights brightened the rearview mirror as the other SUVs pulled up behind them. Vlad studied the dark forest with a frown. The last village they had passed was a good three miles away.

"Are you sure? This looks like the middle of nowhere."

"The other locations turned out to be duds," Cortes pointed out.

Vlad shared the Columbian's reservations. They hadn't found any sign of Oscar nor the Dark Council at the other addresses they had checked out that afternoon and evening.

"All that means is they did a good job of going to ground and covering their tracks," Serena said. "Besides, this is the oldest tip-off on the list. My source said he learned about this place years ago, from a former Dark Council sorcerer."

"I thought sorcerers and witches weren't allowed to leave the Dark Council once they joined up," Mae muttered. "Like, once a scout, always a scout kinda stuff."

Serena's expression turned dry. "I said former, but I really meant defunct."

"If I were a bad guy, this would be the perfect location for a secret base." Lou unclipped his seat belt. "It ticks all the requirements."

Mae made a face. "You mean, isolated, creepy, and ideal for burying bodies?"

"Exactly."

Lou opened the door and dashed over to the marker. Tom joined him from the second SUV. They examined the bushes for a moment before entering the forest.

Rain pounded the roof of the vehicle while they waited for the super soldiers' return.

"Can they see in the dark?" Cortes hazarded after a minute.

"To a degree," Serena replied. "We have nanorobots in our retinae."

A short hush followed.

"Did it hurt?" Mae said quietly. "What was done to you to make you into super soldiers?"

"Most of us don't recall the details." Serena met her

awkward stare steadily. "We were children at the time and we'd spent most of our lives floating inside life pods, attached to feeding tubes."

Mae's face tightened at that.

Lou and Tom emerged from the woods. Lou jogged over to their SUV and climbed in while Tom returned to his vehicle.

"Go straight through. There's an overgrown road fifty feet in."

Tension knotted Vlad's stomach when Serena aimed the SUV at the undergrowth. He hoped they weren't about to embark on yet another wild goose chase.

Vegetation thumped and scraped the doors as they rode over bumps and dips. The ground leveled out after they hit the track. Serena turned west and headed deeper into the forest, the other vehicles in her wake.

A gully appeared. They skirted its lip for half a mile and came to a shallow stream. The rain eased as they crossed over to the other side. The clouds parted, revealing a gibbous moon.

Mae tensed. "There!"

Vlad stared in the direction she pointed. His pulse spiked. Something glinted between the distant treetops to their left.

"Found it," Serena said grimly.

She picked up speed. They'd just come in sight of a pair of dilapidated, wrought-iron gates when Mae barked out a warning.

"Stop!"

Serena slammed on the brakes.

Tarang yowled and tumbled into the footwell in front

of Vlad. Brimstone hissed as he jerked violently against Mae's seatbelt. Hellreaver smashed into the dashboard.

Tires screeched behind them, the rest of the SUVs decelerating sharply.

Vlad shot a worried look at Mae. "What's the ma—?" He froze when he picked up what she had detected. Goosebumps broke out across his skin. He stared out through the windshield. "Shit. Is that—?!"

Cortes's face hardened. "That's black magic."

They climbed out of the vehicle. Violet and Miles's expressions were similarly strained when they joined them along with Tom and the rest of the super soldiers.

An oppressive pressure danced across Vlad in waves. Tarang growled, crimson lighting up his pupils as he reacted to the insidious power pulsing through the air.

Serena frowned at the gates thirty feet ahead, evidently unable to detect what they could feel. "This place is being shielded by the Dark Council's magic?"

"Yes," Mae replied in a clipped tone.

Lou looked around warily. "Are they here?"

"No." Mae's mouth tightened. "I just cast *Nullify* and *Negate*. I can't sense anything else around us or beyond that dome."

Serena stilled.

"There's a dome?" Lou squinted at the shadows ahead. "How can you tell?"

"Because I can see it." Scarlet bloomed in Mae's pupils and around her weapon and her familiar. "Here, I'll show you."

She released a faint pulse of magic.

The silent, red wave rolled up an invisible wall that curved above the treetops. A chill ran through Vlad. Tarang stepped closer to him, the tiger rumbling his alarm.

"Whoa," Tom said hoarsely.

"That's freaky as fuck," one of the other super soldiers stated dully.

"Doesn't that remind you of something?" Miles asked Violet uneasily.

The witch furrowed her brow. "The barrier around Artemus's mansion."

Mae startled. "What?"

"Don't worry," Serena reassured her at the sight of her horrified expression. "The one in Chicago was erected by a goddess."

Cortes frowned. "A goddess?"

A muscle jumped in Lou's jawline. "So, we can't access the place from above either?"

"Doesn't seem like it," Vlad muttered.

Serena frowned. "I don't think anyone's been home for a while."

They looked at her.

She squatted and indicated the tire marks in the muddy trail. "There are no fresh tracks apart from ours. I looked at the weather forecast. It's been raining here on and off for the past month." She studied the gates and the fading red light of Mae's magic. "I'm pretty sure this place has been abandoned for years. If we can get through that barrier without triggering whatever measures the Dark Council may have put in place to warn them of intruders, they'll be none the wiser."

Spell bombs whooshed into life above Miles's hands. "Let's blast a hole through it!"

Mae grimaced. "I don't think attacking it is going to work." She shrugged. "That'd be like, I don't know, deactivating a bomb with C-4."

Lou and several super soldiers cut their eyes to Tom.

"For the last time, I didn't know it was a bomb, okay?" Tom protested.

"Wait," Mae said, shocked. "He *really* deactivated a bomb with C-4?!"

"Luckily, it was inside a bank vault, so the damage was limited to the basement," Serena said thinly.

Vlad inhaled sharply. "That Rio de Janeiro hostage situation? That was you guys?"

"Yeah."

"That could have ended badly," Cortes observed.

"It did," Lou groused. "My hip still aches on cold days."

Tom rolled his eyes. "The reason your hip hurts is because you can't keep your hands off your husband. That poor guy must have the sorest behind in all of Mexi— *ouch!*"

Lou had hit him on the head.

Brimstone huffed something. Hellreaver vibrated.

Mae chewed her lip. "You know, that might actually work."

"What did they say?" Cortes asked.

"That I should try *Absorb*."

Violet sucked in air.

Vlad's stomach lurched as unpleasant memories of their trip to Philadelphia rose at the forefront of his mind.

"*Absorb?*" Lou asked, puzzled.

"It's a crazy spell that allows Mae to consume the magic around her," Violet explained animatedly.

Vlad clenched his jaw.

"I saw what state you were in when you used that spell in Philadelphia," he told Mae heatedly. "I'm not letting you do that again!"

Her expression grew pinched. "The reason I ended up like that was because I used *Assimilate* first. This is different."

He was about to voice another protest when Cortes cut in.

"We're wasting time, Vlad. Let her try it."

The incubus fisted his hands, frustration churning his insides.

"I'll be careful," Mae said quietly.

This did little to comfort him. He startled when she came up to him and kissed his cheek.

Mae pulled back, a faint smile hovering on her lips. "You can bitch about this with Nikolai over a couple of beers after we save him."

"Like I'd drink with that asshole," Vlad grumbled.

"We've been to several bars together," Cortes reminded him.

"Oh." Tom's gaze swung from Vlad to Mae and back. He leaned toward Violet. "So, she has a thing going with him too?!" he whispered conspiratorially.

The witch made a face. "It's complicated."

CHAPTER 24

"YOU SHOULD STAND BACK," MAE WARNED. "I'LL SHIELD your cores so the spell doesn't affect you."

Serena glanced at her team. "We should be okay. We don't have magic cores."

Mae wrinkled her nose. "I assimilated the divine energy in Jared's sword when I last used that spell. It might do something to your nanorobots."

Tom paled.

Serena grimaced. "Shield away."

Hellreaver emitted a crimson aura and moved into Mae's waiting hand. Brimstone transformed, his pupils glowing as he towered over them all. Redness bloomed around the demon fox.

Mae incanted three spells in a single breath. *"Soul Shield! Multiply! Guard!"*

Her magic pierced their bodies, drawing gasps all round. Vlad's pulse stuttered when it wrapped around his core, a hot, unwavering barrier that would protect him come what may.

Lou pressed a hand to his belly, his face pale. "This feels…strange."

"Better strange than seeing your nanorobots get sucked out of you like a popsicle," Tom mumbled.

A scarlet sphere formed around Mae. She levitated into the air and approached the gates. Her eyes flashed.

She raised a hand toward the invisible barrier. "*Absorb!*"

The black magic dome protecting the gates and whatever lay beyond flickered into view again. It shivered violently in the face of Mae's spell.

A vein throbbed in her temple as the Sorcerer King's magic resisted *Absorb*. She lowered her brows.

Brimstone's tails vibrated fiercely, augmenting his witch's magic. Hellreaver quivered violently in her grasp.

Crimson detonated around Mae and her bonds on a thump that made Vlad's ears throb. The pressure wave sent him and the others skidding backward in the mud.

"Shit," Lou cursed.

"Kinda makes you glad she protected us, huh?" Miles said glassily.

The ground trembled. A storm shook the trees. The air boiled around Mae. She shot toward the barrier.

Vlad's stomach lurched when he grasped her intent.

"No!" he barked. "You don't know what—!"

Mae slammed her hand on the corrupt wall. "*ABSORB!*"

A silent implosion bowed the trees toward her. It

sucked the clouds in the sky into a wild spiral centered above her head and cracked the ground beneath her feet.

The jagged line raced toward Vlad and the others.

Golden light blasted into life around Cortes as a burst of negative energy dragged them forward.

He scowled at Vlad. "We should raise our shields!"

Vlad nodded, his heart thumping. He drew on his incubus powers. Redness bloomed upon his and Tarang's flesh. Violet and Miles erected protective walls in front of themselves and the super soldiers.

Serena dug her heels into the ground as Mae's magic pulled at her body. She stiffened in the next instant. Vlad followed her unblinking stare. His breath caught.

A black and red vortex had formed around Mae, whipping up her hair and her clothes. Her eyes glowed with the same sinister light.

"It's working!" Lou shouted.

Vlad's chest tightened. The Sorcerer King's magic was dissipating.

Mae ground her teeth, power throbbing around her with a force that made him lightheaded. In that moment, he wanted nothing more than to lay claim to her heart.

It took over a minute for the barrier to vanish. The tempest settled, leaving a deathly hush. The silence was broken by the sounds of the forest as it came slowly back to life.

Mae panted, sweat beading her forehead. She dropped lightly to the ground, turned, and startled. "What happened to the cars?"

Vlad turned.

The SUVs had come to rest haphazardly in the mud after being hauled dozens of feet across the ground.

"You happened to them," Cortes snapped.

"Oh."

❄

A BAROQUE PALACE EMERGED FROM THE TREE LINE AS THEY navigated the rutted driveway beyond the gates. It rose against the starlit sky, a pale presence lined with dark, foreboding windows.

It radiated the kind of oppressive silence that made it clear it had been abandoned for a while.

Lou shuddered. "That's reassuringly creepy."

Mae couldn't agree more. Unease swirled through her as they pulled up into a courtyard brimming with weeds.

Why did Nikolai never tell me about this place?

By the sounds of it, he would've been a child when it was last in use, Brimstone observed.

They disembarked from the vehicles, Hellreaver humming nervously. He moved closer to Mae as they passed an elaborate fountain featuring gargoyles and demons eating each other in a never-ending cycle of death.

Shallow steps led to a portico flanked by columns and littered with debris and puddles of water.

The main doors were bolted closed, the padlock securing them rusted over. Just like the gates, they didn't seem to be wired with any alarms. Serena crushed the lock with one hand and removed the tarnished metal chains wrapped around the handles. She pulled the doors open.

They creaked ominously, like the jaws of a freshly roused beast.

A chill coursed through Mae. She followed the super soldier into a cavernous entrance hall. It was cold and gloomy, the decor more frugal than she'd imagined it would be despite having witnessed the austere interior of the Dark Council's mansion in the city.

"Charming," Serena muttered.

She put her hands on her hips and examined the distant cupola crowning the four-story-high vestibule. Moonlight streamed through the grimy, stained glass in the vaulted ceiling. The fractured shards illuminated the grand staircase dominating the foyer. It bifurcated on a main landing before rising to the upper floors.

"We should split up," the super soldier said.

Vlad tagged along with Mae as she headed up the stairs, her crimson spell bomb lighting their way. Though he didn't say anything, she could tell he was still vaguely annoyed with her for using *Absorb*.

"Do you think we'll find anything useful here?" the incubus asked when they started down a corridor in the west wing.

Tarang peered at the shadows, his tail swinging lazily.

"I don't know." Mae's gaze swept the dust-covered surfaces around them. She wasn't sure if it was just her imagination, but she could almost feel Nikolai's presence in the air. "There's nothing to lose checking the place out."

They passed rooms containing furniture overlaid with sheets and a somber ballroom with dark, marble floors.

An imposing library overlooked the overgrown gardens at the rear of the palace. The shelves were bare and the fireplaces cold and empty.

Mae wondered if Nikolai had spent time here, hiding in the many nooks and crannies it offered, poring over stories that brought him joy and brief moments of peace in a palace full of cruelty.

It wasn't until they reached a spartan suite at the end of a dank, narrow corridor on the second floor that Mae's stomach started churning. She sensed Nikolai's existence keenly in the place.

Graffiti covered the walls of the living room. It was the first she'd seen in the palace. Vlad cursed as he read it.

"What does it say?" Mae asked in a strained voice.

Brimstone pressed against her leg when he sensed her growing distress. Hellreaver whined softly.

"You don't want to know." A muscle jumped in Vlad's cheek as he scanned the suite. "This was where Nikolai and his mother lived."

Mae's heartbeat boomed in her ears as she explored the first bedroom, the spell bomb floating behind her shoulder casting long shadows on the floor.

It had belonged to a child.

The mattress on the narrow bed had been vandalized, the pale stuffing unrecognizable where it dotted the floor beneath in dirty clumps. The desk and chair near the window were scored with deep grooves where someone had attacked the wood savagely with some kind of blade. A paltry selection of clothes hung in a wardrobe. They had been mangled, likely by the same person who had damaged the rest of the room.

She found a smashed photo frame behind a chest of drawers. Her throat tightened when she picked it up.

Vlad appeared in the doorway, his grim expression telling the tale of what he'd found in the other bedroom. "What is that?"

He came over, Tarang keeping close to him. Mae wiped away the dirt covering the cracked glass with trembling fingers. Her breath caught.

It was a picture of Nikolai and his mother. He was sitting on her lap and looked to be about ten. Happy smiles brightened their faces despite the dark circles under their eyes and their thin frames.

Though starved and abused in the grandiose palace where she had lived as a prisoner, Gabriela Stanisic had been breathtakingly beautiful.

Mae's heart broke when she turned the picture over and saw the inscription visible on the back of the photograph through the broken frame. It had been written in English and said, "Happy Birthday, my sweet Niko."

Her vision blurred.

Vlad laid a gentle hand on her shoulder. "Let's go, Mae."

She stayed still for a moment, struggling to contain her pain and her anger. She took a ragged breath, removed the photograph from the frame, and tucked it in her pocket.

They bumped into Lou on the landing.

"You should see this," the super soldier said in a deadly voice.

Mae shared a troubled look with Vlad. They followed him.

CHAPTER 25

LOU LED THEM TO THE UPPERMOST FLOOR OF THE PALACE. It housed a fraction of the number of rooms on the lower stories. Mae discovered why when they entered the grandiose space that crested its southern half.

It was an arena. One with a domed roof that was currently open to the elements.

Ice trickled through Mae's veins.

This is where Nikolai fought Oscar during the Trial of Blood. *This is where Gabriela Stanisic died!*

Though Nikolai had never gone into detail when he'd described the event where his mother had lost her life at Oscar's hands, Mae knew instinctively this was the place where the tragedy had unfolded. She could smell the lingering scent of death in the stale air.

Serena, Cortes, and four super soldiers crowded around something at the far end of the arena. Brimstone slowed and growled, his hackles rising.

Mae startled. "What's wrong?"

Brimstone did not reply. Dread knotted her stomach at her familiar's silence.

Hellreaver quivered agitatedly. *It might be best you not see this, my witch. You are not in a fit state to—*

Mae moved.

Her breathing quickened the closer she got to Serena and Cortes, the twigs and leaves snapping under her feet loud in her ears. She was trying to make sense of what she could see between their legs.

Serena glanced over her shoulder, her face expressionless. Cortes scowled beside her, Popo silent and drooping on his shoulder.

Mae's steps faltered. Horror rounded her eyes when she finally caught sight of what they were standing over.

Vlad flinched beside her.

"No." The denial left Mae's lips on a low mumble.

It was a pile of skulls and bones.

From the size of the smallest remains, the youngest body had belonged to a child no older than ten years. The shape of the forehead told Mae she'd been a little girl. Her left temple bore a nasty depression amidst a spiderweb of fractures. Her femurs and tibia were broken in several places. The other skeletons showed similar injuries.

A silent scream locked the air in Mae's throat.

They had died a brutal death and had been left to rot in the open, with no grave to honor them and no one to offer prayers and flowers to remember their passing.

"Do you know who they are?" Serena said quietly.

Mae tried to speak but couldn't.

Vlad wrapped an arm around her shoulders and replied in her stead, his tone brittle. "They were the children of the Sorcerer King, Nikolai's half siblings. They were murdered during a ritual where they were forced to fight to the death to prove their worth to their father."

"The *Trial of Blood*," Cortes spat out in the fraught hush. He glanced at the incubus, gold burning in his pupils. "I didn't want to believe you when you told me about it."

Someone gasped behind them.

Violet pressed a hand to her mouth as she slowly crossed the amphitheater, a pale-faced Miles next to her.

"Are those—?" the sorcerer mumbled.

"Yes," Vlad said curtly.

The rage Mae had been holding back overspilled her veins and lit up the air. Everyone grunted and dug their heels into the floor as a powerful pressure wave detonated around her, pushing them back.

"Mae," Vlad whispered in a tortured voice.

She barely heard him.

My witch, Brimstone whimpered.

Hellreaver let out a forlorn hum.

A veneer of incubus energy enveloped Vlad as he closed in on her. He took her in his arms and pressed her rigid face to his shoulder. "Let it out. Or else it will eat you up."

Mae shuddered and sagged, her hands clenching his jacket, his warmth a solace she did not deserve but was eternally grateful for. Just like the time when he'd held her in the church where they had lost Nikolai to the Dark Council, she raised her face to the sky and howled out her sorrow and wrath.

❄

Nikolai was dreaming again. In the dream, he crouched in a dark forest and performed the *Aura of the Moon*, a scrying ritual that would allow him to locate the body of the woman in whom a powerful soul would soon awaken. A soul he hoped would not just prove to be his salvation, but help him avenge his mother's death and save the world of magic from evil.

The dream shifted, as fluid as a river. He found himself on a high-rise in New York, pouring all of his and Alastair's power into the magic circle he had inscribed into the rooftop. It was a spell meant to forcibly rouse the soul they had come to the city to seek. Dazzling white light engulfed them as *Soul Storm* took effect.

He blinked. He was on another building now, this one wrecked by the battle he had unwittingly brought about. He was holding an unconscious woman in his arms, his stomach churning at the devastating power he had just seen her wield and the sight of the demon she had confronted.

His heart lurched when he looked upon her face. Though she was pale and hurt, the Witch Queen's beauty took his breath away.

He expected to feel hatred for her. The hatred that had consumed his insides whenever she had come to mind after he'd returned to the Dark Council. But the only emotions that filled him in that instant were remorse at what he had done to her and an attraction he could not deny.

He moved through more memories, a ghost swimming through an endless ocean he had once known.

He saw a battle in a cemetery, where the Witch Queen had laid her best friend Rose to rest, only to discover that the demon who had killed her had taken control of her body. He witnessed her coming into possession of the weapon he had stolen from the Dark Council and brought to New York for her to use. He experienced gratitude when the New York coven accepted him into their fold despite the fact that the Sorcerer King's blood ran through his veins. He relived the defeats he had helped them and the Witch Queen inflict on his brother and father in the months that followed.

His chest tightened as more intimate moments rose before him.

He was in Mae Jin's apartment. They were having breakfast. She laughed at something he said, her eyes sparkling. He fought the urge to lean over the table and kiss her.

There *were* kisses. Heated moments when the passion that had ignited between them threatened to burn them both.

His throat closed up as the vision of the last time they had been alone played before him. They stood on the rear porch of a clapboard house, under a setting sun and a rising Harvest Moon.

"Choose me," he'd whispered to her. "I will make you happy."

She'd swallowed, emotion darkening her eyes.

Then their hands were on one another and their

mouths clashed and the kiss they shared made his very soul tremble.

✳

HE WOKE UP WITH TEARS ON HIS FACE. ALASTAIR MADE A miserable sound in his sleep beside him.

It took Nikolai a second to register where they were.

A dying fire glowed in the hearth in his bedroom, inside the keep where the Dark Council had gone to ground. The sun was halfway to the horizon through the windows on his left.

Shit. I lost another day?!

Nikolai sat up slowly and dragged a hand down his face, careful not to rouse Alastair.

The crow inched closer to him. He smiled softly and laid a gentle hand upon his familiar. Alastair relaxed under his touch. Nikolai could tell from the silence that there was no one else in the suite with them. A chill danced down his spine.

He couldn't remember much about what had happened last night after Vedran had discovered the precious *Book of Shadows* he had strived so hard to find was a fake. Which meant he'd probably blacked out again. He wondered what Vedran had made of his latest collapse.

If he even reacted to it.

In truth, his father had been so lost in his rage he probably hadn't been aware of much else.

Nikolai gave a brief thought to who'd carried him to his room. He doubted it was Oscar. The last time he'd seen his brother, the sorcerer had been gasping for air. He sneered at the recollection.

Surprise jolted him at his reaction. It was followed by an awareness that shook him to the core.

The contradictory feelings that had wrought havoc on his mind and upon his heart after he'd awakened in the infirmary yesterday were no more. The loathing he felt toward Mae Jin was now an irritating emotion he could ignore. Instead, he found himself experiencing a growing animosity toward the ones in this castle with him.

Whatever it was Vedran had done to him and Alastair to modify their memories had started to lose its effect.

Nikolai clenched his jaw.

He was willing to bet it was Illusion Sorcery. The same Illusion Sorcery his father had accused Mae Jin of using against him. His frown deepened when he called to mind what Oscar had said about the Dark Council eliminating most who could cast that magic.

It all makes sense now. They probably forced the rest into their servitude.

He was pretty certain that the spell Mae Jin had placed inside Oscar in New York had been intended to break the illusion he was under. She'd known Vedran would ask him to help his brother.

But the spell had only cracked it. The fact that he had experienced it indirectly through Oscar's core likely had a bearing on this.

It looks like my father's out-of-control black magic last night undid more of it.

He curled his hands into fists. He needed to completely

undo the sorcery crippling him if he wanted to be in control of his own actions and fate.

I have to find a way to get in touch with Mae. She's the only one who can rid me of it!

His chest tightened with remorse and longing when the Witch Queen's face floated before him. He wanted to kiss her again. Even though she probably loathed him for all he had done to harm her and their friends since being deceived into rejoining the Dark Council. He wondered whether he would ever have the opportunity to beg her forgiveness.

A soft sound had him looking around. Alastair was awake and watching him closely. Nikolai stroked the crow's head with a knuckle.

"Do you remember her too, Al?" he mumbled.

Alastair crooned and butted his hand, regret pulsing across their bond.

Nikolai stilled.

Barquiel. His pulse quickened when he recalled the demon's behavior the night before. *He didn't want Vedran to find the* Book of Shadows. *In fact, he looked pretty damn pleased when I took that fake tome out of that portal.*

CHAPTER 26

THE SORCERER KING STOOD AT THE WINDOW OF HIS OFFICE and stared out at the mid-afternoon sky. His anger chilled the air, so much so Barquiel saw Oscar shiver out of the corner of his eye.

He couldn't sense the cold himself. Demonic souls never experienced any extremes of temperature. He could, however, feel emotions.

The relief he had experienced last night when he'd seen the fake *Book of Shadows* Nikolai had extracted from the portal he had opened with Dietrich's artificial compass still made him weak. He was conscious of how perilously close he'd come to losing the only chance he had to revive the person he cherished most in the world.

Barquiel frowned. *For once, I have that bastard Azazel to thank for this fortunate turn of events. He must have planted a fake to fool whoever wished to find the book and use it for unscrupulous means. In fact, there's probably not just one fake, but several.*

"One of our Dark Council contacts has informed me that Mae Jin has been spotted in Budapest," Vedran said coldly. "She's likely trying to find Nikolai."

Barquiel stiffened at his words. Oscar startled. He flinched when his father whirled around.

"Go to New York and find the *Book of Light* by any means necessary," Vedran ordered the sorcerer in a hard voice. "She won't be able to stop you if she's in Europe."

Shit. Barquiel kept his expression detached out of sheer habit.

Oscar paled. "What?"

"Do not make me repeat myself!" Vedran barked.

Oscar recoiled. His lynx whimpered and darted behind his leg.

Barquiel watched the vein throbbing in the Sorcerer King's temple. *He's losing control of his emotions. We definitely can't have that.*

"I believe you should reconsider," the demon said calmly.

Oscar flashed him a grateful look.

Vedran's gaze burned into him. "I shall ask for your counsel when I need it, demon!"

Irritation made Barquiel's skin itch.

"I have allied myself to every Sorcerer King since the first man to take that throne," he said tightly. "Each one listened to my guidance when it mattered the most. This is a mistake. I doubt the *Book of Light* is still in New York. You should—"

Black magic tinged with dark red flames saturated the air on a ripple that made the demon blink.

"*Shut your mouth!*" Vedran bellowed.

Barquiel grunted in surprise when he was shoved back a foot by the power emanating from the Sorcerer King.

Oscar cried out and fell onto his bottom. He clutched his chest, the blood draining from his face.

Barquiel's belly knotted at the incredible force battering him. *Those flames! Are they—?!*

Drabek screeched, the lynx's cry matching her sorcerer's tortured expression.

Vedran stilled at the sound. He closed his eyes and took a shuddering breath. The oppressive weight bearing down on the chamber eased. Oscar gasped and wheezed.

Barquiel's muscles quivered as he fought the urge to stride across the floor and rip Vedran's heart out of his chest for daring to challenge him so. The only things that stopped him were the fact that he still needed him and what he had just witnessed.

That was definitely Nikolai's Hellfire Magic!

Vedran opened his eyes. His gaze landed on Barquiel. "Go with Oscar."

His tone was composed once more, as if the fury he had just shown them was a lie. The demon was not fooled. He could see the darkness bubbling in the man's eyes.

Soon. Soon I will obtain what I need and kill you myself.

Vedran turned on his heels and looked out of the window, unaware of the silent promise the demon had just made to himself. "Bring me that book."

Barquiel quelled his murderous compulsion and headed for the exit. Oscar followed him.

The sorcerer didn't speak until they'd left the tower. Though the corridors of the castle were pretty much empty, most of the Dark Council sorcerers and witches still recuperating in the infirmary after being subjected to the Sorcerer King's debilitating magic the night before, they both knew the walls had ears.

Oscar hugged Drabek to his chest, his voice trembling slightly. "What's gotten into him?"

"Your father is desperate." Barquiel glanced at him. "He believes the sooner he gets his hands on the *Book of Shadows*, the closer he will be to realizing his dreams."

A mutinous expression tightened Oscar's face. "Like you said, there's no guarantee that damn book is *in* New York."

Barquiel couldn't be certain of that. He'd told Vedran the artifact was likely not in New York to buy himself time.

Mae Jin would not be so foolish as to leave it unprotected, would she? He narrowed his eyes slightly. *Then again, if the artifact is in New York, then this might represent the perfect opportunity to obtain it. And to kill Oscar without Vedran's suspicion falling on me.*

"We have no choice in this matter," the demon told the unsuspecting sorcerer. He paused when he reached the junction that would take him to the northeast tower. "Meet me on the roof. We leave in two hours."

Oscar watched him leave with a brooding expression.

Barquiel's steps quickened as he approached his quarters. *I want to see her.*

He slammed the door shut after him, transformed, and opened a rift to the region of Hell Deep he had long hidden from Satanael's eyes, too overcome with the urge to lay his eyes upon the woman who occupied his every thought to institute his usual safeguards.

Sulfur clouds engulfed the demon when he emerged in the valley that led to the cave where he had concealed his most precious secret. He spread his wings and arrowed toward it.

✳

Nikolai faltered as he approached Barquiel's suite.

I must be out of my mind.

Alastair made a soft sound on his shoulder. The crow didn't seem to be discouraging him from what he was attempting to do.

Maybe we've both lost our minds.

Alastair pecked his ear at that.

He grimaced. "Alright, I'm sorry."

Alastair ruffled his feathers.

Nikolai stopped in front of Barquiel's door. He looked up and down the corridor with a faint frown. He hadn't seen anyone on his way here.

I bet they're all in the infirmary.

He steeled himself and knocked. There was no answer.

He knocked again, louder this time. "Hey, are you in there? I want to talk."

Alarm fluttered across his bond with Alastair, startling him. The crow was peering intently at something on the floor.

Nikolai followed his familiar's gaze and saw what had drawn his attention. His pulse spiked. Crimson light bled onto the marble through the faint slit under the door. It was coming from the demon's suite.

What is that?!

Nikolai swallowed. He hesitated before reaching for the doorknob and twisting it. To his surprise and mounting dread, the door opened under his hand. An acrid stench burned his eyes and nostrils when he pushed it. He froze.

A scarlet rift pulsed in the middle of Barquiel's suite.

A memory came to him then. He recalled seeing something similar in the cemetery where Oscar and the demon had tried to capture Mae with a binding ritual. He'd witnessed the same phenomenon at the abandoned factory on the Brooklyn waterfront where they had gone to confront the Dark Council and rescue Mae's sister and grandmother.

Barquiel had opened portals to Hell on both occasions. And those portals had looked identical to what he was looking at right now.

Nikolai crossed the threshold and locked the door behind him before he could change his mind. His instincts were telling him he should find out what Barquiel was up to. His heart thrummed a wild tempo in his chest.

Still, it's not as if I can just stroll into Hell. I'm human!

Alicia had told him and Mae several of Astarte's human allies in Chicago had once ventured into the Underworld to rescue one of their own. Which meant the air had to be breathable, at least.

Something resonated with his core, rooting his legs to the ground.

Alastair flinched.

Nikolai's eyes widened as he registered the familiar sensation. He pressed a hand to his belly, shock making him dizzy. It was a pulse of magic. One he knew intimately. It was the same power that lived inside him and the ley lines of every nexus he had ever tapped into.

This is white magic. Pure, unadulterated white magic!

The pulse came again. Nikolai's gaze locked on the scarlet rift.

It's coming from there! But—how?! How can there be white magic in Hell?!

Alastair sank his claws into his shoulder. Resolve hardened Nikolai's stomach. They had to find out what this was. Even if it meant venturing into a place no human should technically visit alive.

Nikolai cast a silent prayer to any deity that was listening, drew on his and Alastair's combined powers, and shrouded them in a potent layer of white magic. A thought came to him.

Dark red flames sizzled into life, overlaying the veneer of white magic. Somehow, he suspected Azazel's Hellfire Magic would protect them in the Underworld.

He took a deep breath and stepped inside the rift.

He and Alastair were immediately sucked into the vortex of a scorching wind. The crow clung desperately to him as they fell headlong into a spinning, crimson maelstrom.

Bile rose in the back of Nikolai's throat. Things swam in and out of view beyond the blurry walls of the portal. Things that screamed and howled with hunger and agony. They clawed at the rift when they sensed him, trying to break through to get to him.

He shut his ears to the horrors he was witnessing and focused on the dark spot growing ahead.

That's the exit!

Nikolai tried to decelerate as he approached it, to no avail.

Shit!

He shot out of the portal, flailed wildly when he found himself some ten feet in the air, and hit the ground hard.

CHAPTER 27

ALASTAIR ALIGHTED GRACEFULLY ON NIKOLAI'S BACK.

Nikolai stifled a groan. He pushed up onto his hands and knees and peered around warily. He could see the vague walls of a chasm rising on either side of him. Foul, yellow fumes swirled through the air, obscuring his view of pretty much everything else.

A distant animal shriek raised goosebumps on his flesh. Alastair made a nervous sound. Nikolai recalled the hellbeasts they had fought before.

He flinched when the sulfur clouds stirred on his left. Something glowed and bubbled some eighteen feet away. The billows cleared, revealing a lava pit.

Nikolai swallowed. *Good thing I didn't land in that.*

Alastair clicked his beak and took flight, Hellfire Magic brightening his feathers. Nikolai climbed hastily to his feet and followed the crow's red wings as he arrowed toward the base of a distant cliff.

It was where the white magic they had sensed was coming from.

It took him a good ten minutes to reach the far end of the gully. Demonic energy brushed across his skin when he approached the bluff. Nikolai slowed.

That's Barquiel's power.

Alastair dropped down on his shoulder and stared intently at a spot ahead of them. Nikolai frowned. All he could see was a dark rockface.

"Is there something there, Al?"

The crow squawked.

Nikolai hesitated. He released a weak pulse of Hellfire Magic. It sparked against something. The wall wavered.

Nikolai's insides twisted as the entrance of a cave glimmered into view. It disappeared just as swiftly. His heart thundered against his ribs.

Barquiel shielded this place!

The white magic that had drawn him and Alastair to Hell throbbed strongly from the cliff, as if whoever or whatever was emitting it was angry.

Nikolai's mind raced as he tried to come up with a way to cross Barquiel's barrier. A memory jolted him. His pulse stuttered. He recalled the spell Mae had created to disable demonic energy, when the demon had attacked them in Philadelphia.

Negate can get me through this wall!

Bitterness tightened his jaw. The countermeasure Vedran had invented to neutralize Mae's powers had involved analyzing the structure of *Nullify* and *Negate* and combining his black magic with Nikolai's Hellfire Magic to create a spell that could cancel them out.

His nails bit into his palms. *I'm sure I can recreate it.*

Alastair clutched Nikolai's shoulder tightly as he reached for their magic. He closed his eyes and brought up the shape of Mae's conjuration.

Another recollection flashed across his inner vision. His heartbeat accelerated. *That's right! I helped Mae design a spell to undo the black magic Vedran had placed inside the core of...*

He frowned, his memory failing him as he tried to remember whom it was they had helped. He gritted his teeth.

It doesn't matter. I can visualize the process!

Nikolai's heartbeat boomed inside his skull as he slowly put together his own version of *Negate,* just as he had crafted that other conjuration. Sweat was pouring down his face by the time he completed it. He panted, his pulse racing.

His fingers trembled as he raised his hand and invoked the spell. *"Negate!"*

The air quivered. Barquiel's barrier split open. Nikolai and Alastair darted through the crack. It closed behind them with a hiss of corruption. He turned and found himself in the mouth of a dark tunnel. His scalp prickled.

No. It's not completely dark.

A light pierced the shadows in the distance. Though faint, it was enough to guide him when he added the gleam of his own Hellfire Magic. He headed toward the pale glow, the thread of white magic that had drawn him and his familiar here resonating strongly within their cores.

Nikolai walked for what felt an eternity, though it was

likely no more than a mile. The tunnel bifurcated over a dozen times, the rivers of lava and bottomless chasms he had to navigate past slowing him down even more.

At least there are no hellbeasts down here.

Alastair clicked in agreement.

Just when he thought they would never get to the end of the interminable passage, the light started to brighten. Nikolai slowed. He could hear faint voices.

He pressed his back against the wall and crept forward silently, Alastair as still as stone on his shoulder. The tunnel curved. He dropped down and inched his way around the bend. A cave gradually came into view. One filled with a dazzling radiance that blinded him for an instant. His vision cleared.

His breath caught.

A sarcophagus sat on a plinth in the middle of the circular chamber. Floating above it, within a dome of powerful demonic energy, was an ethereal figure.

It was a woman who reminded him strongly of the Witch Queen. Her hair was longer and her face more mature. Right now, she was frowning at the demon who stood before her prison.

"Cease this madness, Barquiel! In the name of the friendship we once shared, you must free me and relieve yourself of the body you stole. Abandon the Sorcerer King and return to Hell. Your rightful place is here, not on Earth!"

Nikolai swallowed convulsively. *Is that—Ran Soyun?!*

He couldn't think who else would look like Mae and possess such strong white magic.

"But I am close to reviving you, my love." Barquiel's

eyes shone with fanatical devotion. It was as if he hadn't heard a word the woman said to him. "Soon, I shall get my hands on the *Book of Shadows* and retrieve the other half of your soul from its pages. And once I gift you the first Sorcerer King's soul and the core inside Mae Jin's heart, you shall return and reclaim your throne as the most powerful Witch Queen who ever—!"

Brightness seared the chamber, making Nikolai wince. He blinked away the black spots filling his sight.

His heart raced wildly. Fierce white magic surrounded Ran Soyun. Her eyes burned with the same otherworldly light enveloping her as she glared at Barquiel.

"And like I have told you a million times before, I shall reject everything you offer me! I am sick of you repeating the same thing over and over again, Barquiel. I will not have you sacrifice my daughter's life for your foolish plans. I will never be yours, demon!"

"Yes, you will." Barquiel's face hardened. "I will bring you back to life. And you will be my wife, like you would have been had that bastard Azazel not stolen you from my grasp!"

His roar echoed around the chamber.

Nikolai's eyes rounded. *What?!*

Corruption clashed against white magic as the demon's wrath made the air boil.

"You shall never have my heart," Ran Soyun promised in a deathly tone.

"I shall be content with your soul, witch!" Barquiel grated out.

Nikolai's stomach churned. *So, all this time, he's been*

coming down here to see Na Ri's mother? He's kept her alive all these years so he can revive her?!

His gaze locked on the stone coffin. Horror drenched him in a cold sweat as the truth dawned.

No. He kept her body down here, so that both her mortal remains and the half of her soul that Azazel spared could not escape his grasp!

Barquiel's next words turned Nikolai's blood to ice.

"That fool Vedran will be at his most vulnerable when he initiates the *Inheritance Ceremony* and attempts to absorb Davor's soul. I have to make sure the conditions are perfect, so I can overpower him. That's why he cannot find the *Book of Shadows* yet. Not until my plans are ready." He paused. "I'm pretty certain he intends to assimilate Nikolai's white magic core so as to make himself the god he wishes to be."

A nasty chuckle left the demon. "It seems he's forgotten the hard lesson he learned when he tried to absorb Gabriela Stanisic's core. But...he might actually succeed this time around." His tone turned bitter. "He's been consuming that boy's Hellfire Magic."

Ran Soyun flinched.

Nikolai's ears buzzed, his heartbeat so loud he was shocked Barquiel could not hear it.

"I saw it myself, today," Barquiel said sourly. "Vedran's powers are even stronger now that he has acquired some of the magic Azazel himself feared." He met Ran Soyun's shocked gaze. "He intends to force the *Marriage of Magic* on Mae Jin and bind her to his heir so he can control her powers. I cannot let that happen. I need her core and

Davor's soul." His expression softened slightly. "I have to go. I will be back soon, my love."

He turned and headed for the exit.

Nikolai's belly twisted as the demon closed in on his position. *Shit!*

"Wait." Ran Soyun's voice froze Barquiel's steps. "There's something I wish to ask you."

The demon twisted around, surprise widening his crimson eyes.

"This is the first time you have stopped me from leaving," Barquiel said quietly. He hesitated before retracing his steps. "Tell me what you want to know, my love."

Though it was infinitesimal, Nikolai caught the fleeting look Ran Soyun shot his way. White magic flared in her eyes and throbbed through his core.

Nikolai nodded shakily at her silent message. He rose, ran blindly through the tunnels until he reached the mouth of the cave, and bolted past the fire pits dotting the chasm. His breaths came in hard pants as he approached the portal, Alastair gliding fluidly above his head.

Magic warmed his belly. *"Moon Storm!"*

The spell exploded around him and lifted him up. His heart thundered against his ribs as he leapt inside Barquiel's crimson rift. The return was swifter and he emerged into the demon's suite within seconds.

Nikolai staggered to a halt in the middle of the room, Alastair circling above his head before landing on his shoulder. He turned and stared dazedly at the fluttering portal. The enormity of what he had just witnessed made him shudder.

Everything Vedran and the demon who had allied himself with the first Sorcerer King had ever done now made horrifying sense.

Alastair squawked a warning. An echo of Ran Soyun's white magic pulsed through their cores.

Barquiel must be on his way back!

He turned, stumbled out of the demon's suite, and didn't stop until he reached his chambers. A single thought occupied his mind as he slammed the door shut behind him and leaned shakily against the cold, hard wood.

I have to find a way to reach Mae!

CHAPTER 28

Mae stared at the ceiling of the bedroom she was sharing with Violet and Serena.

They were in a safe house owned by Gideon Morgan, in a village north of Budapest. Sunlight streamed through the windows at the far end of the room. Birds chirped outside.

Their cheerful brightness was in sharp contrast to her mood.

It had taken her a long time to fall asleep last night, as it no doubt had everyone else. The ride back into the city had taken place in fraught silence, everybody lost in their own thoughts after what they had witnessed in the forgotten palace in the middle of the forest.

Mae couldn't stop reliving the awful scenes of the prison where Nikolai had spent his childhood. The anger that had simmered through her yesterday resurfaced.

It lost its wind somewhat in the face of a series of disjointed snores.

She sighed and sat up.

Trixie lay on her back atop Brimstone at the bottom of the bed. High-pitched whistles ruffled her lips and her left hindleg jerked spasmodically at something she chased in her dream. A bubble grew out of Brimstone's left nostril and deflated with every breath he took, the sounds he made that of an idling Boeing engine. Hellreaver's snores bore an uncanny resemblance to a chainsaw in a horror movie. He was sprawled on the sheets beside Mae, his blades askew.

The bathroom door opened. Serena came out, looking as fresh as a daisy.

The super soldier studied Violet with a faint frown. "How can she sleep through that?" She clocked Mae's accusing stare. "What?"

"You look like you just got twelve hours of shuteye."

"It's the nanorobots. Super soldiers can go days without sleep."

A metallic sound drew their gazes. Hellreaver smacked his teeth and resumed his sawmill impression.

"He looks like some old guy who's about to snort and scratch his belly," Serena said drily.

"You think so too, huh?"

Violet woke up with an unintelligible grunt. She lifted her face off the pillow and looked at them blearily.

"You sleep like a dead person," Serena said as the witch sat up and wiped drool from the corner of her mouth.

"Thanks." Violet yawned. "What time is it?"

"It's just past three."

Someone knocked on the door.

"Are you okay in there?" Lou said worriedly through the wood. "We can hear some kinda...noise."

"It's open," Serena called out.

Lou came in. He stopped and swept the bedroom with a wary gaze.

Tom peered over his shoulder. "Where the heck is that racket coming from?"

Serena indicated exhibits A, B, and C on Mae's bed.

"Jeez," Lou mumbled. "We thought you were being murdered."

Serena narrowed her eyes. "And your first reaction was to knock on the door?"

Lou grimaced. "I know what you're capable of. Besides, she's here." The super soldier cocked a thumb at Mae, only to freeze when he got a good look at her pajamas. He squinted. "Are those bunnies?"

Mae's tone grew cool. "It was a gift from my sister."

Vlad poked his head around the door. "You still wearing those old things?" He frowned. "What happened to the nightwear I gave you?"

Mae's lips pressed into a thin line. "Nikolai donated them to charity. He said they were the work of the devil."

The incubus curled a lip. "Mark my words, that guy will have you dressing like a nun the minute you get together."

"Who's dressing like a nun?" Cortes appeared behind Vlad. He gave Mae's outfit a questionable once-over. "I didn't realize rabbit-infested pajamas were the current vogue among the sisterhood these days."

Mae scowled. "How about you all go away?"

She emerged from the bedroom a quarter of an hour

later with Brimstone and Hellreaver and followed the enticing smell of fried eggs and bacon to the large, farmhouse kitchen at the back of the dwelling.

The super soldiers were helping themselves to the veritable feast laid out on the table. Vlad stood at the range cooker with Lou and Cortes.

Tarang was inhaling a plateful of steaks next to them. The tiger raised his head and huffed out a greeting to Brimstone and Hellreaver. His tail swung languorously as he pawed at the dishes holding untouched mountains of meat beside him.

The demon fox and the weapon headed over briskly.

Vlad caught sight of Mae. "Do you want your usual for breakfast? Although I should really be calling this a late brunch."

Her stomach growled loud enough to raise eyebrows. She flushed at his smile. "Yes, please."

It was Cortes who brought up the subject of their next move after they'd eaten.

"What do we do now? We still have no idea where the Dark Council went to ground." He sipped his coffee and indicated Mae with a wave of his hand. "Since *Reveal* doesn't appear to be working, we can safely assume Oscar was nowhere near the places we checked out yesterday."

"I've been thinking about something," Serena said pensively.

"You have?" Mae asked.

Serena met her puzzled gaze. "There's no way for us to find Oscar and the Dark Council. But there might be a way to find Dietrich."

Vlad furrowed his brow. "How?"

"Gallium."

Mae blinked. "Gallium?"

"As in the rare metal?" Cortes said. "The one that's a liquid at room temperature?" The Columbian's mouth thinned at their stares. "So sue me, I paid attention in chemistry class."

"Oh." Lou's face brightened. "It's one of the elements making up our nanorobots."

Tom blinked. "It is?"

This earned him dirty looks from several super soldiers.

"You're just a pretty idiot, aren't you?" one of them muttered.

Tom grinned. "Why, thank you."

"I was thinking we should track down recent orders of Gallium to Europe," Serena explained. "You need a license to import the stuff. Dietrich would have had to get his hands on a lot of it to use on those devils."

Vlad drummed his fingers on the table.

"That's assuming the Dark Council used legal methods to obtain it," he said with a frown.

A dangerous half-smile curved Serena's mouth. "Don't worry. We know a couple of black-market experts who can trace pretty much anything."

"Oh." Mae stared. "Are you talking about those guys Jared called last month? What were their names again?" She chewed her lip for a puzzled moment. Her face brightened. She slammed her fist into her palm. "That's right! Howard and Jordan."

Serena shot a faint frown at Violet and Miles before

fixing Mae with an inscrutable stare. "You know about them?"

Violet grimaced. "We only mentioned them in passing."

"It's true," Mae said.

"Who are they, exactly?" Vlad said in a hard voice. "Jared seemed pretty quick to rely on them last month, so they must be powerful in some way."

"You might as well tell them at this point," Lou grunted at Serena.

A resigned expression dawned on her face.

CHAPTER 29

"HOWARD IS THE CEO OF STAEGH CORP," SERENA SAID. "Jordan Banks is a genius who works for Dimitri Reznak, one of the Immortals who helped rescue us when we were children." She hesitated. "Dimitri negotiated the first peace treaty between the Immortal races when they were still at war, hundreds of years ago."

Surprise jolted Mae. "There was an Immortal war?!"

"Yes." Serena's tone turned embittered. "Most humans are unaware of it, but it has shaped their history for over a millennium."

"Wait." Cortes's eyes had shrunk to slits. "Howard Titus? As in the tech tycoon?"

Serena dipped her head. "He's an Immortal."

Vlad exchanged a guarded look with Cortes. "No wonder the guy looks like he doesn't age."

Lou removed a laptop from a bag and switched it on. "Jordan should be up. I'm not so sure about Howard, but I'll try him anyway."

It was Howard Titus who answered first.

"Hang on a minute!" he shouted down the line. "Let me find somewhere quiet!"

Serena frowned at the music and brouhaha reverberating through the speakers. "Is he at a party? Isn't it six-thirty in the morning there?"

Violet checked her phone.

"Yup," she informed them with a fatalistic air. "According to his social media feeds, he was at some billionaire's shindig in Malibu last night."

The scenery changed to a bright exterior. It looked like the Immortal had stepped out onto a terrace near the ocean.

Howard gazed curiously at his phone, the rising sun turning his blond hair to spun gold and giving him the appearance of some kind of Greek god. "Oh, hi guys. I see the whole gang's there. And a few new faces."

"Shouldn't you be in bed?" Serena said critically.

"Hang on a minute," Lou interrupted. "I'm getting Jordan on the line."

The second call connected.

A man in jeans and a T-shirt appeared. He sat eating doughnuts at a workstation. An enormous, concrete and glass computer lab was visible around him.

"Hi, Lou. What can I do for you?" Jordan Banks said distractedly, his spare hand moving rapidly across a keyboard.

"Howard is on this call, Jordan," a melodious female voice interjected.

Brimstone's ears pricked up.

"He is?" Jordan paused, a fresh pastry halfway to his

mouth. He squinted at the screen and scowled. "You're right. Why is that asshole in a tux? Isn't it early morning in L.A.?"

Howard grinned. "Still sore about our last match, I see."

Jordan flipped him the middle finger.

"You should mind your manners in the presence of our guests, Jordan," the female voice reprimanded him.

Brimstone raised his head from where he lay at Mae's feet. *That is not a human, my witch.*

"Who is that?" Mae asked Serena warily. "Brim says she's not human."

Serena looked at the fox. "He can tell?"

Brimstone panted smugly, bushy tail sweeping the floor.

"That's Eva, Jordan's sentient AI creation."

Cortes furrowed his brow. "They have a sentient AI?"

"Why, yes, Enrique Cortes, formerly Beau Bonaparte Cortes," Eva said smoothly.

Cortes froze.

"Beau?!" Miles whispered to Violet.

"Bona—Bonaparte!" Tom choked.

Popo bobbed excitedly. "Beau and Popo rhyme!"

Cortes grabbed his beak.

Vlad's shoulders trembled. Mae bit her lip hard.

"Don't," the sorcerer growled. He glared at the computer camera. "You appear to know a lot about me, Eva."

The AI was either oblivious to his murderous undertone or blatantly ignoring it. "I most certainly do, Enrique. You are the second-in-command of the infamous

Bacatá Cartel, although I must confess I cannot find any evidence of recent crimes attached to your name since you met the Witch Queen and joined the Medellin coven. By the way, did you know your chances of becoming the High Priest of your coven are currently estimated at 99.95 percent? That's a drop of 00.04 percent from last month's estimate."

Eva paused. "I see you entered into a relationship with one Anya Mendes around that time. Maybe some of your coven members believe you will join Ms. Mendes's faction. Also, I'm sorry to say, but it appears Ms. Mendes is currently extremely upset with you about something, given the conversation I'm overhearing right now."

Cortes was speechless for once.

"Damn," one of the super soldiers mumbled. "Talk about striking a guy when he's down."

Eva was silent for a moment while she processed this comment. "I'm sorry, Enrique." The AI sounded apologetic. "I did not mean to hurt your feelings. Just so you know, there is a sixty-two percent chance that Ms. Mendes will forgive your transgression."

Serena pinched the bridge of her nose while Cortes's face reddened. "Not that it isn't highly entertaining watching you freak people out Eva, but we need your help." She frowned at Jordan and Howard. "I'd normally ask Gideon to do this, however, your knowledge of the underground networks operating in Europe is more extensive than his, what with you two being several centuries old. We need to trace large orders of Gallium to Europe in the last, say, six months."

There was a short pause. Howard and Jordan

exchanged a strange look.

"Ten minutes," Howard said with a self-satisfied expression.

Jordan sneered. "You're on."

Serena stared, nonplussed. "What?"

Howard ignored her and raised an eyebrow at Jordan. "You know you're not allowed to use Eva, right?"

Jordan swore.

Serena's mouth slackened.

"Did they just make a bet?" she asked Lou.

"Yeah," Lou replied glumly.

"By the way," Howard said as he tapped rapidly on his phone screen, "is that pretty lady the Witch Queen?"

He shot a seductive smile at Mae. Vlad's face tightened.

"You must be pretty confident in winning if you're flirting," Jordan ground out, his keyboard clattering noisily.

Serena narrowed her eyes. "That guy would flirt with Death itself."

It took Jordan five seconds less than Howard to bring up a list of the largest Gallium imports in the time period they were interested in.

"I win!" Jordan exclaimed.

Howard made a face. "It was close. Plus, I've been up all night."

Jordan smirked. "Just take the loss."

A sultry female voice called out to Howard in the background. "Hurry up, Howie! We're starting the next game of strip poker!" She giggled. "We're playing in the jacuzzi this time."

Howard flashed a dazzling smile at the unseen woman.

"Coming." He looked at the camera. "I've gotta go." His grin widened. "I'm looking forward to seeing you, Mae."

He disconnected.

"Why do I feel like I'm the one who lost the bet?" Jordan said stonily in the ensuing hush.

"It's alright, Jordan," Eva comforted him. "You will always be my favorite. Despite the fact that you've lost 40:60 to Howard so far."

"She has a mean streak," one of the super soldiers observed while Jordan entered into an argument with the AI.

"Is this it?" Serena was scrolling through the data the Immortal had sent through, a frown marring her brow. The list was short. "There are only three companies?"

"I believe you should focus on the last one," Eva said. "No, Jordan. You definitely ceded that chess game to Howard last month. Your memory is failing you. Maybe you should stop inhaling doughnuts and start eating more fish. I think your brain needs the omega-3. You're also growing a paunch."

Vlad grimaced. "Remind me never to upset her."

Serena pursed her lips. "Eva, is there any particular reason why I'm looking at that address?"

"Because I have a satellite view of that location."

An image blossomed on the computer screen. Eva zoomed in.

Mae's pulse quickened. It was a parking lot.

"New York is about three hundred square miles." Serena looked at Mae. "Think you can use *Reveal* over that surface area?"

"Yes."

CHAPTER 30

Bryony put her cup down on the desk.

"Stop doing that," Abraham said.

He was sitting at his table at the other end of the office.

"Stop doing what?" she said sharply.

"Your knee. If you keep moving it like that, you're gonna dislocate something," the aide muttered. "Nobody wants to see a High Priestess on crutches. Besides, Penley looks like he's gonna be sick. He's been watching your leg for five minutes and I swear I saw his eyes roll just now."

Bryony stopped bouncing her knee and looked down at her familiar. The black cat seemed distinctly queasy.

She narrowed her eyes at Abraham. "You know, you've grown rather gutsy lately."

The sorcerer signed a paper and put it in his out tray. "Better gutsy than a wall flower."

His owl Shiloh pulled another document out from a pile with her beak and placed it dutifully in front of him.

Bryony's expression tightened. "It must be that Raven's influence. You never used to be so shameless."

"How about you leave my girlfriend out of this conversation?" He sighed at her crabby expression. "Look, I get that you want to help Mae, but the best thing we can do right now is stay out of her way. You said yourself she can trust those super soldiers. And Vlad and Cortes are with her. She'll call for us if she needs us."

The old-fashioned phone on his desk rang before she could come up with a suitable retort. Abraham picked it up.

"Hello?" The sorcerer stilled. He narrowed his eyes slightly. "They are?" He glanced at Bryony and seemed to arrive at a decision. "It's okay. Let them in."

"Who was that?" Bryony said warily.

"Friends of yours. They might cheer you up."

Bryony sniffed. "I don't need cheering up. I'm not a child."

"There, there." Abraham guided her out of her chair and into the coven meeting chambers. "I'll make us some drinks."

The doors at the far end banged open.

Regina barged in, her jackrabbit Daws hopping beside her. "Howdy, Bry-bry!" She beamed at Bryony. "We came by to see if you wanted to go for lunch."

Bryony pointed an accusing finger at the Vegas coven High Priestess and glared at Abraham. "You said they would cheer me up!"

Erik and Anya trailed in tiredly behind Regina, like casualties in the passage of a storm.

"You need cheering up, Bry?" Regina dropped down on

a couch and patted the spot next to her. "What's got you blue? Come, tell your big sis."

"I'm two years older than you," Bryony said between clenched teeth.

"You are?" Regina looked shocked at that. "Sorry, I keep forgetting." Her tone turned sympathetic. "Even though you have so many more wrinkles than me."

Bryony's eye twitched. Abraham swallowed a snort. Erik groaned.

Anya perched primly on the edge of a chair with Sable and pretended to examine a painting.

"You know what you need?" Regina ignored Bryony's dark look and leaned forward, her voice dropping to a conspiratorial whisper. "A young lover!"

Anya's eyes bulged. Abraham dropped a cup.

Regina started making hand motions. "Someone with a long, thick—*mmmph!*"

Erik had clamped a hand over his mother's mouth.

"Stop talking, I'm begging you!" the sorcerer pleaded.

His Rottweiler Ross huffed worriedly.

Abraham picked up the cup and cleared his throat loudly. "How about we change the subject?" He brought over a tray of coffee and tea and addressed Anya. "Have you heard from Cortes?"

Anya's face tightened. She avoided their gazes.

"They had a spat," Regina said at Abraham and Bryony's puzzled looks.

"He never told her what he did for a living," Erik explained diplomatically.

Sable made an annoyed sound.

Bryony sighed and offered the younger witch a tea.

"Enrique is not a bad man. He's just a victim of his circumstances. He would never have entered a life of crime had it not been for his aunt."

"Still." Anya's fingers clenched on the cup. "He kills people for a living," she finished miserably.

"I can't deny he has blood on his hands," Bryony said quietly. "And neither would Enrique. But he's not just a cold-blooded killer. Did you know he donates money to orphanages and charities in Medellin?"

Anya's eyes widened. "I didn't."

"The *Bacatá Cartel* has a vicious reputation for sure, but they also give a lot back to the community. And they keep the more nefarious gangs on a leash, hence why their primary goal is to put the fear of God in everyone. I suspect many of the stories surrounding them are made up. It's the same with the *Black Devils*. And even though the authorities would never say so publicly, syndicates like the ones Cortes and Vlad belong to make crime manageable in our society."

Anya swallowed. "Thank you. I...never thought of it that way."

Sable crooned and rubbed her head against her witch's hair.

Bryony froze. Her scalp was prickling with a forewarning born of years of experience. Regina stiffened, her eyes narrowing as she swept the chamber with her gaze.

"What's wrong?" Anya said, puzzled.

Sable screeched, startling her.

Erik jumped to his feet. "*Shield!*"

His bracelet shifted into a spear. Blue-green magic

brightened his eyes and weapon as he erected a dome around them a second before violent tremors started shaking the building.

Bryony stood up unsteadily, her heart racing. Her ring morphed into a sword. Penley's pupils flashed green.

"Is it—is it an earthquake?!" Anya shouted.

An alarm started blaring. Corruption oozed into the air.

"That's Barquiel's power!" Regina growled.

Abraham removed his cell from his pocket and tapped the screen. He stumbled and caught himself on a chair. A scowl darkened his face.

"The Dark Council's in the foyer!" He cursed. "All the camera feeds just died!"

"Let's go!" Bryony barked.

She led the charge as they ran out of the meeting chambers and made their way to the reception, the ground trembling alarmingly underneath their feet.

A group of sorcerers and witches had taken refuge under the desk in the waiting area. Brent Perkins, the man who managed the floor, gave Bryony a frightened look.

"Evacuate the building!" she ordered. "Get as many people out as you can!"

Perkins nodded tremulously.

Bryony took the stairs, Regina at her side.

"What do you think they're after?" the Vegas coven witch said in a hard voice.

"I don't know." Bryony clenched her jaw. "I guess we'll find out when we get to the bottom."

It felt like a lifetime before they reached the first floor.

Acid burned the back of Bryony's mouth when they

emerged into the entrance lobby. Bodies littered the floor, some dead, most thankfully only injured and unconscious.

"Where is it?!" Oscar screeched. He was holding a struggling sorcerer by the throat in the middle of the concourse, black magic bubbling around his fingers and in his eyes, his lynx familiar hissing at his feet. "Where is the *Book of Light*, you insects?!"

So, that's what they're after!

Fury filled Bryony's veins and ignited her core. An emerald blaze whooshed into life around her and Penley. She concentrated it into a powerful spell bomb.

"*Release him!*" she bellowed.

Her attack smashed into Oscar's flank. He cursed, his grip slipping on the sorcerer he held as he was shoved aside. His lynx whirled around and bared her teeth at Bryony.

"*Contain!*" Abraham incanted furiously.

A golden bubble formed around the barely conscious man who fell from Oscar's grasp.

Oscar straightened and glared at them. "You think that's enough to stop us, witch?!" He scanned the foyer and the dozens of Dark Council sorcerers and witches filling it before fixing Bryony with an ice-cold sneer. "I can bring this building down on your heads with a snap of my fingers. So, how about you give me what I'm looking for and I might just do Mae Jin a favor and not kill all of you!"

Eerie magic washed across Bryony, raising goosebumps on her flesh. She glanced over her shoulder.

Blue flames sizzled in Anya and Sable's eyes and around their bodies. The witch's face was contorted with rage. The Illusion Sorcery she unleashed exploded across the lobby with a thump that made Bryony's ears throb.

Bryony whirled around as screams rent the air.

The Dark Council sorcerers and witches clutched their throats and dropped to their knees with cries of agony, their familiars collapsing beside them.

Oscar grunted and grabbed his chest. His lynx whined beside him.

Bryony frowned. *Somehow, I'm not surprised to see him still standing!*

"What—" the sorcerer clenched his jaw, sweat coating his face, "what did you do, bitch?!"

He glared at Anya.

"I'm making you believe you're breathing fire, you dumb shit!" Anya snarled.

"Vlad was right," Regina murmured. "Trash talk doesn't suit her."

Erik swore. He raised his spear and erected a shield above his and Anya's heads a heartbeat before Barquiel emerged from a rift and brought his demonic sword down upon them.

The barrier shuddered. Erik grimaced. His face reddened as he poured all of his magic into his shield. Blood spurted from his mouth.

"You're good," Barquiel scoffed. "But not good enou—!"

A barrage of gold spell bombs struck the demon, blinding him for an instant.

Power blasted from Regina on a wave that made Bryony gasp.

"Get away from my son, you winged buffoon!"

CHAPTER 31

ANOTHER WALL OF SPELL BOMBS BURST INTO LIFE IN FRONT of Regina. She cast the missiles at Barquiel with a roar. Daws bared his teeth at the demon.

Frustration churned Bryony's stomach as she and Abraham followed through with their own attacks. *This isn't enough!*

She saw the same realization dawn in Abraham and Regina's eyes as the demon remained unscathed by their magic. Dread made her throat ache.

The only one who has a chance against him is Mae!

The vile energy that thickened the air in the next instant stole her breath and made her knees sag. Abraham gasped and would have fallen had she not grabbed his arm. Regina ground her teeth and dug her heels into the floor.

Demonic power throbbed around Barquiel as he floated above the foyer and observed them like insects. He glanced at Oscar.

The sorcerer was still struggling under the effect of Anya's Illusion Sorcery, foul curses wheezing out of him.

Barquiel focused a crimson stare on Bryony. "Where is the *Book of Light*? Tell me and I shall spare your wretched lives."

Penley pressed against Bryony's leg, lending her his magic. She lifted her chin and glared at the demon.

"Like I'd tell you!"

Barquiel lowered his brows. "So be it, then."

Bryony barely had time to blink before the demon was upon her.

Abraham and Regina shouted out her name as he grasped her by the throat, smashed a hole into the floor with his sword, and dragged her into the jagged opening with him, his talons scoring thin cuts into her flesh.

Bryony caught a glimpse of Penley as Barquiel raised his sword to cleave an opening in the next floor. The familiar leapt over the edge of the breach, his pupils aglow with wrath and magic.

Horror widened her eyes. *No!*

Penley landed nimbly on the demon's blade, shot down it in a flash, and alighted on his shoulder with an angry yowl. He sank his teeth and claws into Barquiel's right pinion.

The demon tossed him off with a flick of his wing. Bryony's blood curdled as Penley went flying toward a wall. The cat twisted, kicked off the surface, and flew at the demon. Barquiel snarled and slapped him away with the back of his hand.

Bone cracked. Penley's pain echoed across his bond

with Bryony as he was airborne once more, his small body heading helplessly toward a metal cabinet.

She crushed the despair threatening to overwhelm her and reached for her magic. Heat blossomed in her belly.

"*Contain!*" someone barked before she could utter the spell.

A golden sphere locked around Penley. It bounced off the cabinet before hovering in mid-air, the cat bobbing unharmed inside it.

Bryony cast a grateful look at Abraham as Barquiel pulled her down through to the next story.

The sorcerer was on his stomach, his outstretched hand manipulating *Contain* where he hung over the edge of the hole in the foyer. He met her gaze, his own wide with panic.

Regina jumped past him, her expression furious. "I'm coming, Bry!"

Daws landed on his witch's shoulder.

Bryony blinked as Regina's skirts billowed up around her. *I can't believe she's wearing silk bloomers!*

By the time Barquiel reached the basement, Bryony was covered in cuts and bruises and a thick layer of concrete dust coated her skin and eyelashes.

The only thing that had stopped her skull and her bones from breaking was the veneer of magic she'd erected around her body while the demon made his way through all six floors underneath the lobby with her riding helplessly along.

Barquiel blasted open the steel doors lining the corridor they found themselves in one after the other with sheer demonic energy.

"Where is it?!" he roared. *"Where is the damn book?!"*

Bryony's legs kicked at the floor as he dragged her along by her hair, his talons slicing into her scalp while her nails scored the scales on his wrist.

"Go to hell, demon!" she snarled.

He lifted her up and smashed her into the wall, knocking the breath out of her. Scarlet bloomed on her dress as he pressed his sword to her chest, the tip piercing her skin.

"Unless you want me to carve out your wretched heart and feed it to you, you best give me what I want!" he hissed inches from her face. "And it won't just be you, I shall do the same to your—!"

He froze, his pupils flaring.

He looked down the junction to their right. Bryony's heart sank.

Barquiel sneered. "I can smell your magic, witch!"

He unleashed a torrent of demonic energy that blasted several walls to smithereens.

Dammit! He's going to bring the whole building down at this rate!

A savage smile stretched Barquiel's mouth when the target he sought finally appeared. It was a vault shielded by powerful layers of magic.

Bryony flinched. A dark miasma had erupted around Barquiel's hand. It sheathed his sword with a sound that made her flesh crawl.

The demon stormed over to the strongroom, debris crunching and flattening under his feet, the black magic he wielded rendering her weak. He sliced through the defensive barriers she had erected with an ease that made her insides twist.

The vault door exploded inward when he kicked it. The metal hatch crashed onto the floor and slid across the repository holding the New York coven's most precious treasures.

Barquiel released Bryony. He ignored the magic-shielded lockers in the chamber and marched toward the black safe at the far end.

Fear choked Bryony's breath. "No!"

She pushed up onto her hands and knees and stumbled after the demon. Someone shouted her name in the distance.

Bryony ignored them and forged ahead, heart racing and magic blooming on her hands. *I can't let him get his hands on the* Book of Light!

A smug expression dawned on Barquiel's face when he reached the safe. "I win, Witch Queen."

He wrenched the door off its hinges.

Bryony stumbled to a stop. She closed her eyes and shuddered.

I'm too late.

A curse had her eyes snapping open.

Corruption swallowed Barquiel. He heaved his sword and smashed the safe again and again with a roar of pure fury, crushing it.

A white card fluttered out and landed at Bryony's feet. She stared.

It was a note. It said "Kiss. My. Ass." and was signed "The Witch Queen."

Bryony looked up, shock making her dizzy. Even

though the strongbox was barely recognizable, she could tell it was empty. Hysterical laughter bubbled up her throat.

Barquiel glared at her. Bryony sobered.

A muscle jumped in the demon's jawline. For one heart-clenching second, Bryony thought he would kill her.

A crimson portal hissed into life at his command. The demon disappeared inside it, his expression murderous. The corrupt magic that had signaled the Dark Council's presence in the building faded a moment later.

Debris shifted behind her. Bryony turned.

"Bry!"

A pale-faced Regina was clambering over broken concrete and smashed-up furniture, Abraham in her wake.

He overtook the witch, stormed across the vault, and grasped her shoulders. "Are you okay?!"

Bryony startled when he squeezed her to his chest. She sagged and clung to him, relief making her tremble. "I'm okay."

Abraham pulled back and scanned her. He scowled. "You're bleeding!"

Bryony patted his arm. "It's nothing that won't heal."

Some color returned to Regina's cheeks. "Glad you're alright, old gal."

Abraham turned and raised a hand. A golden sphere bobbed into view and approached.

Bryony's mouth went dry.

"Penley," she mumbled.

Abraham ended *Contain* and gently handed her the cat.

Bryony hugged the familiar gingerly, careful not to

squeeze his broken leg. Penley meowed and licked her face.

"You silly cat." Emotion choked her throat. "You're getting too old for that kind of stunt."

Abraham looked away as she wiped at a tear.

Regina wasn't as subtle. "I really thought both of you were goners back there."

Bryony pursed her lips. "I saw your bloomers."

Regina smirked at her mildly disapproving tone. "Want me to tell you where I buy them from?"

She winked and dug an elbow in Bryony's ribs. Bryony winced.

"What's this?" Abraham said.

He bent and retrieved the card from the floor. His jaw dropped open when he read it. He met Bryony's gaze.

"She—she didn't?!" he spluttered.

Regina looked curiously over his shoulder. The witch sucked in air.

"She did." Tension knotted Bryony's belly afresh as she examined the empty strongbox. "She must have retrieved the compass before she left New York. I only hope it's somewhere safe."

The distant wails of sirens reached them as they listened to the building groaning around them.

CHAPTER 32

UNEASE SWELLED INSIDE MAE AS THEY LEFT KRAKÓW Airport.

She couldn't pick up *Reveal*.

Serena glanced away from the road and shot a tense look at her. "Still nothing?"

Mae shook her head.

She caught Vlad's worried look in the rearview mirror.

It had taken two hours to fly into Poland from Budapest. She'd expected *Reveal* to show up on her internal radar the closer they'd gotten to Kraków. The spell had remained stubbornly silent so far.

They reached the outskirts of the city and drove around Old Town. Dusk was falling by the time Serena pulled into a parking lot between a hip hotel and a private clinic, close to the city's train station. It was the location Eva had identified as the one most worthy of their interest.

Mae climbed out of the vehicle while the rest of their convoy piled in behind them.

Her stomach churned. *Did Vedran manage to get rid of my spell?*

Maybe there is another reason why you cannot sense it, my witch, Brimstone hazarded.

The fox accompanied her as she walked to the middle of the car park.

Mae drew on her core. *"Reveal!"*

Her magic returned nothing. Hellreaver hummed nervously against her chest.

Serena and Vlad joined her, Cortes and Violet in their wake.

"You think the Sorcerer King undid your magic?" the incubus asked, his tone mirroring her trepidation.

"Either that or we're at the wrong location."

"My gut's telling me this is the right place," Serena said quietly.

A cell phone chimed behind them. It was Miles's.

The sorcerer answered it. "Hi, Brent."

He froze.

A chill danced through Mae as she watched the blood drain from his face. He met her gaze, his own stunned. His hand fell limply to his side when the call disconnected.

"The New York coven is under attack!" he said numbly.

"What?!" Violet gasped.

"Anya." Dread widened Cortes's pupils. "She went there today!"

Popo made an anxious sound.

"Dammit!" Mae cursed.

Her insides twisted at this unexpected turn of events. *Why now?!*

"Oscar must be in New York," Serena said coldly. "That's the only logical explanation for why you can't pick up *Reveal*."

Mae's nails bit into her palms. "I think you're right."

"That's gonna make finding out where the Dark Council is holed up harder," Lou grunted.

Vlad frowned. "Maybe Dietrich has contacts in this city."

Serena's expression tightened. "It'll take time to root them out, if there are any. And I have the nasty feeling time is of the essence right now."

Touch the ground...

Mae's scalp prickled. She looked around wildly. "Did you guys hear that just now?"

Vlad shared a wary glance with Serena. "Hear what?"

Touch the ground, my daughters...

Mae's heart stuttered.

Na Ri's presence swelled inside her subconscious. *Mother?!*

Ran Soyun's warmth filled their souls. *He is trying to find you...*

It took Mae a heartbeat to register the meaning behind the faint words. Hope stole her breath. She dropped down and pressed her hands against the asphalt, her pulse racing.

"Mae?" Vlad said, startled.

She ignored the incubus and closed her eyes. *Please! Please, let this be what I think it is!*

Her chest tightened painfully when a faint pulse of

white magic laced with Hellfire Magic brushed against her fingertips.

Mae swallowed a sob, relief rendering her weak.

"You're scaring me," Vlad mumbled, his voice taut with fear.

She looked up at him fiercely through her tears. "It's Nikolai! I can feel his magic! He's looking for me!"

Serena traded a sharp look with Lou. He nodded curtly.

"Think you can follow it?" she asked Mae.

"Yes."

"This could be a trap," Vlad warned stiffly.

Mae rose and wiped her eyes with the back of her hand. "It isn't."

The incubus lowered his brows. "How can you be so sure?"

"Because Ran Soyun told me so."

The trail led them thirty miles south of Kraków, into a mountain range that crossed over into Slovakia. Stars peppered the night sky as the SUVs raced up tortuous roads that soon turned into dirt tracks. Dark gullies where rivers gleamed appeared from time to time beyond vertiginous drops.

"We're close," Mae said.

Her fingers dug into her thighs as she focused on the thread of white magic she could sense. She could only imagine what Nikolai must be going through right now. The fact that he was looking for her and Ran Soyun knew about it was something she couldn't wrap her head around.

Only one thing was clear. She had to get to him.

Brimstone's growl made her scalp prickle. Hellreaver released an angry hum. Mae blinked. Something had just resonated with their cores.

A scowl furrowed her brow. "I can feel *Reveal* up ahead!"

Serena floored the gas. They crested a peak minutes later.

Mae's eyes widened. "Stop!"

The tires raised a shower of dirt and pebbles as Serena braked. The SUV skidded to a stop on the side of the track, everyone inside cursing. The other vehicles decelerated with sharp screeches behind them, Lou's bumper stopping inches from Cortes's door.

"You know, you really need to give me a bit more warning than that," Serena said darkly.

Mae opened the door and jumped out, her heart in her throat. She walked past the edge of the trail and headed for a cliff a short distance away. A shadowy valley opened up beyond it.

Trees shrouded the flanks of the depression. The forest stopped on the edge of a lake as still as a mirror in the light of the rising moon.

An island stood in the middle of the expanse of water.

Straddling it was a castle.

❄

"WHAT DID YOU JUST SAY?"

Vedran stared at Barquiel like he'd grown another horn.

The demon met his furious gaze, the anger that had

237

ignited inside him in New York simmering in his veins still.

"The compass isn't in New York. Even Bryony Cross looked shocked when she saw the empty safe. Mae Jin must have it with her."

Vedran remained frozen for a moment. A vicious snarl left him as he wiped the contents off his desk with a sweep of his arm, his features contorted in an enraged mask.

An antique clock smashed onto the floor and rolled toward Oscar. The sorcerer swallowed. He flinched at the black magic throbbing across the chamber.

"Then, we must find her," Vedran growled. "Find that damn witch and get that compass!"

"How?" Oscar mumbled.

"We don't even know if she's still in Budapest," Barquiel said stiffly.

"Use Nikolai as bait."

Surprise jolted the demon. "What?"

"You heard me the first time." Vedran's eyes burned with a darkness that seemed to absorb the light in the room. "If he won't cooperate, make him. I don't care what you do to him, as long as his core remains intact."

Barquiel's pulse quickened. *He's lost his fucking mind. Nikolai is an asset neither he nor I can afford to lose!*

Oscar's eyes widened as his father's meaning sank in. "Wait. Are you saying the Illusion Sorcery he's under is failing?!"

He shrank back when Vedran fixed him with a glare.

The Sorcerer King took a shuddering breath and regained a measure of control over his emotions. "I'm beginning to suspect the reason he blacked out when he tried to remove her magic from your core was because he regained some of his memories. Which makes me think she put a spell inside you to combat the Illusion Sorcery he was under."

Oscar blanched. His hand trembled as he touched his belly. Barquiel could tell the sound of that scared the living daylights out of the sorcerer.

"Forcing him to open the fake compass so soon after that first insult undid more of Anya Mendes's magic," Vedran continued bitterly. He paused. "That was my fault entirely. I was in too much of a rush to get my hands on the *Book of Shadows.*"

Barquiel masked his surprise. *I never thought I'd see the day this man would admit to his mistakes.*

"Does that mean he's no longer of any use to us?" Oscar said in a brittle tone.

Barquiel could see the sick excitement building behind his eyes. Having to play the role of nice older brother to Nikolai in the past month had enraged him to no end. He was obviously looking forward to being able to beat the sibling he hated to a pulp again, like he used to when they were children.

Except he doesn't realize how much stronger Nikolai is now, the fool.

"Oh, he is, so don't go getting ideas," Vedran warned his heir.

He removed something from a drawer. It was a stone, its smooth surface inky but for the sizzling blue runes scored into it.

Barquiel's pulse quickened. He recognized the item.

A sinister expression tightened the Sorcerer King's face. "Once I put this inside Nikolai's core, his hatred for the Witch Queen will eat him alive and he will do my bidding once more." He blinked, as if an idea had just come to him. "In fact, why don't I just do that now. It will make getting him to bait Mae Jin that much easier." He eyed Oscar coldly. "Go fetch him."

But try as he might, the sorcerer could not find his brother.

CHAPTER 33

SERENA SLIPPED SILENTLY OUT OF THE WATER. HER nanorobot suit shifted color, adapting to their new surroundings. Tension tightened Mae's limbs as she emerged from the lake with Brimstone and joined the super soldier behind the bushes where she crouched. Vlad, Tarang, and Cortes were seconds behind her, Popo flying low next to his sorcerer.

Water dripped off the wetsuit Serena had given Mae. Hellreaver lay still against her chest. Like Brimstone, the weapon's attention was focused on what he could sense through their bond.

Nikolai's magic throbbed urgently against their cores.

He's close, my witch, Brimstone said.

Mae swallowed. *Yes.*

Flaming torches and lanterns dotted the grounds and the walls of the keep. They could see Dark Council sorcerers and witches patrolling the area.

The sounds of a commotion reached them just as the

Nolan cousins and the rest of the super soldiers surfaced, Lou and Tom bringing up the rear.

Mae's shoulders knotted. "Do they know we're here?"

Serena raised a hand to silence them and cocked her head. "No."

Mae could tell her enhanced hearing was enabling her to pick up the conversation between the guards near the entrance and the flustered witch who'd just run out of the castle.

The super soldier furrowed her brow. "They're looking for Nikolai."

Mae's stomach lurched.

"He's hiding from them?" Cortes said.

The Columbian was less distressed than he had been in the parking lot in Kraków. If anything, his fear for Anya had morphed into a laser-like focus to make the ones responsible for threatening her pay for their transgression.

Abraham had called them on the drive to the mountains.

The New York coven had suffered twelve fatalities as a result of the attack on their headquarters by Barquiel and Oscar. Considering the damage the building had sustained, it was a miracle there hadn't been more victims. The coven headquarters had been condemned by the city's engineers, the damage to its foundations pronounced too severe to fix.

Ice had filled Mae's veins when she'd discovered the reason for the attack and what Barquiel had done to Bryony and her familiar.

"They were after the *Book of Light?!*" she'd mumbled, her worst fears realized.

"Yes." Abraham's tone had turned stern. "No one was amused by the note you left in the safe by the way, especially not the demon."

"What note?" Vlad had said, nonplussed.

"Oh." Mae had fidgeted under their stares. "You guys found that, huh?"

Serena's lips had twitched when Bryony's aide described what Barquiel had discovered in the New York coven's vault.

"Incidentally, when exactly did you do it?" Abraham had asked suspiciously while Vlad pinched the bridge of his nose and Cortes muttered something under his breath.

"The day I came to the coven, after the incident in Concord," Mae had replied guiltily. "Nikolai knew where it was, after all."

A heavy sigh had traveled down the line.

"I just hope wherever you've hidden it, Barquiel and the Dark Council can't get to it," Abraham had said somberly before bidding them good luck and disconnecting.

Serena's voice brought Mae back to the present.

"If I had regained my memories and was trying to get in touch with my allies, I wouldn't flounce around in enemy territory."

"Where could he be though?" Vlad muttered. "It's an island."

Hellreaver quivered. Brimstone's ears pricked up.

My witch, he warned.

243

Mae's pulse spiked. Something was rising through the ground. Her belly clenched on a wave of awareness.

It was a power she knew as well as her own.

Cortes startled when he sensed the magic bubbling beneath them. "What the—?!"

Crimson flashed in Vlad's eyes.

He reached for Mae a heartbeat before *Transmigrate* sucked her, Brimstone, and Hellreaver into the earth.

❄

NIKOLAI GRITTED HIS TEETH AS THE SPELL ROARED AROUND him with a violence that rattled his bones. Blazing rivers cascaded into the dazzling, infinite space where he crouched, their power amplifying his and Alastair's cores.

The air trembled some fifteen feet ahead of him. It exploded with a *whoomph* a second later.

His breath locked in his throat when Mae appeared, Brimstone at her side, and Hellreaver around her neck.

She staggered before regaining her balance, the waves of pulsing energy in the nexus making her dark hair ripple and brightening her skin where it was exposed outside her wetsuit. Her gaze found him as he climbed unsteadily to his feet. Alastair issued a hesitant croak on his shoulder.

Tears bloomed in Mae's eyes. Her face crumpled. "Nikolai!"

His vision blurred. He wiped his eyes, not wanting to miss a single moment of their reunion.

"I'm sorry," he rasped. "I didn't—I didn't know what I was doing!"

Mae closed the distance to him, clasped his face, and tugged him down for a kiss that scorched his soul.

Happiness. Relief. Sorrow. Anger. Love.

The emotions wrapped him in a storm that threatened to wreck his heart and tear his mind apart. His only anchor was the woman in his arms, her heat cocooning him as she wrapped her arms around his neck and pressed against him, the passion in her touch and her lips making his body burn.

It was a while before he lifted his head and pulled back. He gazed into the Witch Queen's bright eyes and said the words he should have told her a long time ago.

"I love you, Mae."

She sobbed and clenched her hands on his shirt.

Brimstone whined. Hellreaver trembled.

"I—I love you too!" Mae blubbered.

Nikolai chuckled at her messy face. He wiped snot from her nose with his sleeve. "You're an ugly crier."

She punched him in the gut. He gasped, laughter bubbling up his throat. He grabbed her fingers and stayed her hand as she made to lift it off his belly.

"Erase the rest of the Illusion Sorcery." He pressed his forehead against hers. "Make me the man you fell in love with, Mae."

Her breath caught, her skin hot against his.

"Okay," she said tremulously.

Nikolai reached up and steadied Alastair. Heat seeped into his flesh as she drew on her magic. Redness flared in Brimstone's eyes. Crimson bloomed around Hellreaver.

"Are you ready?" Mae asked.

Nikolai steeled himself and dipped his chin.

She inhaled and invoked the conjuration. *"Dissever!"*

A crimson fire laced with white magic and gold runes blazed through his blood and Alastair's until it reached their cores. The vestiges of the Illusion Sorcery they had inadvertently fallen under shattered and disappeared as the spell blasted it to smithereens.

Every memory Nikolai had lost returned in a kaleidoscope that made his head spin and his chest tighten with a remorse so deep he feared it would drown him. Alastair shuddered under his hand.

The last images drew a tortured sound from them both.

All the horrific things they had done to Mae, Brimstone, and Hellreaver in that church in Concord blazed through Nikolai's mind. He didn't realize he was weeping until Mae kissed his wet cheeks and hugged him to her.

"I'm sorry!" he cried brokenly in the crook of her neck. "I'm so sorry I hurt you, Mae! Your leg!"

"It's okay," she whispered. "It's all healed up."

She held him for a long time, her tears soaking into his hair.

Alastair drooped, his body trembling. Brimstone made a soft sound. The crow hesitated before flying down. The demon fox nudged him gently with his snout before sitting and curling his tail around him.

Nikolai finally raised his head, his jaw set in a hard line.

He grasped Mae's shoulders. "I have something to say to you." He swallowed and looked at Brimstone and Hellreaver. "All three of you."

Mae's eyes flared when he told them about Barquiel and the rift. Disbelief drained the color from her face as he described whom he had seen in the cave, deep inside the Underworld.

Crimson detonated around the Witch Queen and her bonds when he recounted what Barquiel intended to do and Vedran's dark goals.

CHAPTER 34

VLAD'S HEART POUNDED IN HIS CHEST, HIS IMPULSE TO storm into the Dark Council's stronghold and burn the place to the ground making his skin itch.

It had been ten minutes since Mae had disappeared.

"Calm down," Cortes warned in a low voice. "That spell was *Transmigrate*. Which means she's in a nexus right now, probably with Nikolai. Since this place isn't on fire, we can presume they're not fighting."

Serena kept her eyes on the keep.

It was clear from the shouts they could hear and the way people were frantically searching the castle and the grounds that they hadn't found any sign of the missing sorcerer yet.

"They'll come check this area soon," Lou warned.

"I know." Serena looked at Tom. "How close are you?"

"It's done."

A nanorobot drone the size of a ladybug landed on

Tom's wrist and was absorbed into his suit. He slipped a tablet out of his waterproof backpack.

A three-dimensional map of the castle and the island appeared on the screen after he booted it up. Tom rotated it with his fingers and superimposed an infrared satellite image. Red silhouettes glowed into life in and around the property.

Cortes stared. "You guys are getting live satellite intel?"

"The Immortals have their own array," Serena murmured, her attention on the display.

Tom indicated the lowest level of the keep, a hundred and fifty feet underground. "From the nanorobot energy signatures the drone picked up, it looks like our targets are here."

Serena leaned forward. "Expand that."

She pointed. Tom did as she instructed. A dungeon grew in size, beneath the southern shore of the island. It looked to be attached to some kind of underground lab.

Fast-moving shapes swarmed the cells inside it.

Lou frowned. "Is it just me, or does that look like way more devils than we saw in New York?"

Serena's face tightened. "It's not just you."

Tarang growled a warning. The hairs lifted on the back of Vlad's neck. He whirled around in time to see Mae reappear with Brimstone and Hellreaver. His stomach lurched.

Nikolai and Alastair were with them.

The sorcerer raised his hands slowly in the face of the guns leveled at him. The giddy feeling that swept over Vlad at seeing Mae back safe and sound was swallowed by rage. He rose and strode past her, his teeth clenched so tight his face hurt.

"Vlad, wait—" Mae started in a strained voice.

He ignored her plea and punched Nikolai in the jaw.

"You bastard!" he hissed. "How could you do that to her?!"

"Er, guys?" Lou lowered his gun in the awkward hush. "We really don't have time for your threesome drama right now."

"Give them a minute." Serena sighed and tucked her weapon in her holster. "This is important."

Vlad practically vibrated with anger as he loomed over Nikolai. The sorcerer straightened and looked at him steadily.

"It's good to see you again," he said quietly. "Thanks for being there for Mae." He faltered. "And I'm sorry. For everything."

Vlad didn't miss the meaning behind his last words. He fisted his hands. *This asshole might as well just crow about the fact he's won Mae's heart!*

Tarang nudged his leg.

Vlad noticed Nikolai's red eyes and the tear stains on his face for the first time. He recalled the horrors the palace outside Budapest had revealed about the sorcerer's past. A bolt of remorse churned his belly.

Alastair hopped onto the ground and greeted the other familiars with a nervous sound. They crowded around him and butted him gently, the tiger sending the bird bowling over twice.

Cortes came up to Vlad and placed a hand on his

shoulder. "It's clear he regrets what he did. No one can fight an Illusion Sorcery as powerful as Anya's."

"I've forgiven him," Mae told Vlad stiffly. "I hope you can do so too."

There was an edge to her voice that hadn't been there before. One the incubus didn't like. Serena seemed to notice it too.

What happened down there?

He took a ragged breath, conscious he'd lost this battle.

"We good?" Nikolai said.

"I haven't given up on her," Vlad snapped. "And you're still an asshole." A thought came to him then. "Did she tell you she moved in with me?"

Mae pretended to stare at the ground.

Nikolai narrowed his eyes slightly. "No, she didn't."

"How about we save the rest of this for later?" Serena indicated the map on Tom's tablet. "What's the fastest way of getting in there undetected?"

❄

Violet eyed the opening of the culvert with a doubtful look. "Isn't this the sewers?"

"It used to be, before they installed plumbing," Nikolai said.

He bent slightly and headed inside the conduit. Mae followed.

Nikolai had skirted the woods at the edge of the island and brought them to the rear of the castle. Mae could feel Vedran's black magic and Barquiel's corruption somewhere above them. They made her fingers twitch.

From the tension thrumming through Brimstone and Hellreaver and the anger burning through Na Ri, they were as eager to confront their enemy as she was.

Distant shouts echoed down the tunnel minutes later.

"We're close," Nikolai warned.

They emerged into an empty chamber where several culverts met. Boots clattered noisily on a metal grating some ten feet above them.

A familiar voice had Nikolai's shoulders knotting and Mae clenching her jaw.

"Find him! Find that bastard!" Oscar screeched somewhere close by.

Serena spoke. "You know, the five of you could leave with Nikolai."

Mae turned. The super soldier was studying her with an inscrutable look.

"Your goal was to rescue him." Serena indicated the sorcerer with a tilt of her head. "We can probably extract Dietrich without the Dark Council being any the wiser."

"She's right," Lou murmured.

Nikolai frowned. Mae had told him about the super soldiers and their mission before they'd left the nexus.

"I'm afraid that's going to be impossible," Mae said in a lifeless voice.

Serena frowned at her tone. "Why is that?"

"One, we don't abandon our friends. Two, there's a demon up there who intends to carve out the core in my heart so he can revive my dead mother and a sorcerer who wants to kill his own son so he can become a god."

Vlad's pupils flared with redness. Cortes grew deathly still.

Violet shared a shocked look with Miles.

"What do you mean?" the witch mumbled, pale-faced.

Mae had to fist her hands to stop them from shaking while she told them what Nikolai had discovered only that day.

"Your mother is alive?" Serena said.

Mae gathered from the super soldier's surprised expression that the Immortal seer she was close to had not foreseen this.

"Alive is a questionable status."

Serena hesitated. "I'm sorry." She gazed at the grille above them before looking at a culvert facing south. "We should split up. Dietrich is down there with his modified devils."

Mae furrowed her brow. "You should take someone who can use magic."

"I'll go," Violet volunteered.

"No." Vlad's incubus energy washed across Mae. A crimson ball flared on his fingertips. "This will be more useful against those devils."

"Are you sure?" Serena shot a glance at Mae. "I thought you'd want to—"

"I'm sure." Vlad faced Mae. "We'll finish this and come back you up."

Her belly clenched as she watched him. She knew what she was feeling was selfish. She'd just reunited with Nikolai. She had no claim on Vlad. But she couldn't fathom what it would do to her if she lost the incubus.

I might not be in a position to give him my heart. But that doesn't mean I don't care for him deeply.

Mae swallowed and forced herself to say the words he needed to hear. "Be careful."

Vlad smiled faintly. "I always am, Princess." His smile faded as he looked at Nikolai. "I'm counting on you."

"Don't do anything stupid," the sorcerer muttered.

CHAPTER 35

BARQUIEL PACED HIS SUITE, HIS HANDS FISTING AND opening at his sides.

Things were starting to fall apart.

Nikolai putting on a disappearing act was one thing. Vedran losing control over it was a whole other matter.

Never mind what happened in New York!

He snarled and punched a wall at the memory of the Witch Queen's note. Stone cracked beneath his fist.

Barquiel marched over to the windows. Lanterns moved in the gloom as the Dark Council continued to scour the grounds for the missing sorcerer. He gnashed his teeth.

This is why humans are useless! Had Vedran kept a closer eye on his precious progeny, things would never have gotten this bad!

Nikolai was too important for him to overlook in his schemes. Stopping Vedran from absorbing his core was only one reason. The sorcerer might prove useful once Ran Soyun was revived.

His white magic complemented hers, which meant he could act as a source of power for the newly arisen Witch Queen.

Where the hell could that little rat have gone?! It's a goddamn island!

A thought came to him then. He lowered his brows.

Maybe I should send some demons out to look for him. Or even better, Dietrich's devils.

He turned, intent on making his way to the Immortal's lab. Something brushed against his senses as he took a step toward the doors. Barquiel stiffened.

The energy he'd just felt was growing exponentially.

His eyes widened when he finally put a name to the presence approaching his chambers at a phenomenal speed. *No! That's impossible! She couldn't—!*

The doors imploded on a blast of crimson magic that knocked him off his feet. Barquiel snapped his wings and braced in mid-air before he could strike the wall, his heartbeat accelerating.

❄

MAE'S BLOOD BOILED WITH WRATH AS SHE STEPPED INSIDE the suite, Hellreaver in her grasp and Brimstone towering above her in his nine-tailed form. The magic pulsing through their bond rattled the windows and shook the floor.

She'd lost track of Vedran's magic on her way to the southwest tower, where Nikolai had told her his office was. The Sorcerer King had probably vanished at the first sign of trouble.

Mae had decided to go after her second target.

To her chagrin, she hadn't encountered as many Dark Council members as she would have liked on her way to Barquiel's chambers. Smashing the faces of the few she had crossed paths with hadn't even put a dent in her thirst for revenge.

She scowled at the demon. *Punching this asshole might!*

"Be careful, my witch," Brimstone warned.

"You!" Barquiel hissed.

The air split open beside him. He withdrew his dark broadsword from a rift, his expression furious.

Mae watched the crimson-tinged crack close with clenched teeth. *I doubt that's the portal Nikolai saw.*

"It isn't, my witch," Brimstone said, his gaze on Barquiel. *"That window only accesses an interdimensional pocket."*

Confusion flitted across the demon's face at their exchange. His lip curled. "How did you find this place?!"

Mae could barely see for her rage. "Why does it matter how I found the hole you've been hiding in, you impotent bastard?! More importantly, where is my mother? *Where is Ran Soyun?!*"

Na Ri's voice underscored her bellow.

Shock flared in Barquiel's eyes.

Mae moved.

Sparks exploded when Hellreaver made contact with Barquiel's sword. The voices of a thousand enraged fiends left the weapon on a deafening ululation. He bit down, his serrated blades throbbing with a power so pure it made him glow.

Mae slammed a hand against Barquiel's stomach as he struggled to free his sword from Hellreaver's grasp. Magic surged through her veins.

"*NEGATE!*"

Barquiel gasped, the spell taking a chunk out of his demonic energy. A thin crack appeared in his sword. He bared his teeth in a snarl, kicked Hellreaver, and retreated a beat. His figure blurred.

Brimstone caught him with a giant paw as he shot under Hellreaver and came at Mae, the fox's magic-tipped claws carving the demon's scales and scoring red lines across his chest before he sent him flying into a wall.

Glass exploded as Barquiel struck a mirror with his back.

"*Answer my witch's question!*" Flecks of drool fell from the demon fox's jaws as he growled at their nemesis. "*Where is my former queen?!*"

Barquiel looked down and touched the dark blood trickling down his flesh. His expression grew thunderous. Corruption exploded around him.

Mae ground her teeth, the crippling pressure weighing her down. Her knees sagged. Hellreaver howled in her grip as he slumped under the demon archduke's powers. Brimstone bared his fangs, his body bowing.

Barquiel froze when they slowly straightened.

"How—?!" The demon's crimson eyes rounded. "How are you doing that?!"

The power of three blazed in Mae's bones, the runes of the spell she and Na Ri had concocted on the drive to the mountains melding together.

"I realized something interesting when I took down

Vedran's barrier yesterday, outside that awful palace in the forest."

Barquiel flinched.

Mae sneered. "If you combine *Absorb* with *Negate*, it has an interesting effect. Want to know what that is?"

Dread tightened Barquiel's face for a moment. A determined scowl creased his brow. Darkness bubbled in his eyes and bloomed around his body as he called forth the black magic he had obtained through Vedran and Dietrich.

"Yeah, I don't think that's gonna work!" Mae growled. Fire throbbed across her bond with Brimstone and Hellreaver as the incantation came to life. *"REVERSE!"*

The hellish power congealing the air dissipated with a thump that made Barquiel gasp. He clutched his chest and groaned. Panic contorted his features.

Mae knew he'd just realized the invocation was absorbing his powers even faster than *Negate*. She closed the distance to the demon, blood pounding in her skull with every step she took.

"Now, tell me where my mother is, you scumbag!"

"My witch!" Brimstone barked.

Mae's pulse stuttered.

A crimson portal had opened behind Barquiel. He tipped backward into it, a mocking light brightening his pupils.

Horror turned her blood to ice. *No!*

Na Ri's presence filled her mind. Power burned her cores, freezing her breath.

The incantation left Mae's lips unbidden, her first incarnation instinctively invoking the one spell that could

259

stop Barquiel where he was headed. A spell their demon father had taught them.

"*CHAOS SEAL!*"

Demonic magic seared the air. An incoherent scream escaped Barquiel as the portal twisted around his falling body.

It closed with a hiss.

❄

NIKOLAI'S PULSE THUMPED WHEN HE ENTERED THE CASTLE foyer from a side passage. His gaze found Oscar on the landing where he stood barking orders. It took everything he had to hide the revulsion churning his stomach at the sight of his brother.

It was a moment before the closest Dark Council sorcerers and witches clocked his presence. A hush fell across the foyer and spread into the gallery overlooking the entrance. Alastair tensed at their stares.

Oscar turned.

Nikolai crossed the hall at a casual pace. "I heard you were looking for me."

His voice echoed in the strained silence.

Oscar frowned heavily. "Where did you go?! We've been searching everywhere for you!"

Nikolai shrugged. "I went for a walk."

Low murmurs started around him. His answer turned Oscar's expression ugly.

"Are you messing with me right now?!" the sorcerer snapped.

Nikolai spread his hands, his tone innocuous. "Why ever would I do that?"

He started up the stairs, magic warming his belly.

Oscar went still as he approached. "Father was right." His eyes shrank to slits. "You remember, don't you?!"

Drabek hissed around his ankles.

Nikolai slowed fractionally, a tell Oscar didn't miss.

Black magic bloomed around the sorcerer. His pupils and those of his lynx shifted to obsidian.

Moon Shield detonated in front of Nikolai, blocking the spell bomb Oscar hurled at him in a blur of motion.

The sorcerer flinched when his attack bounced off the shimmering barrier. It took a chunk out of one of the stone columns supporting the gallery. The sorcerers and witches next to it shrank back with startled cries.

"How?!" Oscar retreated a step as Nikolai drew closer, his eyes rounding. "How did you do that without saying the spell out loud?!"

Nikolai's heart raced, Alastair's surprise mirroring his own. It was only in that moment that he'd managed to invoke his first wordless spell. He looked at his hand and flexed his fingers. The magic in their cores felt infinitely stronger.

Is it because we've just been inside a nexus?!

Alastair ruffled his feathers. Nikolai swallowed.

No. It's because my soul has acknowledged Mae again, just as hers has accepted mine. This is the power granted to me by virtue of being her consort.

There was no time to ponder the humbling truth he'd just grasped.

Nikolai lowered his brows and said the words he knew

would infuriate Oscar like little else. "It's because I'm more powerful than you are, brother."

Rage brought a rush of color to Oscar's face.

"Bring this bastard down!" he roared at the Dark Council.

More sorcerers and witches had appeared from the innards of the castle. Black magic spell bombs bloomed into life in the entrance hall and around the gallery. They sailed toward him, a barrage of corrupt spheres.

Alastair's core throbbed in tandem with his own. Heat scorched his veins.

"Moon Fire!"

CHAPTER 36

WHITE FLAMES BURST INTO LIFE AROUND NIKOLAI AND Alastair. They roared across the foyer and swept through the gallery in the blink of an eye, neutralizing the Dark Council's attacks. The men and women yelled and cursed as the fire engulfed their clothes and raised blisters on their skin.

Those who had been spared recoiled.

Cortes, Violet, and Miles had emerged from the shadows around the lobby. Magic throbbed around them and their familiars.

Nikolai glanced at Cortes. "Did you take care of what I told you to?"

"Yeah." The Columbian's stony gaze remained focused on their enemy. "We sank their boats. They're not getting off this island unless they swim. And they'll die of hypothermia before they reach the other shore."

The Dark Council sorcerers and witches exchanged frightened glances.

"It doesn't matter!" Oscar glowered at Nikolai from behind the black magic shield he had raised. Sweat beaded his face. "Barquiel can rift us out of here!"

Nikolai had to hand it to the sorcerer. That he was managing to maintain his defenses in the face of *Moon Fire* was an impressive feat.

He indicated the ceiling with a cocked thumb. "Do you hear that?"

Oscar looked up. Tension knotted his shoulders. Booms echoed dimly from the direction of the northeast tower. They shook dust from the ceiling.

"That's Mae, kicking Barquiel's ass," Nikolai said with a faint smile.

"Wow, she'd really going at it, huh?" Violet muttered. She caught a glimpse of a sorcerer trying to slip away and brought him down with a spell bomb. "No one gave you permission to leave, asshole!"

Fury reddened Oscar's face and corded the muscles in his neck as she engaged the Dark Council with Cortes and Miles.

He glared at Nikolai. "I won't let you get away with this!"

A chill coursed through Nikolai at the black magic boiling in the sorcerer's eyes. It overspilled his skin, mottling his face with inky lines. Drabek flinched and looked up at her sorcerer.

Nikolai clenched his jaw. *That fool. Even his familiar knows that power will consume him!*

Maybe it was a vestige of familial attachment that made him reach out to the man glowering at him. Oscar was as much a victim of circumstances as he was.

Had he grown up in a different environment, he might not have embraced the path of evil.

"Our father's madness must stop, Oscar," Nikolai said quietly. "Please, withdraw from this battle, brother."

Oscar stilled.

For a moment, Nikolai thought he'd gotten through to him.

The sorcerer's face distorted in a mask of outrage.

"You are not my brother!" he screamed. He raised a trembling hand. *"ROT!"*

Moon Fire flickered.

Oscar moved, the flames around his barrier retreating. He took something out of his pocket and approached Nikolai. It was a stone glimmering with fiery, blue runes.

Nikolai's mouth went dry when he recognized his brother's intentions.

"That's right, you bastard of a whore!" Oscar spat. "Soon, you'll be licking my boots and doing my bidding. That includes killing that little bitch of yours!"

A red mist descended in front of Nikolai. He scowled and grabbed the sorcerer's wrist as he made to drive the Illusion Sorcery stone containing Anya Mendes's spell inside his body.

Power ignited his and Alastair's cores.

The crow squawked, eyes and wings blazing with all the colors of the magic they wielded. A conjuration they had used only once before blazed through Nikolai's mind.

"RUPTURE!" he snarled.

The stone cracked and disintegrated, the magic it contained winking out. Oscar screamed as his arm crumpled and shattered. Drabek screeched.

Nikolai ignored the familiar's cry of pain. He pressed a hand to Oscar's stomach and met his shocked gaze. The second spell left his throat on a hiss.

"*Subjugate!*"

Drabek fell and convulsed. Oscar threw his head back and screamed. Vessels burst in the whites of his eyes. Blood oozed out of his nose. He thrashed in Nikolai's hold, desperate to resist the spell he and Vedran once used to overwrite Anya Mendes's bond with her familiar.

But Nikolai's magic was stronger.

❄

BLOOD SPLASHED VLAD'S CLOTHES AS HE FELLED A DEMON. Tarang brought down another and ripped its head clean off before spitting it on the floor, his pupils a bright scarlet.

The fiend's skull rolled and bumped into Tom's boot.

The super soldier shuddered. "Ugh! I hate these things!"

Lou grabbed the throat of the fiend coming at him and shot him in the eye. The creature slumped in his grasp, the holy-water-impregnated and divine-power-coated bullet melting its brain.

Serena removed her dagger from a demon's heart and rose. "Looks like he's hiding back there."

Vlad followed her gaze to the iron-clad door some fifty feet away, at the end of a tunnel.

Dietrich had evidently been clued-in on the attack on the keep. He'd closed himself off in his lab, but not before releasing a bunch of demons first.

There were ten left. They stood between them and the door.

Mae's magic brushed Vlad's skin, raising goosebumps on his flesh. He looked up, his pulse quickening. He could tell she was fighting someone powerful.

I need to get to her!

Incubus energy flooded his veins and lit the air with a crimson glow. He ground his teeth and opened himself up to the darkness that always lived within him. Tarang's muscles bunched, hackles rising and redness flashing in his eyes.

It had gotten easier for them to wield the devastating power they rarely unleashed, lest they lose control and go on a rampage.

That's probably because of Mae.

Serena squinted at him. "Look, I don't know what you're thinking, but things are pretty tight down here, so you should probably—"

"Let's do this, Tarang!" Vlad bit out.

They swept across the corridor, a storm of blades, fangs, and claws glinting in a macabre dance as they dispatched the demons in their path. They twisted, jumped, bolted up walls, and ducked beneath talons, their aim true and their movements lightning quick.

Dark blood painted the walls and floor in the passage.

Vlad and Tarang landed in front of the door seconds later, their chests heaving.

"Or they could do that," Lou told Serena dully.

She sighed.

Vlad tried to cut the lock with his diamond-edged swords. Something buffered the attack. He flinched as a wall of black magic and demonic energy glimmered into view.

"What the hell is this?!"

Serena approached, frowning. "Let me try."

A light caught Vlad's gaze. A golden glow fluttered on the super soldier's daggers. He blinked. Her skin was shining with the same radiance.

Is that the divine power Mae was talking about?!

He stepped aside to make way for her. Serena stabbed the weapons in the invisible barrier. It resisted her.

Her pupils brightened, the divine energy within her lighting up the nanorobots at the back of her retinae. She clenched her jaw, dug her heels into the ground, and tried to power through.

Sparks exploded when the blades punctured the shield.

Vlad sucked in air as the door's defenses tried to blast her off, the force of the recoil making his hair flutter.

"You'd better stand back," Serena warned in a deadly voice.

He retreated to Lou's side, Tarang following.

A vein throbbed in Serena's temple. The muscles on her arms and legs bunched. She roared and cut through the barrier, her boots digging indents into the ground.

"Now!"

Lou fired at the exposed lock. Vlad carved through the bullet-riddled metal with his swords. Serena stepped back and kicked the door with her foot.

It fell slowly inward. A vile stench flooded the tunnel as it clattered noisily onto a stone floor.

Tom heaved. Tarang growled. Vlad narrowed his eyes. He could smell death coming from the shadows beyond.

They entered and looked around, senses on high alert.

Furnaces glowed here and there, the light they gave off outlining myriad glass equipment and complex machines atop the work benches. Cold cabinets stood against one wall, their low hum drowned out by the generators powering them.

"Serena," Lou warned.

Vlad looked in the direction the super soldier was staring. A human bone still covered in flesh and gristle lay on the floor. More became visible as his eyes adjusted to the gloom.

"Fuck," Tom muttered.

Serena's face tightened. "Well, it's not as if we weren't expecting something like this."

"No," Tom said hoarsely. He showed them the tablet in his hand. "I mean, *fuck!*"

Vlad's eyes widened. The cell doors in the dungeon behind the lab were rising. Red dots filled the screen.

Serena scowled. "Shit!"

Divine power flashed in her pupils. She grasped her blades in a white-knuckled grip and assumed a defensive stance, her gaze locked on the distant wall.

Acid burned the back of Vlad's throat as he braced. Tarang lowered his head, haunches tensing and fangs gleaming on an unholy growl.

The rear of the chamber exploded. A black cloud carrying the reek of Hell burst through the debris. A sea of red-eyed devils emerged from it, nanorobots gleaming on their teeth and talons, their blood lust corrupting the air.

Vlad knew immediately that they were in trouble.

Because these devils looked different to the ones they'd fought in New York.

CHAPTER 37

"Stick him, Enrique!" Popo screeched. "Stick him in the cojones!"

Cortes impaled a Dark Council sorcerer in the chest and scored the eyes of another with his whip. He glowered at his overzealous familiar while the men fell back with groans and screams.

"How about you let me do the fighting, flea brain?!"

Popo sucked in air. "That's mean! I groom myself every day!"

"This is kinda making me glad Trixie can't talk," Violet said dully.

"Same," Miles muttered. "FYI, that bird has an unhealthy fixation with human genitalia."

Nikolai cursed and shielded them against a barrage of spell bombs with *Moon Storm*. He stepped into the fray, his focus unerring as he delivered fatal cuts and stabs to their enemy, his spear blurring in his hands. The last witch grabbed her neck and gurgled before collapsing onto her back, blood pouring through her fingers.

Nikolai's heart raced as he straightened and looked around.

Most of the Dark Council members in the castle had converged on the entrance hall. Though he and the others were surrounded, they were still winning, if too slowly for his liking.

Just a little more, then I can go find her!

Unease trailed cold fingers down his spine. He hadn't detected Mae's magic in a while.

I really hope she hasn't gone after Vedran on her own.

His eyes cut to Oscar where the sorcerer huddled against a wall to his left. He was holding Drabek and mumbling incoherently to himself behind the *Contain* spell Nikolai had erected to imprison them, his expression glassy.

The lynx still hadn't regained consciousness.

A harrowing scream cut through the din of the battle, distracting Nikolai. He whirled around. His stomach plummeted.

Vlad, Lou, and some dozen super soldiers had backed into the south of the lobby from a corridor. They were fighting something Nikolai couldn't see. A Dark Council sorcerer close to them shrieked before exploding in a mist of blood and gore.

Nikolai's mouth went dry. The man's head and torso disappeared inside the maws of two massive, nanorobot-enhanced devils. Another one gulped down his limbs with loud crunches before licking its lips and focusing its crimson eyes upon his group.

"Great," Cortes snarled. "Like we didn't have enough on our hands!"

Vlad and Lou regrouped with them with the rest of the super soldiers.

"What the hell happened to 'we'll finish this and come back you up?!'" Nikolai barked.

"There was a change of plans, alright?!" the incubus snapped. "These devils are on a whole other level!"

Violet looked past Lou.

"Where are Serena and Tom?!" the witch asked in a strained voice.

"They've gone after Dietrich."

"Are they gonna be okay?" Miles said anxiously.

"I wouldn't worry about Serena." Lou grimaced. "And Tom may be our group clown, but he's our third-in-command for a reason."

"That guy has nine lives," a super soldier muttered.

Lou reloaded his gun and fired repeatedly at a devil as it launched itself at his head from a stone column, his expression hard.

The monster screeched, chest caving under the deadly volley of bullets. By the time it landed on the floor, its injuries were repairing themselves.

"Dammit!" Lou cursed. "Serena was right. The only way to put these monsters down is to strike at their brainstems!"

Nikolai's scalp prickled a heartbeat before a suffocating storm of black magic throbbed the air. Cortes grunted, knees bending. Violet clutched her throat and grimaced.

The Dark Council witches and sorcerers still standing

dropped to their knees and wheezed, most fainting. Horror widened Nikolai's eyes as he looked at the stairs.

He could feel Mae's magic clashing with Vedran's in the distance.

"Go!" Vlad yelled.

❄

Mae entered the Sorcerer King's suite warily.

Nikolai had explained where his father's chambers were before they'd parted. He'd also warned her not to go there on her own.

She fisted her hands. *I couldn't just wait.*

She hadn't sensed Barquiel's demonic energy since the portal closed on him. Wherever he'd ended up, she hoped the bastard was suffering.

Brimstone sniffed the air cautiously as they crossed a dark living area. French doors overlooked a terrace to their right. Moonlight made the stonework outside glow.

Mae scanned the shadows, tension tightening her limbs. "Anything?"

"No, my witch," the demon fox grunted.

Mae scowled. *Where the hell has he gone?!*

Hellreaver froze where he was bobbing in front of her. Crimson detonated around him. He dove for the floor with a snarl.

He's here, my witch!

Mae barely had time to reinforce the *Soul Shield* she'd erected inside the three of them before the ground opened up and swallowed them whole.

They tumbled headlong into a black hole.

She landed on something invisible seconds later, her breath knocked out of her. She jumped to her feet and whirled around, *Devour* brightening the air with a red glow where it sizzled above her hand.

A feral sound rumbled out of Brimstone as he loomed protectively beside her, his crimson gaze sweeping the darkness.

"Can you see anything?" Mae asked, her heart thumping against her ribs.

"Not yet, my witch."

Hellreaver gnashed his teeth as he hovered defensively before her. *I can taste his scent, my witch! It's all around us!*

A chill coursed through Mae.

Hellreaver is right, Na Ri said. *This darkness is more than just an absence of light. This is pure black magic!*

Mae could feel her first incarnation's blood lust. It was like a living beast roaring through her mind. A thought came to her. She swallowed.

"Could this be the portal Vedran manifests?!"

Vedran's voice oozed out of the shadows on their right. "How clever, Witch Queen."

Mae jerked around. *"Nullify!"*

The spell revealed nothing. She ground her teeth.

Of course it wouldn't! He's using his black magic and Nikolai's Hellfire Magic to mask his presence!

Heat flooded her veins as she drew on her cores and the power of her bonds.

"REVERSE!"

Something flickered in the gloom to their left. They whirled as one.

"That one actually stung, witch."

275

Vedran's tone turned Mae's blood to ice. Not only was it coming from a different direction to where they'd just glimpsed movement, it had an edge to it she hadn't heard before. One that made her stomach roil.

Vedran sounded insane.

"Obliterate."

Mae barely had time to register what the Sorcerer King had said before his spell swept over her. Corruption tainted with Hellfire Magic robbed her of air and sucked at her magic. *Soul Shield* trembled.

Brimstone roared, his tails quivering with a violence that made the air vibrate. Hellreaver blurred as he cut desperately at the inky veil, leaving crimson trails where he passed.

Mae's throat ached when she tried to inhale. Her vision swam. Despair numbed her senses.

Dammit!

Fire filled her cores.

Together, Na Ri grunted inside her.

The spell formed with a slowness that made Mae's chest tighten.

"Ab...sorb..." they invoked.

It suddenly got easier to breathe.

Brimstone shuddered and shook himself, the dimming light in his eyes brightening anew. He flinched, his head swinging.

The air shifted behind Mae. Something clamped around her neck. Her magic winked out.

"My witch!" Brimstone yelped.

Horror filled her as she grabbed at her throat. It was a

collar like the one Oscar had used on her at the warehouse in New York.

Hellreaver carved the space at Mae's back with an unholy sound.

But Vedran was already gone.

Mae swayed and dropped to her knees, Brimstone and Hellreaver's cries resonating in her ringing ears. Vedran's insidious magic was drowning her consciousness. Tears burned her eyes.

I can feel Nikolai's Hellfire Magic in this too!

She was starting to lose hope when golden light bloomed on her left wrist. She blinked. Her pulse thrummed as she stared at the bracelet Serena had given her. Artemus Steele's divine energy warmed her cold skin. She tugged at the collar. It came apart in her hand.

Vedran bellowed in rage, the sound echoing all around her.

Whiteness sparked at the edge of Mae's vision.

❄

NIKOLAI'S BREATHS CAME IN SHARP PANTS AS HE SPRINTED toward the Sorcerer King's chambers, Alastair's claws digging into his shoulder. He'd stopped sensing Mae's magic and Vedran's corruption a minute ago.

Fear churned his stomach when he saw the open doors. *No!*

He crossed the threshold and stumbled to a stop, his heart in his throat. The suite was empty.

Panic made him dizzy.

Where are they?!

Something resonated with his core. Nikolai froze. He touched his belly with trembling fingers. It was a faint trace of Hellfire Magic.

Blood thundered in his veins as he stared in the direction where he could sense an intangible connection. *There's something there!*

Alastair flapped his wings. Nikolai scowled, drew on their cores, and dropped down on one knee. Dazzling light detonated around them as he pressed his hands to the floor and tapped into the nexus where he had hidden mere hours ago.

A roar left his throat. He brought a tidal wave of white magic to the surface of the earth and straight into the Sorcerer King's chambers.

❄

THE BLACK HOLE MAE HAD BEEN TRAPPED INSIDE disintegrated with a hiss of corruption. She lurched as she found herself back inside Vedran's suite, the remains of the magic-infused nanorobot collar disintegrating around her.

Nikolai caught her in his arms before she could fall.

The spell concealing Vedran wavered, revealing his figure where he stood by the French doors.

Alastair squawked threateningly.

Brimstone and Hellreaver framed Mae and Nikolai, demonic magic throbbing around them as they bared their fangs at the Sorcerer King. Mae shuddered, her cores slowly coming back to life. Her bond with Brimstone and Hellreaver reignited with a thump.

Vedran stared at Nikolai. "You canceled *Void*."

It wasn't so much a question as it was a statement.

Mae swallowed.

Though Vedran looked fairly stunned at what had just transpired, he recovered his composure quickly, his face shifting into a vacant mask that chilled her to the bone.

Nikolai stepped protectively in front of her, his pupils aglow with Moon Magic and his knuckles pale where he gripped his spear.

Vedran glanced at the night sky. "Ah. I see the full moon is amplifying your powers."

His voice sounded dead.

Mae, Na Ri warned.

I know. Her nails bit into her palms. *Something's not right.*

Goosebumps covered her flesh in the next instant. Nikolai cursed. Shadows were forming next to Vedran.

"Is it another portal?!" Mae said.

Brimstone's eyes shrank to slits. *"That isn't a portal, my witch!"*

Horror widened Mae's eyes as the darkness condensed into a sword made of black magic.

"What the hell is that?!" Nikolai growled.

Mae's heart stuttered. She'd just picked up on something. Something that didn't make sense.

There was a soul inside Vedran's weapon. One she could make out because of Na Ri's presence. Bile burned the back of Mae's throat.

Is that—a familiar?!

Na Ri's horrified revulsion bled into her consciousness. *Yes.*

Vedran vanished. Time slowed.

Mae twisted on her heels, her heart thudding sluggishly in her chest, *Decimate* a half-formed spell on her lips. Nikolai turned, eyes rounding and Hellfire Magic blooming slowly around him and Alastair.

Brimstone reared back, his head smashing the ceiling and his tails moving agitatedly as he batted at the enemy who'd appeared in front of him.

Vedran slashed the demon fox across the face, his features contorted with a rage that turned his eyes a bubbling obsidian.

"*Give me the* Book of Light! *I know it's inside you!*"

"No!" Mae screamed.

She rose inside a crimson sphere, fury and fear choking her lungs.

Vedran darted out of the way of *Decimate's* deadly bolts and Nikolai's *Hell Flare*. He kicked off a wall and flashed toward Brimstone, his dark sword aimed straight at the familiar's heart.

Hellreaver blocked his path, countering the fatal blow that would have felled the demon fox. The impact rocked through Mae's very being and stole her breath.

Crimson trembled around Hellreaver. A terrible whine escaped him.

The sound he made when he cracked stopped Mae's world.

Brimstone yowled as Hellreaver came apart in two, disbelief dulling the light in his eyes.

The *Book of Light* fell out of the weapon, its edge gleaming as it caught the moonlight. Vedran dove and snatched the artifact.

"HELL FLARE!" Nikolai bellowed.

A black and red firestorm engulfed the Sorcerer King. He cursed and invoked *Void.*

Wrath seared Mae's veins. *"CHAOS SEAL! PURGE!"*

The spells detonated around her, filling the room with a storm of crimson magic. The windows exploded. The walls cracked. The castle trembled.

Vedran grunted as he vanished from view with his dark sword and the *Book of Light,* pain underscoring his voice.

A buzzing sound filled Mae's ears in the aftermath of his disappearance. Her gaze found Hellreaver. He had returned to his pendant form and lay in two pieces on the floor.

"Hellreaver?" she whispered brokenly.

Brimstone nudged the weapon with his snout, deep shudders shaking him, his throat choked with whimpers.

Mae dropped down, stumbled, and fell onto her hands and knees. She crawled to Hellreaver and gathered him with trembling fingers. He lay unmoving in her palms, metal cold and voices silent. Her chest tightened until she could barely breathe. She ground her teeth, drew on her magic, and invoked the spell that had allowed her to heal Nikolai and Vlad's fatal injuries in Philadelphia.

"ASSIMILATE!"

The incantation fizzled into nothingness. Hellreaver stayed still.

A sob left Mae when she felt the absence of his bond deep in her cores.

"No! No! *No!"*

Nikolai knelt behind her and took her in his arms as

she rocked and screamed out her denial, Na Ri's wail of agony echoing through her soul. Brimstone threw his head back and howled.

Vlad stumbled into view in the doorway of the suite, Cortes and the others behind him.

Horror drained the blood from their faces when they saw Hellreaver's remains.

CHAPTER 38

MAE WOKE UP TO NIKOLAI'S ARMS WRAPPED AROUND HER waist. She blinked blearily at the clock on the bedside table of her old bedroom, in her parents' house in Flushing. It was six-thirty in the morning.

She settled down on the pillow and hugged Brimstone to her chest. He stirred, his heartbeat strong and steady against her hands. Like her, the fox had barely slept last night.

They both gazed wordlessly at the small box on the dresser. It contained Hellreaver's remains. The weapon was as still and as silent as the day Vedran had smashed him to pieces.

Mae's throat clogged up. *I miss him so much, Brim!*

The fox whined and licked the tears tumbling down her cheeks. The sound woke Nikolai. He stiffened before relaxing against her.

"Want to go for a walk?" he said softly against her nape.

Mae wiped her face and nodded.

Daylight was peeking over the horizon when they stepped out of the house, the rest of her family still fast asleep. The guards on night watch greeted them with silent nods as they walked out of the front gate.

Even though there had been no sign of the Sorcerer King or the Dark Council in the past week, Noah Tegner and his team were still assigned to Mae's family as their protection detail. No one could be sure there wouldn't be any retaliation for what had happened in Poland.

Mae and Nikolai navigated the neighborhood in companionable silence, Brimstone padding silently beside them while Alastair flew overhead. The streetlights blinked off with every block they passed.

They had gotten into the habit of an early morning walk ever since they'd showed up at Mae's parents' house, on the night they'd returned from Europe. Vlad hadn't said a word when Mae had told him she wanted to be home with her family. She'd kissed his cheek and left him standing on the tarmac in the rain, where they'd just stepped off the *Dante 3*. Cortes had stayed by the incubus's side as he'd watched her drive off.

Yoo-Mi hadn't batted an eyelid when Nikolai declared he'd be staying at the house with Mae.

All the sorcerer had done in the long nights since then was hold Mae in his arms. They had not spoken about the horrible things they had lived through or the wound festering inside Mae's heart. A wound she feared would never heal, unlike the one on Brimstone's face.

Ye-Seul was making breakfast when they returned to the house.

"Is mom still asleep?" Mae asked tiredly.

She brought the fresh pot of tea brewing on the counter to the kitchen table and sat down. Nikolai took cups out of a cupboard and got milk and sugar.

"Yes." Ye-Seul stopped by her chair and kissed her cheek. "How are you doing today?"

Mae gazed into her grandmother's wise eyes and knew she couldn't lie. "Not great."

Ye-Seul patted her shoulder. "Accepting what you have lost is the first step toward finding a way to regain it." She paused. "Incidentally, the bags under your eyes could sink a ship. You should put some cucumber slices on them." She placed a couple of steaks on Brimstone's plate. "Chow's ready, foxy."

Mae stared at her grandmother and pondered her cryptic words while Brimstone jumped up on a chair. The fox's tail drooped as he gazed at the empty spot beside him. It was where Hellreaver would normally sit. She stroked his back.

Murmurs sounded on the landing. Ryu and Noah came downstairs. The doorbell rang.

Ryu headed to the foyer. "I'll get it."

Mae heard the door open and her sister's surprised, "Oh."

She sighed. "Let him in, Ryu."

She already knew who it was. Judging from Nikolai's faint frown, so did he.

Vlad came into the kitchen. He looked as worn out as she felt and was carrying two boxes of *Vetriano's* breakfast pastries. The smell stirred her practically non-existent appetite slightly.

He met her gaze, his face impassive. "Hey."

"Hi," Mae said quietly.

Nikolai studied him coolly. "Who invited you?"

Vlad narrowed his eyes slightly.

"I did." Yoo-Mi walked in behind the incubus. "Hi, Vlad. Want some coffee?"

"Hello, Mrs. Jin. Coffee would be nice."

"I thought you guys could do with some cheering up," Yoo-Mi said blankly at Mae and Nikolai's stares. "Besides, ain't nothing like some competition to get things moving," she muttered under her breath on her way to the coffee maker. "At this rate, I'm never gonna be a grandmother."

Mae blinked. Nikolai furrowed his brow.

A beatific smile stretched Vlad's mouth. "Looks like I have the full blessing of the lady of the house."

Nikolai's frown deepened.

Ye-Seul removed a tray of *Hoeddeok* from the oven and set them on a serving dish. Everyone sat down. An awkward silence descended as they ate, Mae and Brimstone picking at their food. It was broken by Ye-Seul's bombshell announcement.

"I'm thinking of getting a sex transplant."

Nikolai's eyes bulged, his fork midway to his mouth. Vlad dropped his pastry in his coffee. Yoo-Mi looked like she'd turned to stone.

Mae and Noah carried on eating glumly, like this was par for the course.

Ryu pursed her lips. "Do you mean a hip transplant, grandma?"

"That's what I said," Ye-Seul grumbled. "You young ones don't listen properly."

Everyone heaved a sigh of relief.

"And why do you want a hip transplant?" Yoo-Mi said tersely. "You looked as sprightly as a spring chicken when you went dancing with Mr. Choi two weeks ago, at that ballroom dancing competition."

"Their grandmother does ballroom dancing?" Vlad asked Noah *sotto voce*.

"She's a regular showstopper," the sorcerer murmured.

"It'll make me more nimble on the floor," Ye-Seul explained.

"Any more nimble and I'll have a heart attack," Yoo-Mi said thinly.

The doorbell rang again before Ye-Seul could come up with a valid protest.

"I'll get it." Nikolai rose, his expression that of a man who didn't think he'd ever get used to life at the Jins.

A familiar voice reached Mae.

"I thought you were only staying a few days," Bryony said, surprised.

"Did you move in?" Abraham said, suspicious.

"No," Nikolai said, one hundred percent sullen.

"What happened?" Violet said innocently.

"Yeah, you look kinda upset," Miles muttered.

Mae could've sworn she heard Nikolai grind his teeth.

Cortes, Jared, and Alicia weren't far behind. According to Nikolai, who'd been keeping in touch with Abraham, the Reaper Queen had finally reappeared a couple of days ago.

"You should move this to the living room," Yoo-Mi said as the kitchen crowded up. "I'll make more coffee."

Tarang lay down beside a sofa. Brimstone settled on

the floor next to him. The tiger wrapped his tail around the fox. The other familiars crowded around them.

Mae found herself the object of a battery of not-so-subtle, worried glances.

CHAPTER 39

Jared broke the uncomfortable silence. "So, there's still no sign of Oscar?"

Nikolai flinched.

Bryony glanced at the sorcerer, her expression guarded. "No."

By the time the dust had settled after their battle with Vedran and the Dark Council, Oscar had disappeared, leaving his familiar behind. The New York coven had taken Drabek into captivity, although there wasn't much they could do with the familiar.

Unlike Sable, who'd managed to cling to her sanity despite being a victim of *Subjugate*, the lynx had lost her mind.

Mae knew Nikolai harbored a degree of guilt over this, even though it was likely due to the black magic in Drabek's core reacting badly to his spell. She clenched her jaw.

There's also the fact that she'd been abandoned.

Since no one had seen what happened, Mae was unsure if Oscar had deserted Drabek of his own free will or if he had been forced to leave the lynx behind. The only one who knew the answer was the sorcerer.

And probably Vedran. He's the only person who could have gotten through Nikolai's magic.

Rage simmered in Mae's blood at the thought of the man who had robbed her of Hellreaver. Not only had Vedran broken the weapon Azazel had had forged for her, he'd also gotten his hands on the *Book of Light*, which meant he was one step closer to finding the *Book of Shadows* and the soul of the first Sorcerer King.

It was upon their return to New York that Nikolai had told her the shocking truth she had long suspected. Vedran had been siphoning his and Alastair's Hellfire Magic directly from their cores.

Mae didn't realize magic was seeping from her pores until Tarang bobbed past her line of vision. Brimstone, Trixie, and Millie clung grimly to the tiger.

She startled and looked around.

Popo, Shiloh, and Penley floated near the ceiling. Everyone else bar Alicia was barely hanging on to their seats.

Mae retracted her magic guiltily. "Sorry."

The crimson haze filling the air faded. Penley landed nimbly on Bryony's lap. The coven's healers had fixed the cat's broken leg.

Bryony looked relieved as gravity took over. "You haven't done that in a while."

"Yeah, well, I'm a bit vexed these days," Mae muttered.

She looked at Jared. "Did Serena deliver Dietrich to the Immortals?"

"He's under lock and key, awaiting his trial." Jared's face tightened. "I'm pretty sure he'll get the death sentence. That bastard has a rap sheet that could fill an entire room in my precinct. He has six more lives left. He will be executed until his final death."

Mae shuddered. Serena had told her the likely fate awaiting Dietrich after she and Tom had captured the Immortal. Since Immortals could survive sixteen deaths, a death sentence meant they would be killed, allowed to revive, and killed again. It was a gruesome way to go and not a decision the Immortal societies took lightly. Considering Dietrich's crimes over the centuries, it was what he deserved.

Serena had made a gruesome discovery in the bolthole where she and Tom had cornered the Immortal. It had been home to several tanks holding the dismembered remains of decades-old, first-generation super soldiers. It seemed Dietrich had ferreted them away from the primary facility where they had been kept and used them in his macabre experiments.

No one could tell if the super soldiers had still been alive at the time the Immortal had taken them captive.

As for the enhanced devils Dietrich had created, Serena and the super soldiers had spent a couple of days hunting down the fiends who'd managed to escape the island. If not for the Immortals' satellite network, the monsters would have reached the closest village in the mountains.

Cortes eyed Alicia cautiously. "Any sign of Barquiel in the Underworld?"

The Columbian looked more relaxed than before they'd left New York. All it had taken was a near death experience for his girlfriend to forgive him.

The Reaper Queen shot a glance at Mae. "Wherever *Chaos Seal* sent him, it's not any of the places I've searched in Hell Deep."

Tension knotted Mae's shoulders. She hoped Barquiel never resurfaced.

"Do you think he's dead?" Vlad asked Alicia warily.

"No."

The Reaper Queen's answer squashed Mae's vain hopes.

"He's an Archduke of Hell," she continued. "Besides, I would know if he'd perished. And the news would have spread through the Underworld like, well, fire."

Mae licked her lips, her pulse quickening. "What of Ran Soyun and Azazel? Has Astarte's alliance found any sign of where they might be?"

Alicia hesitated. "A demon thought he spotted your father on the edge of Arakiel's domain, a few weeks ago."

"Arakiel?" Nikolai repeated.

"The Second Leader of the Grigori," Cortes muttered. "He's a fallen angel who used to go by the name Earth of God." He narrowed his eyes at their stares. "I was curious, so I read up about them."

Alicia grimaced. "Arakiel's an ornery bastard. I'm planning to check in with him soon."

"And the devils Astarte and her allies had spotted in

Hell Deep?" Abraham asked stiffly. "Have they discovered anything about them?"

Unease clouded Alicia's face at the aide's question.

"That's the weird thing," she said quietly. "We can't find them. Not the devils, not the hundreds of ghouls and fiends faithful to Barquiel."

Dread curdled Mae's blood. She could see the others were thinking the same thing.

"It has to be Barquiel's doing."

Her harsh words echoed in the stilted hush.

Alicia sighed and rubbed the back of her neck. "Look, we're doing our best to find him. You just have to give us—"

"Take me there." Mae fisted her hands. "Take me to Hell."

Vlad's eyes flared. Nikolai's head swung mechanically as he fixed her with a dazed stare. Bryony and Abraham looked like they'd been struck by lightning. Violet and Miles gaped.

Jared sighed and pinched the bridge of his nose.

"Well, that's a fresh approach," Cortes said leadenly.

Brimstone jumped on Mae's lap. He looked into her eyes, his own unblinking and his bond pulsing strongly with her cores.

Are you sure about this, my witch?

Mae nodded jerkily. Brimstone was quiet for a moment.

Alright, he huffed.

He curled up on her thighs and rested his head atop his paws, the matter settled as far as he was concerned.

Mae met Nikolai and Vlad's gazes.

"Come with me." She focused on Vlad, her heart thundering against her ribs. "Your father is the King of Incubi. As such, you will have influence in the Underworld by virtue of your bloodline." Her gaze shifted to Nikolai. "Though you may not know the location in Hell Deep where Ran Soyun is trapped, I know your white magic can help us find her." She swallowed and pinned Alicia with a determined look. "Azazel will know I'm in Hell. He will come find me."

Alicia lowered her brows. The Reaper Queen didn't look at all happy. "You know you're asking for something impossible, right?"

Mae clenched her jaw. "Artemus Steele went to Hell with his friends."

"That idiot is the son of an angel!" Alicia snapped. "And the ones who accompanied him were divine beasts."

Mae jutted her chin. "I have Azazel's blood in my veins." She indicated Nikolai. "He has the strongest white magic on Earth." She pointed at Vlad. "And he's the son of Ilmon."

Alicia turned to Bryony. "Make her see sense."

Bryony's mouth pressed to a thin line as she studied Mae. "I'm flattered that you think I can reason with the Witch Queen."

Mae bit her lip. Alicia sagged.

"There's one more thing," Mae said.

"What's that?" Alicia asked in a defeated tone.

Mae's fingers flexed on Brimstone's fur. "I want you to take me to Armaros."

Alicia's eyes flared crimson. "What?!"

"I'm going to ask him to fix Hellreaver."

✳

Mae, Brimstone, and Hellreaver's adventures conclude in Witch Queen, the final book in the Witch Queen series! Witch Queen will be available to purchase in ebook and print formats in AD Starrling's new online store coming in 2024. Stay tuned by signing up to her author newsletter.

Don't forget to check out Seventeen and Legion, the other series set in the same universe as Witch Queen!

ACKNOWLEDGMENTS

To my friends and family. I couldn't do this without you.

To my readers. Thank you for reading A Fury Of Shadows. If you enjoyed my book, please consider leaving a review on Amazon or Goodreads. Reviews help readers like you find my books and I truly appreciate your honest opinions about my stories.

BOOKS BY A.D. STARRLING

Seventeen Series
Seventeen Series Novels
Seventeen Series Novel Boxsets
Seventeen Series Short Stories

Other series based in the Seventeen Universe
Legion
Witch Queen

Military Romantic Suspense
Division Eight

Miscellaneous
Void - A Sci-fi Horror Short Story
The Other Side of the Wall - A Horror Short Story

ABOUT A.D. STARRLING

Want to know about AD Starrling's upcoming releases? Sign up to her newsletter for new release alerts, sneak peeks, giveaways, and get a free boxset and exclusive freebies.

Follow AD Starrling on Amazon

Join AD's reader group on Facebook
The Seventeen Club

Check out this link to find out more about A.D. Starrling
Linktr.ee/AD_Starrling

Milton Keynes UK
Ingram Content Group UK Ltd.
UKHW012027081223
434064UK00015B/136/J

9 781912 834419